Praise for the nov

"A writer to watch."

—*Publishers Weekly*

"A charming cast of characters, a twisty mystery, and a diabolical killer make *Nothing Ever Happens Here* impossible to put down. A riveting page-turner with a sly sense of humor."

—**Robyn Harding, internationally bestselling author of *The Haters***

"[An] entertaining thriller [that] maintains tension and intrigue through to the satisfying end. The author's fans will devour this."

—*Publishers Weekly* on *The Vacancy in Room 10*

"*On a Quiet Street* [is] a brilliant and twisty tale. A fast-paced, highly enjoyable and compulsive read that may well make you look at your entire neighborhood a little differently..."

—**Hannah Mary McKinnon, internationally bestselling author of *Never Coming Home***

"A twisty thriller in the vein of *The Girl on the Train*."

—*Bustle* on *On a Quiet Street*

"Seraphina doesn't let up this time. In her heart-racing new thriller, she hangs you off a cliff, hits you with red herrings and suspects at every turn, and takes your breath away with her final startling twist."

—**Katie Tallo, internationally bestselling author of *Dark August* and *Poison Lilies*, on *The Vanishing Hour***

"A sly and pulse-pounding murder mystery set in steamy Louisiana."

—**Kimberly Belle, internationally bestselling author of *Stranger in the Lake*, on *Such a Good Wife***

"Unputdownable. I found myself suspecting everyone at some point. Twisty, original and a must-read—highly suspenseful and cleverly written."

—**Karen Hamilton, bestselling author of *The Perfect Girlfriend*, on *Someone's Listening***

Also by Seraphina Nova Glass

Someone's Listening
Such a Good Wife
On a Quiet Street
The Vanishing Hour
The Vacancy in Room 10

NOTHING EVER HAPPENS HERE

SERAPHINA NOVA GLASS

GRAYDON
HOUSE

GRAYDON
HOUSE®

Recycling programs
for this product may
not exist in your area.

ISBN-13: 978-1-525-83672-5

Nothing Ever Happens Here

Graydon House
22 Adelaide St. West, 41st Floor
Toronto, Ontario M5H 4E3, Canada
www.GraydonHouseBooks.com

Printed in U.S.A.

For Kim LaFontaine

Friend, mentor, and the one who encouraged me to write that very first thing all those years ago.

1

Shelby

It's a death omen. The words pierce the evening air and then are lost in the surrounding laughter and chatter. The words are meaningless to me as I hold my wineglass against the light of a flickering candle on the table and examine the hairline fracture in the glass. It's a brisk October night, but in northern Minnesota that means heavy coat weather and a rush to enjoy anything outside before six months of winter, so it's a perfect excuse to have a girls' dinner at Groucho's—the kind of place with a showy outdoor pizza oven and heat lamps on the eclectic back patio with its mismatched tables and chairs and cozy firepit.

When we clinked glasses—cheers to Rowan, soon heading back to Boston after a school break—mine cracked.

"Death omen?" Mack repeats.

"Yeah. If you break a glass during a toast, someone's gonna

die. It's a thing," Rowan says. "I'll take it for you." She holds her hand out for my glass. Mack slaps it down.

"Not twenty-one until September, no you may not, and is this what I'm paying tuition for? You're learning about death omens?"

"Yep," she says, and then a horrified expression blooms on her face when I still sip out of the glass of wine. "Don't drink it for God's sake! You'll shred your intestines. See, death omen. I told ya."

"It's a tiny crack. Shhh. You're freakin' the girls out," I say, because my four-year-old twins sit eating cheese pizza with plastic bibs and coloring mats next to us. Fine, they're paying no attention, but still.

"Right." Rowan smiles and I motion for the waiter to replace my glass. After many years and more of our life savings than we could afford to spare, I finally got pregnant at forty-one. And yes, I absolutely make sure it's known far and wide—from Fargo to Duluth—that those girls are God's most perfect creations. My miracle children. They can joke that it's surprising that I don't have an actual bullhorn to make daily announcements within the town square about how these girls are unfuckwithable. But it's nice, actually. You make a big enough deal about something for long enough and it has a ripple effect. People treat them like they are made of glass, and it's just the way I like it.

"Well, Leo promised to not get drunk at the Royal Oak tonight and to be home on the couch with popcorn popped by the time I get back," Mack says, scanning the QR code on the bill to pay the tab.

"Do you know nothing about PFCs?" Rowan asks.

"Yes, you told me," Mack replies, sipping the last of her wine and standing, so Rowan aims her soapbox lecture at me instead.

"They're the carcinogens in microwaved popcorn bags. You're literally eating cancer when you make that shit."

"Language," Mack says, nodding to the twins. "She's taking an ecofeminist class."

"I see. Well. I think it's past someone's bedtime anyway," I say to the girls, and Poppy shakes her head and looks like she might start to pitch a fit. I give Rowan a side hug. "The wind is picking up too, so get home before that storm gets going." Mack kisses me on the cheek and before they make their way out of the courtyard, suddenly June is in full hysterics because she left Bertha the stuffed badger at the cafe earlier. I flag Mack back over, but she doesn't hear me, so I take the girls by their arms and rush out to the lot before she can drive off. Thank God, because the thought of June without Bertha for the night makes me shudder. She's already pulling away from me to lie face down on the ground next to Mack's car and howl.

"We have a badger situation," I tell Mack. "She put Bertha in a highchair at one of the booths. Sorry." Mack slips the cafe key off her ring with an amused smile and tells me to leave it under the mat when I'm done.

When I pull up to the Firefly Cafe, a chilly wind kicks up dust in the parking lot and makes a whistling sound through the bending trees. I leave the car running with the heat on and whisper to the girls that I'll be back in thirty seconds, even though they are both fast asleep already. I jog up to the front door and use the flashlight on my phone to see the lock. It takes some fiddling before I manage to get it open. The wind becomes so strong, I practically fall into the front entry when the door pushes inward. I see Bertha right away. She's in a booster seat with a plate of blueberry pie still placed in front of her. I'm sure one of the college kids Mack hired must have closed up, because she wouldn't have left all that there overnight just to be cute. I start to rush over to grab the stuffed animal when I suddenly stop cold.

There's a figure behind the register. The file cabinet under the counter is open and papers are pulled out.

"God, you scared the shit out of me," I say, assuming it's Leo. Because who else would have a key? The door was locked. And who else would be going through their files? But the figure doesn't respond. When he steps out of the darkness and into the beam of my phone light, I see he's wearing a thick ski mask and he's dressed in black, and my body begins to tremble uncontrollably. I hold Bertha to my chest and take a step backward. I look to the front door, assessing quickly if I could sprint to it before he could get me, but what if he has a...

And then, with gloved hands, he points something shiny and metal that I can scarcely see in the darkness, but I get enough of a glimpse to know it means I'm seriously fucked.

"Turn that light off!" I blink at him in shock. "Now!" I obey. "Get back there," he says, motioning to the kitchen and glancing toward the front window to make sure nobody is there—no cars are passing.

"Leo?" I say one more time because, for a moment, I think it sounds like it could be him, although the voice is too distorted to tell. His clothes are baggy and oversized so it could be anyone. I can't tell from the shape or size, and for just a brief moment I think maybe this is a joke.

"Fucking go!" he screams, and then the panic officially sets in. I'm not dreaming, and it isn't a joke.

"Please!" I start to plead. "Um... Do you...? What are you looking for? What do you want? I know Mackenzie—Mack. And, and, and Leo—the owners. They'll— I know they'll give you whatever you want if you just don't... If nobody gets hurt. I know they will. Just tell me what you want." He doesn't reply. Instead, he starts slowly walking toward me so I am forced to move—to walk toward the back kitchen like he wants. My whole body shakes as I look out the front window at my car with my babies sleeping in the back seat. I swallow down a sob and put my hands up as he moves toward me. I expect him to just direct me to move, but he suddenly grabs me by the arm and pats me down, looking for a weapon or something like they do at airport security. Then he pushes me hard through the double swinging doors to the kitchen, where I lose my footing and barely catch myself before I fall.

The kitchen is dim, lit only by the small lamp on Mack's desk on the back wall where she keeps her cookbooks and recipe cards. The lamp's base is made of brass and shaped like a mouse reaching up and screwing in the light bulb. It was a white elephant gift that she ended up loving. I stare at the familiarity of it in this strange moment with longing, as if it can somehow help me. As if it can stop whatever terrible thing is about to happen. Adrenaline surges through me. I keep my eyes on the man, confused about what he wants. He seems unsure himself about what he's going to do.

"Take your clothes off," he says suddenly.

"Oh God. No. My babies. My babies are outside," I whisper because the words are barely able to come out of my mouth. The reality of what's happening is choking me.

"Do it. I don't have all night."

"Please," I beg. Tears are starting to roll down my face now. "Please, anything you want. I— Whatever you came for, just tell me and I'll…" He slams the gun down on a steel prep table, and the sound is deafening. He points it at me again, and I think of sweet June and Poppy and how, maybe if I just do what he says, he'll let me go. I can't see his face, so that's good, I think. That means he might let me go, because I could never identify him. That's giving me a flicker of hope, so I have to do whatever he wants. The girls are, impossibly, only feet away from me behind this cafe wall, asleep to the sound of the humming car motor and a sleep story I put on in the car, "The Pumpkin Pie and the Blustery Day." It always makes them sleepy. Oh God, the thought of them makes me start to hyperventilate.

I try to control it. I push away any thought of them waking up and trying to find me. I can't bear to think about them at all in this moment or I'll snap, and that will be the end of me. I'm not the one with the gun. I just have to make my mind a blank space and let this happen as quickly as possible.

I pull off my denim jacket and then, through uncontrollable tears and shaking hands, I pull my black sweater dress over my head and let it fall on the ground. He leans against the baking table, pushing aside Mack's favorite blue mixing bowl, and watches; he doesn't speak. When I leave my underwear on, he just waits me out. He still doesn't say anything, which is becoming more unnerving, making him feel more dangerous and unpredictable to me. I can't see his face. He doesn't grab me or throw me down or anything else that I expect to happen at any second. He just stares until I slowly, painfully take off the rest of my clothes and stand in front of him naked, covering myself with my hands as much as possible, weeping and waiting for the worst.

He walks over to me slowly, looking me up and down. Should I try to fight? If I let it happen, I might see the girls. I might survive this. If I fight, he fights back and then... I might not. This question is on repeat in my mind, along with every possible outcome, and all the thoughts whirl in my head. But it's only a matter of seconds and then he is right in front of me.

He still doesn't grab for me or touch me. He picks my clothes up from the ground, and my head swirls with confusion. He takes a few steps back, and then he laughs. I don't understand what's happening.

He throws my clothes at me, hard, and shakes his head.

"Look at you," he says. "Absolutely sickening. Pathetic. Put your clothes on. Jesus." A stab of humiliation cuts through me—a shame so unexpected, yet so deep, it steals my breath for a moment. I hide myself behind my armful of discarded clothes and have no idea if I should run or scream or beg—what is happening? I have no idea what is happening.

"What do you want?" I ask again, my voice trembling.

"You weren't supposed to be here, and you fucked up my plans," he says matter-of-factly.

"Then just let me go. You can do whatever you—you can… I won't even tell anyone I saw anything. So you can just let me go and…whatever your plans were, you can just…"

"I can't have you reporting seeing someone here tonight."

"I won't. I *promise*."

"Do you know who I am?" he asks, taking me by surprise. I stare again at his size and clothes, and try to discern his voice that's so soft and muffled, it's impossible to decipher.

"I… Leo?" I say again, tilting my head, staring as hard as I can through my tears and dizzying confusion, looking for anything about him that would give his identity away. But it can't be Leo. It makes no earthly sense. He doesn't answer, of course. If it's not Leo, maybe this man will let me go now that he knows I'll report to the police that it's Leo I suspected. Unless it really *is* him, and he's secretly turned into some sort of sick monster. God help me, I'm in a fucking nightmare.

"See, you fuck up the timeline if you report seeing someone here at this time looking through these records. And of course that's what you'll do. Don't keep saying you won't because you want me to let you go. Of course you will, and I'm sorry, but I need to make sure that doesn't happen."

"What? No…what do you mean, I…" I hold up my hands, because he still has the gun aimed at me.

"If you tell anyone I was here, I'll…you know what, I won't even kill you. I'll just make everyone around you pay and make you watch. Ya got that?"

"But I won't—I don't even know who you are! Who would I even tell? I promise, I…"

"I think you know. If you just thought about it, you'd know who I am. You'd know why I'm here." He stares at me, maybe looking for some spark of recognition in my eyes, but there is none, because I don't know. "Fuck it, I can't take that chance."

"No, wait," I whimper, and he picks up Bertha from the floor where I dropped her and looks at her face.

"This is what you came here for, a fuckin' weasel, huh?" he asks, and I nod. And it's stupid that I want to correct him that it's a badger, not a weasel, and that a thought like that is even crossing my mind right now.

"That's too bad. Shitty timing," he says, and then he grabs me by the arm and pulls me to the back of the kitchen past towering rows of plates and wineglasses, past the pantry and the back delivery door with pallets of flour and cane sugar piled against it. I wonder, for a fleeting moment, if I could break away from him and run through it—just push out the back door to freedom in hopes he's just a scared thief and not a murderer. And then I think of getting shot in the back in front of my kids in the car and I don't run. I let him pull me until he stops, and when he does, my heart falls like a stone in my chest and the blood drains from my face, and all I hear is ringing in my ears.

"I'm sorry, but I need to make sure you don't fuck up my plans. You were looking for this," he holds up Bertha and tosses her into the walk-in freezer. "You found her in there when the doors snapped closed behind you. At least that's what they'll assume when they find you, I'm sure. And I was never here."

He pushes me into a small room that's stacked with icy shelves of packed chicken wings, and berries for pies, and ice cream buckets. I scream and try to rush to the door, but everything happens in a blink—in a blur—and I'm trapped before I even knew what was happening. It's negative ten degrees, and he's locked the door behind him.

I stand in shock for a few moments, and then my heart is racing so fast and I'm crying so hard, I can barely see through the tears to pull my clothes on. I shiver and shake violently from the cold as I dress. My feet are already freezing to the metal floor as I try to pull on stockings that will do nothing to protect me from the extreme cold. There is nowhere to hide, no way to escape, no window, no place to even sit and curl up, no one looking for me. Just a metal, airless icebox. I came in to get a stuffed animal. How is this happening?

I scream. I scream and wail, and beat at the door. I scream for so long and so hard that a spattering of blood from my battered throat mists the glossy metal door, but there is nobody to hear. After what seems like hours, but is maybe only minutes, the cold begins to turn my hands colors—a deep purple blue, and I can't bend my fingers. The numbness starts to morph into an ache, a full body weakness, and I have to kneel on the frozen metal floor. I can't pound on the door anymore because I don't have any strength. It's leaving my body.

He's left me here to die, and I think about them. My babies, just outside, sleeping to the sounds of a cozy pumpkin pie story I put on YouTube, holding their new, fuzzy reindeer blankets to their chests, waiting for their mother to come back to them. I touch my fingers to the door.

"My babies," I can barely whisper now, but I cry out to them until there is nothing left inside me. "My babies, my babies." Everything goes dark.

2

Mack

When I drop Rowan off at Julia's house for the night, I get out of the car and make a big production of hugging her goodbye. The two of them will drive all the way back East to school tomorrow and Julia will drop Row off at school on her way up to Syracuse, and I'll find myself wishing we had a dozen more kids to fill the house in her absence. I'm happy Leo promised to be home with popcorn and a gin and tonic tonight, because he knows this is the hardest part: the many goodbyes I have to endure each time she goes, leaving hair bands and toast crumbs and threadbare slipper-socks in her wake for me to find over the coming days, like tiny cruel reminders that she's all grown up and gone.

When she finally pulls free of my embrace and tells me she'll be safe, I wave to Julia's mother, wrapped in a robe on the front porch, motioning Rowan inside. Then I pull away, blinking back tears and turning up an old Shania Twain song to boost my mood. I pass the Firefly on my route back home and see Shelby's car parked outside of the front door, idling. I slow for just a moment, thinking I might stop in because she left a half hour before me and it seems odd she's just getting to the cafe now. But I mind my business, because there are a thousand reasons that, with two little girls in tow, she could have been delayed.

I drive the half mile back to the house and feel a prickle of annoyance when I don't see any lights on inside as I pull into the garage. A marathon of *Kitchen Nightmares* and Orville Redenbacher's was promised, and he's already asleep? Seriously? His car's in its spot beside me, so unless he has candles lit and is waiting for me in the bed draped in a Gordon Ramsay apron, I'm bordering on getting very pissed off.

When I exit my car, something feels really strange. I can't explain it. It's just the same boring garage I see every day, functioning primarily as a path from house to car. Nothing appears different. Leo's Audi is there, the lawn mower and some rakes are in their usual corner. The kayaks are above me in the rafters, and the Christmas decorations are in their plastic containers on the shelves along the side wall, so what is it that feels so off? A chill runs through me and I quickly click the garage door fob so it closes me in, because I am overcome with the sudden, irrational fear of being watched.

I stand in the silent garage now and listen for…what? I don't know. There's nothing but the clicks and creaks a car makes as it cools down, and a weird instinct I can't place. I walk into the house and see a half-empty glass of wine sitting on the kitchen counter.

"Leo?" I call out, dumping my purse and pulling off my coat. The house is quiet. No football game softly playing on the TV upstairs the way I expected. He *is* asleep, damn it.

"Lee?" I say again, flipping on a lamp on an end table and calling upstairs a few more times. No answer. I sigh and make my way up the staircase, stealing quick glances into the dark guest room and hall bath on my way to the bedroom, where I will find him tipsy and passed out. And I guess that's fine, because it's not very often he goes out for drinks with the guys, so I decide not to give him too much crap about it. We can watch Gordon Ramsay verbally abuse people tomorrow.

When I tiptoe into the room, I use the glow of my phone screen so I don't wake him up. It's not until I'm in the en suite bathroom pulling out a makeup wipe that I glance into the bedroom and notice his side of the bed is empty. I feel a jolt of adrenaline rush through me, and I walk back into the room and switch on the lights.

"Leo? Leo!"

I feel the panic start to rise and my face feels hot, my heart speeding up. I rush down the hall flipping on all of the lights. I start to whip open closet doors and look under the bed for some stupid reason, because where the hell could he be? His car is here. I take the stairs two at a time and stand in the middle of our open concept main floor. There aren't that many places to look. From my vantage point, I see the kitchen and dining area, the screened-in porch off the sliding doors of the kitchen, the living room and office. It's all empty.

"Leo!" I call again, to nobody. "Okay, don't panic," I start to mumble to myself. "If his car were gone, you'd assume he was still at the Royal Oak, you wouldn't be freaking out, so if his car is here then what…" I try to think of a "then what," but there are no answers I can come up with. An emergency would mean he'd probably take his car. I would think maybe he took a walk, but in my twenty-two years of marriage, I have never seen Leo walk around the neighborhood for any reason, not even when we had a dog.

I text Row first, casually. Not to alarm her, but to see if she's heard from him. When she answers back "No. Why?" I explain it away and tell her I just wanted to make sure he got a chance to say goodbye before she left tomorrow, and she texts back a heart.

Then I call the two friends he was with at the Oak, Robby and Aaron. Robby answers right away, and I can tell they've had a few too many. It sounds like they're still there, because I hear the white noise of bar chatter and a Red Hot Chili Peppers song playing in the background. Robby speaks too loudly into the phone and I pull my ear away.

"Mack! Hey, ya missed dart league. We lost, but that's because Aaron was busy getting his dick sucked in the bathroom and…" He stops and I hear Aaron shout something, and then laughter. "Naw, naw, just kidding…"

"Is Leo there?" I cut him off.

"What? No. He left ages ago. Said he was going home early tonight."

"He left? When? What time?"

"Uh…a couple hours maybe. Why? Something wrong?" he asks.

"I don't…know. I just… I'll call you back," I say, and hang up. I sit on the arm of the couch in the silence and stare across to the kitchen island and think. There has to be a goddamn reason, so I can't let myself think the worst. It's odd, yes, okay. But there must be a perfectly reasonable explanation that I'm not thinking of.

I'll just—I'll wait a little while. He'll show up.

I do wait. I pace the floor and look in all the rooms again, and pour a drink and take deep breaths and I try not to cry, and then I wait some more, and then I start to drive the dark side roads, uselessly, in search of him. But he never does show up. By midnight, I've called the hospitals and all of his friends, plus the neighbors in case he ran to one of them for help. I have called Shelby twice, but I know she turns her phone down at night when the girls are sleeping, so I don't expect her to get my message until the morning. And she was with me all night, so she probably has no ideas. Same with Rowan; I only left her the one message so as not to scare her. I've called the cafe, but nobody is there. I've called everyone I can think of, even his father in Tampa, to see if they'd had any word from him today. Nothing.

I think of his heart condition and try not to fear the worst: that he wandered off somewhere and had an attack or something and there was nobody there to help him and he's lying in a street somewhere. God!

But no. I don't let this take hold, because the simple fact is that he doesn't wander off on evening jogs, and his things are here, so I try to erase that scenario and think of anything else I could be overlooking. When I have waited as long as I can stand to, I finally report him missing.

It's not until the small hours of the morning, when I have the police out looking all over town for him, that it begins to sink in that something very bad has happened. Like *really* sink in that there is no misunderstanding or simple explanation left. That this has reached a new level of full-on fucking horror show.

When I finally get a call from the police, I pick up desperately hoping they've found him safe, but that's not what they are calling about at all. They need me to come down to the cafe immediately. There's been an incident.

I drive the black back roads with shaking hands and blurry eyes, as fast as I can toward the cafe. What could have happened in the middle of the night that's so important? A break-in? Vandalism? I don't care. It could be burned to the ground for all I fucking care right now. I just want Leo. But Leo has vanished into thin air.

I swallow down the sobs I feel climbing my throat and I kick up dust as I pull into the dirt lot of the cafe and park. It's swarming with cops. What the fuck? Then I see Shelby's car, and her two girls are screaming and crying as a medic kneels down, wrapping blankets around their shoulders. There's a small

crowd of people, and red lights flashing, and people are shouting, and then I see them rolling out a stretcher. A stretcher,
from the front doors of my cafe. Underneath the sheet is the
shape of a body. Dear God, what's happening? Someone's dead.

3

Florence

Fifteen Months Later

I read a story on the internet about how elderly people without hobbies are among the saddest sacks on earth, although I'm sure I have that wrong and they didn't use the word "sacks." Anyway, it went on to say how having hobbies could greatly reduce one's chances of developing dementia. They didn't give a percentage and I would have liked a percentage, because if it's only a one percent chance reduction, well then, why bother? But I guess they wouldn't have written the whole article, in that case, or used the words "greatly reduce one's chances" for that matter either, would they? So I decided I would like a hobby.

So, when I Googled "how to start a hobby" the first advice given was to break it into small steps so you're not overwhelmed. For Christ's sake, I didn't Google how to embezzle diamonds from the Russian mafia, I was simply thinking I might take up cookie making or something. How could I get overwhelmed? Anyway…then I learned that professional cookie decorators call themselves "cookiers" and I just found the term so irritating I gave up on the whole thing.

Then Millie told me I could knit with her and I told Millie that she's shamefully cliché, and how does she not have carpal tunnel by now? And it's not really a hobby, is it? She'd be sitting in front of the television watching *Bonanza* with or without her knitting in hand, so it's quite mindless, and I don't think a hobby should be mindless. Bernie has taken up winemaking, but his room smells like a boiled egg, so I don't think he's doing it right. It's still at the top of my list, though.

Gardening was a contender too. I was quite the gardener once, but the snow won't melt until April, so that seems a long wait. I could be dead by then for all I know. But then Herb said I should make a podcast about gardening and share my wisdom with the world. This intrigued me—because I was once a news announcer on public radio, and in a way it's a perfect idea. My love for plants and helping people learn, hmm. But how would one even begin? I just showed up and talked into a mic at the station, and that was long ago. I would need to figure out a lot of things, but learning it all would keep me busy, and maybe that's a hobby all in itself. I was almost sold on the idea.

But then something very serendipitous happened. I was at Murph Moyer's funeral, which was such a sad occasion since Murph had just had a hair transplant he was very excited about, and had planned a trip to the Bahamas to swim with the pigs. I guess that's a thing… He even bought a bottle of spray tan on Amazon, and then just like that, a fall on the ice on his way down to The Angry Trout for a pint one night and that was it. And now he looks orange in his casket, poor Murph, and he never even got to put his new hair to good use. It's like that these days, though. When you get to be our age, you start receiving invitations to a lot more funerals. And part of you gets used to it, but the main part of you never does.

At the reception, I was chatting with Rosie and Susan by the punch bowl. We were sitting in metal folding chairs and holding little slices of white cake on napkins when I noticed Winny pouring a long pull of scotch into a Santa Claus coffee mug and sitting by herself next to a fake ficus in need of dusting. She was hunched over her drink, and I saw her dot her eye with the corner of a napkin, so I excused myself and went to sit with her.

I could tell it wasn't her first scotch because she had a glassy-eyed look and loose lips, but that's a good thing. It was easy to get her to confide in me and tell me why she'd missed our bridge game last Tuesday and what in the world was the matter. I mean, I know her husband passed only a couple of months ago, of course. But he'd been battling severe diabetes complications and was in the hospital for who knows how long. He was even left unable to speak after a diabetes-induced stroke. Lord help him. It was a mercy, really, him passing. It was very expected. So I am quite surprised at what Winny tells me—that she thinks her husband was murdered and didn't die of natural causes. Well, I had to set my punch on the floor next to me and rest my hand on my heart a moment.

"Sweetheart, why would you say that? Otis was so sick, bless him," I say to her, placing my hands on her knees. I thought she lost the plot, if I'm honest, but I was still going to be sympathetic. She picks at Santa's chipping glitter beard and talks into her lap.

"Something wasn't right there," she says with a haunted look on her face.

"What do you mean, love?" I ask, trying to look in her eyes so she's forced to look back at me, but she continues to mumble. And I suppose I would speak quietly too if I were saying the crazy thing she was about to say.

"Someone there killed him," she whispers.

"At the hospital?"

"Yes, Florence. I… Yes. I'm not just—I'm not crazy. I'm not making shit up."

"Of course you're not, dear," I say, but I don't really mean it. "Well, did you tell the police?" I ask, because what else does one ask in this sort of situation?

"Of course, but they don't believe me. I can tell. They say they'll 'have a look,' whatever that means, but I know when I'm being condescended to. They will not have a look. Plus that old detective Riley has a head full of chipped beef. Has he ever helped anyone solve anything in this town?" she asks, becoming louder and more agitated as she goes. She puts her mug down and takes a deep breath.

To be fair, the only crime I can remember happening in the last few years in this town, besides petty bike theft or drunk fistfights, is the tragedy that happened to Mack and Shelby that terrible night last year, but I can't blame Riley for that. It absolutely baffled everyone. He does have a head full of chipped beef though, I'll give her that.

"Why would you think something like that, love? You know all of the hospital workers," I say, which is a given. She pretty much knows everyone around here.

"You think one of them hurt Otis? That's…" I stop, because I don't know what to say. It's absurd and makes me worry for Winny. I wonder if she's gone around telling other people this sort of thing.

"He told me," she says, and since I know he was unable to speak, now I really zip my lip and just look over at the bottle of scotch on the refreshments table with a longing gaze, wondering how to kindly extract myself from the conversation.

"Something's goin' on around here, Flor. Something is happening. First Shel and Mack, and poor Leo wherever the hell he really is. Now this." It's strange to hear someone say "poor Leo," because the general, mostly unspoken consensus is that he's a rat bastard who ghosted his wife. I hope I'm using that term correctly. *Ghosted*. Anyway, I wonder if it would be rude to lean over and pick a few cucumber sandwiches off of the table while she's talking. I do hate to be rude, but I really am famished, and I know Liddy Wingfield made them, and she uses the pimento cream cheese on them, which is a dream.

Before I can decide, Winny leans in conspiratorially.

"Can I show you something?" she asks.

"Of course," I agree, giving up on my chance for a cucumber sandwich as she motions for me to follow her. The reception is at Dusty Waltman's house because he and Murph were very good friends. I suppose he's a nice enough man, I just can't get past the urge to take a bottle of Pledge and a washrag after him each time I hear the name Dusty. Not his fault, I suppose, and his house is quite tidy, although too drafty for my taste.

Even so, I follow Winny down his front hall with the brown plaid wallpaper and creaky wood floors, and we pull our coats from a pile of other sad-looking black and navy down coats draped over an old steamer trunk near the door and walk out into the frozen air. It's so cold the snow is having trouble trying to fall, and it swirls around the lampposts in light, icy specks. Before I can complain about freezing to death, I hear "My Heart Will Go On" start to play inside, and now I'm happy to be out here, so I give her a minute as I shift from foot to foot and blow on my hands while she pulls something from her pocket. Why do they play songs like that at funerals? Everyone is already sad, and now I can hear sobs from inside. I hope they play "Another One Bites the Dust" at my funeral. And have it at a Dave & Buster's, where everyone will get free mojitos and play free Skee-Ball, and not in a drafty house with peely wallpaper and stale sheet cake.

Winny finally fishes out whatever it is she's been digging for, then shoves the pieces of a ripped-up sheet of paper at me. I take it, examining it and have no idea what the hell she's playing at.

"What is it?" I ask. She takes the papers back, swipes a layer of snow off of Dusty's porch swing, and sits. I sit next to her, and she lays them out on her knees.

"Look," she says, and I do. I see a scrap with the words "Help me" scrawled across it, and another that reads "Trying to kill me." But the words before it are torn away. She stares at me, waiting for a response.

"Well, what is this?" I ask.

"Otis wrote it. Look! This is the clearest one." She puts a scrap on top of the others. It says, "You have to tell someone what's happening here." The last part says, "Warn Mack and Shel…" but the end of her name is torn away.

"See," she says, "and then it stops, like he couldn't finish."

"I don't… Why is this in scraps? Why would he write this?" I'm shivering from the cold, and my words come out in white puffs.

"All I can think is that he was trying to get this note to me. Maybe something happened when I went home that last night, because he was gone by morning and he never had a chance to give it to me. And then I think back to all the people who were in the room when I was there, and maybe he couldn't risk giving it to me then, but I was there so much it's all a blur. I can't keep it all straight. I found it just a few days ago in the wooly sweater he always wore over his hospital gown. It was sitting in a bag for weeks and then I went through it all and… God. He was begging for help. I'll never forgive myself. Maybe he didn't want someone to find he'd written it—someone he was afraid of. I don't know," she says, tears welling in her eyes as she pushes the paper shreds back into her pocket.

"Why else would it be torn up?" she asks before I even have a chance to respond to all this shocking information. "I mean, that's all that makes sense, right? For why it's torn up? It's like he was afraid of someone finding it, I mean why else? He was trying to warn me—to get help, and he was afraid the person who was after him would find it. I know how that sounds, but

I have gone over this a million times in my head, and what other reason could there be?"

"Shit" is all I manage to say.

"My poor Otis, I couldn't help him and he was all alone there with someone trying to hurt him. But who would want to hurt Otis? I mean, who in the world?" she says, and that's exactly what I was going to ask.

"And you told all of this to Detective Riley?" I ask.

"Yeah right. What do you think he'd say—that Otis had a stroke and we didn't know the extent of the damage, so this was probably some delusion or paranoia?" she says, and he would have a point, of course. "But I know my Otis, and he seemed *different* those last days. I know, of course, a stroke makes people different, but I still know him, Florence. I know him, and I saw his eyes change. Now I think it was fear, not just being sick, but…this…" She half motions to the papers in her pocket.

"I can't let it go. I can't have his cries for help literally in my hand and blow it off as paranoia. I need to find out the truth. And fine, people can think whatever they want about me, but what about Mack…and poor Shelby Dawson. It was a warning to them too."

"You think he meant they're in danger?" I ask. She closes her eyes and blows a cone of white mist into the frozen air, shaking her head.

"I don't know," she says. "Yeah. Maybe."

"This could all be connected," I sort of mumble to myself, thinking about any reason why, even if he was suffering from some delusion, he would bring Mack and Shelby into it. That's pretty specific for a delusional man's imaginings. Winny holds her head in her hands and I put my arm around her shoulder. We shiver together for a few moments.

"I believe you," I say.

"You do?" she asks, straightening up and looking at me with wet, desperate eyes.

"If there's some motherfucker out there responsible for this, we're gonna find him," I say. She puts her arms around me and cries while I hold her and tell her it's going to be okay.

And that's the moment everything was set in motion. I didn't know it then, but hunting a killer would become my new hobby, not gardening, as it turns out.

4

Shelby

It's that sad, dead week between Christmas and New Year's where everything feels weird and you are allowed to eat stocking chocolates or cheesecake for breakfast, so I sit inside the front office at work and nibble the leg of a deranged-looking gingerbread man, trying to keep the dark thoughts away.

It took a year of therapy and a couple dozen self-help books to begin to feel grateful to be alive. Gratitude is the only way to escape the spiral down into the depths, they say. So I try to say a list out loud in the morning, counting all the blessings in my life. I am grateful for my girls, for my husband, I am grateful for the heat in my car and my job that I love, I am grateful for the sky, and slipper socks, and the air in my lungs, and gravity, and this fucking gingerbread cookie. And sometimes it helps a little, but it doesn't pull me from the depths as promised.

They found you just in time, be *thankful*. But when I look at my girls, and think about their fear, being locked in the car wondering where I was, there is no gratitude for being alive. There is nothing but white-hot rage. I can erase the terror I felt as the pain turned to numbness and then the world went dark. I can sometimes push the memory away for a whole day on a good day, but when I think about my babies crying in that car, I just… I have to stop the thought before I let it go any further in this moment, so I throw the rest of the cookie in the garbage and try to take a few deep breaths.

I carefully push myself to stand. One foot has a partial amputation. I'm lucky, they say. I can still walk and I lost two fingers on my left hand, what a miracle it wasn't worse. I know they mean well—every lovely friend and acquaintance who tries to say something positive like that, I know that. What the hell can you really say to someone after something like this? But also fuck them for trying to make anything about this positive.

I peer out into the rec room and see Millie sitting in front of the TV watching *Die Hard* and drinking from a jug of sangria, and Florence and Bernie playing chess at a card table covered in tinsel and Hershey's wrappers. I can tell from here that Mort is in a filthy mood by the way he holds his book in front of his face, silently protesting the movie choice, but still peers over the cover now and then to scowl at the screen.

It's the residents at Oleander Terrace who really pull me out of the depths, at least for short spaces of time throughout the day. The Ole is a small assisted living facility I manage where the residents have their own rooms and shared living space rather than their own apartments, but most of them are quite independent and only need limited care. I think most chose this place over fifty-five-plus apartment facilities because of the community. It's not a nursing home. They mostly do what they please. It's small and there's always poker or pottery class or dance nights and just people around in the common area to fill the void, but it still doesn't cure the loneliness. I may be jaded and half-crippled now, but I can still see that much clear as day.

Herb walks into the rec room in shorts and flip-flops despite the fact that it's nineteen degrees below zero outside. He cracks a Miller Lite and sits in a battered recliner next to Mort.

"Christmas is over," he says.

"So?" Millie snaps.

"So I recorded the Giants game, no more Christmas movies for cryin' out loud."

"*Die Hard* is not a Christmas movie, Herb."

"Bruce Willis is literally wearing a Santa hat as we speak," he says, gesturing to the screen.

"Mort, is *Die Hard* a...?" Millie starts to ask, but he cuts her off.

"It's a controversial question. I'm not getting involved."

"Oh, for Christ's sake," she says, refilling her cup from the sangria jug. Florence puts Bernie in checkmate and then sits at the table behind the sofa to continue a jigsaw puzzle that's been sitting half-solved for days. Herb takes the remote and puts his game on, and Millie gives him a passive "Up yours, Herb," as she opens a mini candy cane and starts playing Candy Crush on her phone instead.

I go into the rec room and sit across from Florence. The puzzle is a thousand pieces and features Big Foot walking through the woods. I try to shove a couple of pieces into place.

"I don't know the point of these," Florence says, tucking her white bob neatly behind her ears and blowing on a mug of coffee. "After I put all this work in, then what? Destroy it and shove it back in the box?"

"That's life, Flor. We put all that work in and what's the point? We end up in a box," Herb says without even taking his eyes off the game.

"Oh Jesus. Here we go," Millie mumbles.

"Hey, I wanted to ask you guys something." I change the

subject and I have to be careful with my approach because we lost our security guard, Kenny, who moved to Duluth last month and we're required to have one. And let's be honest, there is nothing more I want than a security guard when I know the psychopath who did this to me is still out there somewhere, but we have no budget for it because we have lost most of our funding and are at risk of shutting down. That is the *last* thing I want any of them to know. I do, however, want to find someone who will work on the cheap; a college student, maybe. The residents have all lived in town for decades, and even though everyone knows everyone around here, they *really* know everyone and Millie usually somehow knows all their personal business too, although I haven't worked out how she does it.

"I need to replace Kenny after the New Year. Any thoughts? I want it to be someone you like having around too."

"Ohhh, what about Griff Barlowe? I saw him down at the Y looking delightful in his swimming underpants… What are those called?" Millie asks.

"Griff is an accountant, why would he be our part-time security guard?" Florence asks.

"She said she wants it to be someone we like having around," Millie says.

"I don't think he'll be wearing his swimming underpants instead of a security uniform around here anyway," Bernie adds.

"No way we're hiring Griff. First off, we're not hiring a guy who wears a Speedo,"

"Speedo, that's it," Millie says.

Herb continues. "He'll literally bore us to death. He probably has tax jokes stored up to victimize us with. No. Plus, he's ugly as a pan of worms. Get your eyes checked, Millie," Herb says, still not taking his attention off of the TV.

"Evan Carmichael is back in town," Millie says, ignoring Herb.

"Right, I heard that. That's an idea," I say.

Now that I think about it, I hadn't thought about him for the job, but I do remember that last week, when I heard that he was back in town, it was one of those rare occasions when I took my attention off of my own problems and sat in a moment of quiet to think about what a lovely thing it is that his father died and left him his old house. That sounds awful, but his father was a raging alcoholic and the fact that he held on until sixty-two is a mystery to us all. He once got so drunk down at Dickie's Tavern, he sold his car for forty bucks to the woman who called bingo so he could buy more booze. I think that was actually the tipping point where he just stopped leaving the house because he had no way around after that and just got sicker and sicker. What a way to go.

I heard through the rumor mill—not that it's reliable, but still—I heard that Evan is going on two years on disability and hates it and would rather be working. Maybe he'd take the gig for the insultingly low rate that we can afford to pay in exchange for a sense of purpose. Of course that's not how I'll spin it to him—that sounds pitying. He could be...very needed here. And who doesn't want to feel needed?

He moved down to Minneapolis after junior college and became a cop, which was surprising to me because he was quite the dork in high school. I could see him becoming a theater arts major or something, but I guess people grow up. I thought he was kind of dreamy in school, actually, but I don't think he ever knew it. I don't know the details of it all, but I know he was shot on duty by a teenager trying to hold up a gas station for the measly eighty bucks in the register. The teen only went to juvie for two years because of his young age and poor Evan had a bullet that took out the vision in his left eye, and he's no longer able to serve.

I think him moving back here where all the folks that care about him are will probably do wonders for him. Maybe I can get Clay to help fix up his dad's house. That place has to be a total shitpile after all these years of a man holing up in there. I heard he ordered a pallet of Colt 45 to his house from Flynn's Liquor once, but that's probably an exaggeration.

"What do we need a security guy for? I was in the navy," Herb says.

"So what? You think anyone is gonna give this loose cannon a gun?" Millie asks the room, pointing to Herb.

"Who said anything about a gun? I got a TenPoint Titan crossbow in my storage unit," he replies.

"Lots of good it does us in your storage unit, genius," Millie says.

"Returning violence for violence multiplies violence, adding deeper darkness to a night already devoid of stars," Mort says from his chair in the corner. He's currently reading his way through all the classics and is having trouble garnering any enthusiasm about this from the rest of the gang.

"Pardon?" Bernie says.

"Who wrote that? Can anyone name the author of the quote?" Mort asks in a soft voice.

"Shel Silverstein!" Herb guesses because he tries to support his friend when he's in the mood.

"You think it's Shel Silverstein?" Mort asks, dismayed.

"Well," I change the subject. "I think trying Evan is a great idea," I say, hearing Heather come into the front office to take over second shift. "I'm bringing the girls to Mack's for dinner. I'll bring the leftover scones for you in the morning," I say, pulling my down coat off the back of an armchair and wrapping a knit scarf around my neck.

"I'd prefer a rack of lamb myself—there's enough sugar around here," Bernie says. I smile at him and tell him I'll see what I can do. I say my goodbyes, wave to Heather, and make my usual rounds. Even though I don't need to, I like to make my way down each hall and check on the folks who like to keep to their rooms. I hear Elvis's "Blue Christmas" play from Lu-

cinda's cracked door, and strings of colored lights flicker from
Wally's miniature tree. There's a creepy Santa statue that has
a motion detector so he waves and shouts Merry Christmas at
you when you pass by, but the mechanism stopped working
and now it sounds like he's choking on something instead. I
finally unplug him and watch the light inside of him dim and
then die, and I bring him outside with me to toss him in the
dumpster. His time is up.

When the frigid air hits me, I decide to just leave him in a
snowbank for now and rush to my car to get the heat going,
but as I approach the car, I see something stuck from under my
windshield wiper. For a moment I think it's a take-out menu,
but who would be out here in this weather passing out menus?
When I get closer, I see it's a red envelope. My hands begin to
shake involuntarily.

The wind howls and snow whips at my face, so I grab the
envelope and jump into my car, locking the doors. I turn on
the ignition and just look around a moment, giving the back
seat a paranoid glance even though the car was locked and no
one could be there. I look up and down the snow-covered two-
lane road on either side of the building. Nobody.

I look at the envelope in my hands and can't imagine what
it could be except maybe a Christmas card from, I don't know,
Chris, the janitor who left earlier. Something, *anything* that
would just make perfect sense and have me laughing at my
paranoid self in a minute, but my gut is telling me something
very different.

I open the envelope with my heart in my throat and read the
words scrawled on the small square of thick paper tucked inside.

*"I told you what would happen if you went public. I won't kill you,
I'll make everyone around you pay, remember?"*

5

Mack

The snow never seems to stop. There are flurries this morning as I pull on my parka and push my feet into snow boots. I take a deep breath before I step out into the dark, frigid 5:00 a.m. air. My feet crunch and squeak over the packed snow on the sidewalk I haven't had the energy to shovel because who can keep up? I sit shivering in the driver's seat of my car, blowing on my hands, waiting for it to warm up and then drive the short ditance to open the Firefly.

When I get to the cafe, I plug in all the strings of fairy lights hung over the window frames and click on the flameless candles on each table. Even though it's early January and Christmas is over, I keep the cozy feel people have come to expect from the place year-round—the wood tables and chairs and roaring gas fireplace in the corner next to stacks of hardcover classics. That was Leo's idea—make the place an experience—

fuzzy blankets on the leather couch near the fireplace, throw pillows, dark, moody colors. If an Irish castle and a New York bookstore and a ski chalet all had a baby it would be this place, he'd say. It never made much sense and never mind asking him how all three of them would achieve procreation together, but nonetheless, it is the coziest place probably in the tristate area, and that's a comfort to me now.

I preheat the ovens and turn on some Billie Holiday that pipes softly through the speakers. Before I take off my coat, I make the first pot of dark roast, pour myself a generous mug, and sit in front of the fire to thoroughly warm up before getting to work.

I stare at the flames and think about Leo the way I do most mornings. The tears don't come anymore, though. Now that it's been over a year and I learned what I have come to learn about him, the tears have just stopped, which is worse, I think. At least crying was a short-lived catharsis, and now...there's a stir of something inside that builds with nowhere to escape. I can't tell if it's anger or unthinkable loss, or the deep, unsettling torment of not knowing what the hell happened.

He left us broke and I haven't even managed to be able to really, fully admit it to myself, let alone tell anyone. I haven't even told Shelby, God help me. Twenty years ago, fresh out of college, we opened our first pizza place. I was a baker. He majored in business and finance, so it was kismet. We opened a few more locations, and then sold them five years later for a hefty payday. A comfortable life. Then, he opened a few other businesses and did some investments, but this cafe was my baby, so I ran it. I was happy to settle into one place and we were stable enough for him to dabble in other businesses because we kept a solid nest egg and that was the deal—the promise. We were happy, we were looked up to.

I didn't know right away. Mercifully, I got to go through the initial stages of shock and police and interviews completely ignorant of his theft and deceit. But then a few weeks in, auto payments on household stuff were missed, and I started trying to delve into the finances myself until we could find him. Because of course we will find him. What a shock I was in for. I found credit card statements—secret cards that he went into debt on to pay bills and payroll on the two pizza shops he bought. Everyone knows he lost those businesses a couple of years ago, but that was post-COVID—that was the same hardship every restaurant dealt with. At least that's what everyone thinks. Thank God that's what they think, because it seems nobody knows about his gambling addiction and that he lost all of our savings, retirement, and multiple businesses and hid it from everyone.

Sometimes I wonder if he ran because it was only a matter of time before I found out we had nothing left. I've spent months and months wondering and sobbing into pillows and hating him, then forgiving him and begging God for him to come back and that we would work through anything—that he had an addiction and we can get help and make it right... and then the next day I think of Rowan and what he's done to her future, and I hate him again, and it's all so exhausting I can barely breathe.

I close my eyes, sip my coffee, and take a nice long sigh before walking the creaky wood floor to the back kitchen to start gathering ingredients for cranberry scones and apple turnovers. I top off my coffee and pop a very small Lorazepam under my tongue to get my nerves through another day. I touch my fingertips to my favorite blue bowls—porcelain delftware, and feel a sort of indescribable ache. Maybe it's gratitude that it's still mine—that the house and cafe were paid off, and so far I can't dig up any second mortgages or incurred debt I don't know about. But I fear every day that some other shock like that could surface. The length he went to steal and hide it all is astounding. He cooked the books like the finance expert he was and took out payday loans. For Christ's sake, he actually borrowed from loan sharks, which I thought was something that only happened in B movies. Or maybe the aching feeling is simple hatred for a man who lied to me for years and stole everything I ever worked for out from underneath me.

I hear the bell above the front door jingle and Mort and Herb from the Oleander's shuffle in, shivering beneath their giant overcoats. They sit on the burgundy leather couch in front of the fire, and Mort picks up the paper.

"Hiya, Mack," Herb says, pulling off a scarf and shaking snowflakes out of it into the floor.

"Morning." I smile. They don't need to order. A black coffee, and a chai tea with milk. A cheese Danish for Herb, and a plain bagel for Mort because he could do without the diabetes, thank you very much.

"Twenty-two below zero this morning, oofta," Herb says as I place their usual on the coffee table in front of them.

"You're wearing flip-flops," I say, staring at Herb's feet.

"Well, but I got the socks on with 'em," he says, biting into his Danish.

"You sure do," I say, and pat his arm before making my way back to the coffee bar. A few very cold patrons rifle through the door and take a window-front two-top. I used to run this place like an owner, and now I'm waiting tables and making lattes with hearts on top, and earning tips every day until I have to bring in a few sparse staff for lunch rush. But I try not to think about that now. I don't need to put on a happy face; but I need to arrange my features in an acceptable way as to not scare off the customers. Small towns are funny. I have the undying support of many, but still a lot of folks who feel uncomfortable and don't know what to say to me because I am a reminder of tragedy. The fact that it's all still out there unresolved makes people uneasy. And there are probably a few who think I killed him and am bound for an episode of *Snapped*, but today I am trying to just get through today.

On my way to bring a teapot to the window table, I see Shelby barrel in the front door with the twins. She tells them to pick something from the pastry case and continues to peer out the front window, sporting pajamas under her parka with her hair standing in a wild side ponytail. It's her usual fashion statement these days, so that part's not shocking, but she looks frazzled.

I know coming here at all has been a slow process for her. She waited six months to step foot back inside these doors, but in true Shelby style, she wasn't going to let some psychopath take her away from her best friend's business *and* the place the girls practically grew up in. He didn't get to have that, take that away from her, so she's done a better job than I would have of coming back and compartmentalizing the trauma.

Still, it can't be easy, even after all the time that has passed.

"What are you looking at?" I poke her on my way back to top off Herb's and Mort's drinks.

"Billy Curran."

"Everyone's always looking at Billy Curran—he has a nice peach," Mort says, and we all look to Mort. "That's what Millie tells me anyway."

"He's in the construction business, why would he have any peaches?" Herb asks.

"It means his heinie, his butt, Herb. You should read a book sometime," Mort continues, reading the copy of *The Wind in the Willows* he plucked from a shelf.

"You read about guys with nice peaches in those books? No thanks."

"Why are you looking at Billy Curran?" I ask.

"Because I saw him go into The Angry Trout and I said, 'It's not even 7:00 a.m., a little early, don't you think?' And he said he's doing some renovations. Did you know about this? He said he's taking over the bar. I didn't even know he was back. He lives in Milwaukee. Linda Curran told me that Lou would rather be buried alive than step down from running the Trout." Shelby walks away from the window, exasperated, and looks at what her girls are pointing out in the glass case. She sits them at a table with apple muffins and pours herself a cup of coffee.

"No school today and they're still up with the roosters," she says, chugging the first few sips of coffee. "So, seriously what the hell? It's gotta be big news that nice-peach Billy is back. I haven't heard a thing. Lou didn't die, did he?" Shelby asks, propping herself on a bar stool, pouring stevia packets into her mug.

"No," I say. "Billy's been in and out of town a lot for the last year or more, helping out. Lou can barely see anymore and Linda is never at the bar. It's overrun by college bartenders they hire, giving away shots by the dozen, so it's probably a good thing he's finally stepping in."

"Yeah, all that is good and well," Shelby says, "but it's weird. Why would he leave the city and his job…and does this mean Nora is gonna be at the bar now? Christ. It's the only good bar in town. She'll ruin it for everyone. Oh Lord. She'll probably talk him into turning it into a nail salon," she scoffs. "Get a napkin, Poppy, for goodness' sake. That's your school jacket." Poppy hops over to the coffee bar and wipes hot cocoa off her collar. I sit next to Shelby on a bar stool.

"Well, Nora will not be moving back." I smile conspiratorially, relishing in having any bit of gossip before Shelby gets a hold of it.

"Shut up!" she says, hand to heart.

"She left him for an anesthesiologist she works with…that was like two years ago."

"How the hell do you know that?" she asks, her mouth gaping open.

"He told me. We have businesses facing each other. I've run into him a few times."

"Stop" is all she says, waiting for more.

"I guess the times he's in town, he's keeping to himself while going through the divorce without needing commentary from everyone. He just decided to come back full-time and take it over recently—like a few weeks ago. That's all I know."

"Well," Herb pipes in uninvited. "Linda used to show up at the Trout without her teeth and wearing a jungle-print house-coat. So get Billy with his nice peach in there and I think the whole town will appreciate that." Shelby notices the pair of them, smirks and sits on the arm of Herb's couch.

"I didn't know you two snuck out so early. You know we have coffee at the Ole?" she says.

"Mmm-hmm," Mort says, not looking up from his page.

"Did you know Billy Curran was obsessed with Mack in school?" she teases.

"Stop telling them stuff like that. He was not," I snap.

"He looked quite smiley this morning for a guy in subzero weather before the sun came up. I guess if I stopped working a hard manual labor job and handed draft beers to folks for a living instead, I'd be feeling pretty smiley too. Annnnd get-ting to gaze through my neon Bud Light sign in the window at my long-lost love across the lane."

"You're ridiculous," I say, picking up the small plate of crumbs leftover from Herb's breakfast and walking back to the counter when I see Billy Curran walk through the door. I stop midstep, surprised to see him, and of course Herb, Mort, and Shelby all stare. He is immediately self-conscious. He closes the door and looks down at himself, then back at us.

"Um, hello." He looks over each shoulder and again, back to us. "Everything okay?"

"Yes!" Shelby says. "You're just lettin' in all the cold air, is all."

"Oh, sorry," he says.

"Can you turn around?" Herb asks, and Billy raises his eyebrows at him.

Mort nudges Herb and shakes his head. "He has a parka on, you won't be able to see it." Herb silently agrees and goes back to his coffee. Billy shakes off a confused look and comes up to the counter.

"Morning, Mack," he says, smiling. Shelby bounds over and sits on a stool next to the register.

"Morning, can I get you something?"

"A couple of black coffees," he says, taking his card out of his pocket. Shelby gives me a "see, I told ya" look and holds up two fingers and mouths "Nora," rolling her eyes.

"Actually," he says, "I've been meaning to ask if you'd consider, I don't know, taking a look at the bar, offering an opinion."

"I've seen the bar," I say, handing him his coffee.

"Well, I'm trying to make some changes. I mean, it has a singing trout on the wall and the carpets have been there since the '70s."

"I would argue that that's what people like about it," Shelby says, butting in.

"Maybe. But in my attempts to remove the smell of stale beer and pee, I need to update a few things at least. You have the vibe here everyone likes. I thought you could offer some ideas—I'd pay you, of course." He sort of shakes his head like it's a stupid idea, and I'm about to say no.

"Of course, Billy. Not a problem." Because of course I can offer him this small kindness even though it comes with a smirk from Shelby.

"Oh, great," he says, and before he can utter another word, Shelby stands and walks behind the counter.

"Go ahead, I'll watch the register."

"Uh, I don't think he meant now, but thanks," I say giving her a "what the hell are you doing" look.

"No one's in this early anyway," she says, giving the few that are a dismissive hand gesture like they're the weird exceptions. Billy shrugs.

"I am painting today, so...but I know you have lot on your plate, so no rush, really," he says, and I wonder what he means by that. Most people think I started working nonstop to keep busy and take my thoughts away from an empty house and my missing husband; they don't know that I need to work just to pay the staff and my own bills. Does he know more than he's letting on? He probably meant nothing by it and it's just a thing people say, but I tend to overanalyze everything these days.

"It's really no problem," I say, taking off my apron and pulling on my coat that swallows me in its massive faux fur hood. I ignore whatever look Shelby is trying to throw at me and follow him out. It's still dark outside and the sharp air is a shock no matter how many times a day you get punched by it. I smile to myself when I think about Leo's description of the bar—if Applebee's and a dumpster had a baby, that would be The Angry Trout. I can't imagine there is much I have to offer, but it can't hurt to be nice for a few minutes.

We walk into the dim, silent space. All the chairs are piled upside down on tables, and it's warm and familiar. The red, tacky carpet is disgusting as ever with its dark gum stains and beer spills, but it's sort of soothing and nostalgic at the same time. The jukebox that's been there since I was a kid still lights up the corner, the karaoke machine on a tiny stage looks sad and lifeless in daytime hours, and the vinyl bar stools are still torn and ancient, really just the way people like it. This place hasn't changed in decades, and it's a nice comfort for folks.

He switches on the light above the pool tables and another behind the bar that illuminates the rows of glass liquor bottles. Then suddenly, I feel my shoulders being grabbed from behind. I scream and whip around, swinging my fist.

"What the fuck!" I yell, my heart in my chest…until I realize that it's Billy's father, Lou, and that I've hit him. In the face.

"Oh God!" Billy rushes over. Lou holds up his arms defensively and makes a whimpering sound that makes me feel worse than I thought possible.

"I'm sorry. I thought you was Billy. I…I wasn't trying to…" Lou stutters, cowering.

"Oh, I'm so sorry!" I say. "Oh my God, you…are you okay? I'm so…"

"It's okay," Billy says, helping his dad straighten up. Lou adjusts his glasses and blinks at me.

"I'm fine. I wasn't expecting anyone in here."

"Here," Billy says and helps Lou to his chair in the small office that's really more of a closet with a desk in it off to the side of the bar. He gets Lou back in front of the computer monitor, the desk piled with dusty files, crumpled paper, and Pepsi cans.

"Everyone's fine," he says, but I'm still holding my heart, equal parts terrified I was about to be attacked and mortified that I hit an eighty-seven-year-old man.

I pick up the coffee Billy set on the bar that must be for Lou and bring it to him.

"Here, God, Lou. You sure you're okay?" I ask, offering another apologetic look to Billy over the top of his head.

"Eh, I got worse from Linda when I walked in on her on the can the other day," he says, and that's when I see it.

Hovering over Lou's shoulder, in this grimy closet office, on an antiquated desktop computer, blinks a handful of file folders labeled "security footage." One says January to March 2018, April to June 2018…there are three months' worth in each file, all the way up to the present, January 2024.

"Oh my God!" I blurt.

"He's really fine," Billy says. "We can go ahead and…" He starts to move out of the office, until he realizes I'm pointing at the screen with my hand cupped over my mouth. He looks to where I'm looking.

"You have footage of that night," I say, not as a question but a statement because I know the camera on the front door faces the street and catches my cafe. "How?"

"What night?" Lou says, squinting at the screen through the thickest glasses I've ever seen.

"Dad," Billy says, placing a hand on his shoulder. Lou looks up at Mack and makes the connection.

"Oh, yeah of course. Sorry. 'Course I have footage of that night," he says matter-of-factly.

"All this time. Why didn't you give it to the police? What's on it?" I ask, my hands shaking, my heart speeding up. I can't read the look on Billy's face, but it's a mix of discomfort and embarrassment, if I'm right.

"The police asked about my camera, and I said there was nothing on it. That was it," he says, pushing his coffee aside with a curled lip and cracking open a Pepsi.

"What?" Billy asks, but he doesn't seem totally shocked. Is that because Lou is sort of flaky in general and it doesn't come as a surprise?

"So you told them you didn't have footage?" I clarify.

"No, I looked through it all when I heard what happened and didn't see anything on it, so when they came around, they didn't press me. They just casually asked about my camera and I said I got nothin'."

"And that was it?" I ask in disbelief. "This was Detective Riley, I guess, since he's assigned the case."

"Yeah, what's the problem?" he asks, clicking on his Tetris game and then thinking better of it and turning back to me with his arms folded across his chest.

"Lou," I say as gently as I'm able, although I would like to smack him again for his apathy right now. "Would it be okay if

I take a look through it myself?" I ask. I feel like Billy is about to protest, and he passively does.

"If he says he didn't see anything, are you sure you wanna—"

"Knock yourself out," Lou interrupts, standing. "Linda's got some Egg McMuffins she put in the glove box for me." He gestures to his chair for me to sit. "Ain't nothing there, though. I have hawk eyes." With that, he heads out to his truck for his glove box breakfast. I look at Billy, who has an indiscernible look on his face. He gives me a tight smile resembling concern, and I sit in Lou's chair and shakily hover the dusty mouse over the October–January file and click it open.

My breath catches when I see the date there, several rows down: October 19th. Each day is labeled. I click, and wait. The camera just sits there on the front of the Trout, mostly useless in general—just picking up cars passing, patrons coming in and out, hours of nothing.

"Why would he keep all of this—years back?" I ask Billy who's perched on the edge of the desk, sipping his coffee.

"He doesn't get rid of anything," he says, looking around as if I should be able to tell that from the state of the place.

I continue to fast-forward through that day's footage until I find 10:00 p.m., then I slow down and click frame by frame around the time Shelby was attacked. The camera sits on the front of the bar, and you can see my parking lot and front door, and I'm hoping for any clues—anything that shows someone breaking into the cafe. Maybe it's so I can know once and for all it wasn't Leo losing his mind and having some psychotic break that night the way people say—if nothing else, I'll take that.

I know Lou didn't see anything out of the ordinary, but I still feel tears forming behind my eyes and hear my shallow breath. This was the moment my life fell apart—and there's nothing there except a crow on a telephone line in the frame.

I sit back in my chair and sigh. I pick up Lou's untouched coffee and take a sip and then look to Billy with wet eyes and palpable disappointment. He pulls up a file box and sits on it next to me.

"I'm sorry," he says. But then I see movement out of the corner of my eye. I slam the coffee down and my hands flutter to the keyboard to rewind the frames.

"What was that?" I ask, breathlessly. "I thought Lou said he saw nothing."

"Well, in all fairness he can't see shit and this is the first I'm hearing about this."

I replay it, frame by frame, and then stop cold when I see a figure. I gasp. I rewind again. Out of nowhere, someone steps into the frame of the parking lot. My lot. Jeans and a hoodie, and they are just too far away to make out much more than that—I can't discern stature or age. They pull the hood of the sweatshirt over their head a fraction of a second after they walk fully into the frame and then disappear behind the cafe to the back door.

"Who the fuck is that?"

6

Shelby

I don't tell anyone about the note on my car. My instinct was to go right to the police, of course, but what will they say? It's a handwritten note. There's no way to connect anyone to it, and there's absolutely nothing they can do about it. The idea of fingerprints left behind crosses my mind, but the notion that Riley would dust for them is far-fetched. Someone going out of their way to threaten me and be that careless is also unlikely, so I decide to keep it for now. I need to think. The police have done jack shit to protect me thus far, so I just need to figure out what to do myself. What's the best way to proceed?

I thought it was over. The thing is, I never told anybody the whole story. They know an intruder locked me in...left me there, but they don't know the part before that. The humiliation. I can't even bear to tell my husband. I can't think about it. I just wanted it to be over. It *was* over.

But now he's back. Whoever it is, he's the only person who would know those cruel words threatened that night. If I tell anyone about him, he would make the people I love pay. He must have really thought I knew who he was, and after all the time passed, realized I don't, otherwise I would have had him arrested long ago. He thought I would die. To be fair, he didn't do a good job killing me and I was found. But it doesn't matter. He hasn't been caught, so why now? After all this time, why torment me now? What the hell did I do? It's pathetic to hear myself say why me, but really...why me?

I keep the note in my bag. I'll tell Clay or Mack and see what they think I should do, but it brings everything back and I just can't face it—I can't comprehend why someone is after me. Wrong place, wrong time is the only thing that makes any sense. It's hard to talk to Mack about it because of all the whispers about Leo. Did he have some mental breakdown? Was it him?

I walk the main hall of the Oleander's. Lois is untaping garland from the door to her room, Arnie chuckles from the recliner in his room in front of an episode of *Three's Company*. Everyone is safe, I keep telling myself. Everyone is fine. *I'm* fine.

I have Heather showing Evan the ropes around the place. He's agreed to a part-time evening shift, and I'm delighted. Heather does not have a reputation for being the sharpest knife in the drawer, but she's sweet as pie...so I make sure to pop in a few times and ensure it's all going smoothly.

She's looking at him with googly eyes, although he's far too old for her. He's my age and she's twenty-six, but by the Jim Halpert looks I have caught him expressing to her in return when she's not looking, I think we're in the clear there.

I come back into the rec room, which is really the main open area inside the front door next to the small office. It has a kitchenette, a Ping-Pong table nobody uses, a big community table and chairs, a plaid couch and scattering of mismatched armchairs. It's not the spa-like community living facility I wish we offered. It looks more like my parents' basement in the 1980s—a stack of board games and puzzles stacked precariously on a bookshelf, an old dartboard on the wall, a minifridge. It's tacky and kitschy, but we have all found a home here, so I guess nobody is really complaining.

I see Heather chatting to Evan at the card table where someone has finished the Bigfoot puzzle with the exception of one missing piece, which I am certain has Mort in fits. Heather's introducing everyone; they're all excited to have new blood in the place. I perch on the edge of the sofa next to Florence, who's plucking away at a laptop I've never seen her use before, and I pop open the foil off a leftover Santa chocolate from the candy bowl on the coffee table. Millie walks in and hands Evan a crumply reindeer gift bag, smiling proudly.

"Oh. Uh...thank you," he pulls out a rainbow-colored blob of yarn. "Wow."

"It's a pot holder," Herb says, trying to help explain.

"It's for you," Millie beams.

"Cool," he smiles, examining it.

"This is Millie. She likes to give a pot holder to everyone she meets," Heather says, patting Millie's arm, oblivious of Millie glaring back at her. I can see the words "up yours, Heather" practically forming on Millie's lips, but we have company so she just goes and sits down instead.

"It's the only thing she knows how to knit," Herb adds. "And she's flirting with you."

"Oh, take a pill. It's not like I'm walking around here in my bra and panties," Millie says.

"And the world breathes a collective sigh of relief," Herb replies, and I stifle a giggle.

"And this is Erb," Heather says, gesturing to Herb.

"Herb," Herb corrects, shaking Evan's hand, an unlit cigar hanging from his lips.

"Erb is a cigar collector," Heather says. Evan's eyes flit over to me, and I give a quick closed-eye shake of my head to indicate it's not worth asking. Heather was corrected by a teacher once in high school, after calling things like basil and cilantro "herbs." She was told that the *H* is silent. They are "erbs" and she's applied this knowledge to the first Herb she's met, and no one can tell her otherwise.

"Cigar aficionado, really," Herb says. "You a cigar guy? I got a few gems recently. Nicaraguan Perdomo if you're interested."

"You don't have to say yes," Florence adds, still clicking away on her computer. "Nobody wants to stand out by the dumpster in the freezing cold with you to smoke cigars, Herb." Then back to Evan, "Seriously. You can get cancer just smelling him."

"And that's Florence." Heather smiles, eternally ignoring the bickering. At that, Heather stands, smooths the front of her pants, and excuses herself to go and finish her office work. She possesses not one iota of a sense of humor, bless her.

"You can smoke a cigar with Herb or play video games with the guys or whatever you like really, you don't need to man the front door like a royal queen's guard or anything. We're just happy to have a little security—someone to keep an eye out," I say, and chills run along my arms thinking about someone out there in the frigid night—someone who's watching me.

"It's nice to be halfway needed again," he says. "And my father's house is so depressing and needs so much work that it'll give me a little break from all that."

"I can imagine it's a lot," I say, "but it's good to have you back."

"Good to be back." He smiles and picks at the edge of Bigfoot's ear, but I can imagine losing his big-city dreams and collecting disability while living in his neglected childhood home feels very far away from "good to be back," but I don't say that. I put the third foil chocolate I was about to unwrap back in the bowl and stand to go. We've already done all the boring paperwork, and I'm ready to get out of here and see my girls, so I pluck a strand of hair off of my sweater and tell him to call if he needs anything.

"And you're technically on shift from 5:00 to 10:00," I add "but Heather does overnights, so if you ever need to leave a little early or anything, I mean just let me know. We wanna keep you happy." I think about asking him not to tell anyone what time his shift is because I don't want anyone to know when we don't have security. I don't want them to know when we're vulnerable, but if someone was in my lot placing a threatening note on my windshield, I have the sinking feeling that I'm so fucked no matter what that none of this even matters—none of us are safe. His words "I won't even kill you. I'll just make everyone around you pay and make you watch," echo in my mind. I try to shake the thoughts away.

I head to the office and finish up a few items of paperwork, and after an hour, I hear Herb's distinct giggling, so I peer out to see what no-good he's up to when I see him pouring out a Windex bottle in the sink and washing it out. He hands it to Evan, who fills it halfway with his bottle of blue raspberry Gatorade and they poke each other as Heather walks through. I see Herb give a nod over to Evan, trying to control his snort-laughing, and Evan takes a drink of the Gatorade from the Windex bottle, sending Heather into a howl, and the whole gang in the rec room begin roaring with laughter. I know right away that Evan will fit in at the Oleander's.

I don't need him making everyone paranoid guarding the front door, like I said. I'm just happy to have a former police officer around who could shoot somebody if we really need him to...but the friendship he's quickly making with the gang is more than I could have ever hoped for. I find myself smiling as I walk to my car until fear sets in again—something primal that stops me in my tracks. I look at my car sitting alone on the packed snow that covers the lot, the streetlight above it illuminating the blowing snowflakes in a beam of light above my lonely-looking Nissan. I imagine all of the horror stories

I heard as a child—a man waiting in the back seat to wrap a cord around my neck and strangle me when I sit in the driver's seat; a man waiting underneath the car to sever my Achilles' heel with a steak knife when I approach. Or maybe he's lying in wait in a dark SUV a block away, ready to follow close behind and run me off one of the rural roads home. And there's nowhere to run—it's all thickets of trees and black two-lane highways for miles, and it's below zero outside.

I look back to the glowing triangle of light from the front door and feel a rush of panic—a feeling of being watched. I run back inside the way I used to run up the basement stairs as a child after convincing myself there was a monster at my heels, and rush through the front doors. Everyone looks up at me.

"Forgot my keys," I say, and then I go into the front office with my head down, knowing everyone is aware I probably had another panic attack. Heather's not in there now, so I close the doors and try to calm down. I can feel hot tears run down my face, and I can't afford to just break down. Clay has a shift later tonight and I need to pull it together and take care of the girls.

I'm not getting in that fucking car right now though, that's for sure. I call Clay and make him pick me up instead. He doesn't grill me on the phone. He just says that he'll pick up takeout from Dragon Wok and we will swing over and get the girls when their ballet lessons end at six. I wait for him at the front glass doors, telling everyone my car battery died and holding back tears until he arrives.

On the dark and quiet drive to the dance school, I crunch on a wonton and flip through radio stations. He doesn't press me because he knows I have…episodes…ever since the "tragic event." And I don't press him because I know how helpless and angry the topic can make him—he couldn't help me, and there are a few fist-shaped holes in the garage drywall to prove how much he wants to kill the person who hurt me. To add insult to injury, he's also taken on night shifts at the hospital again;

just front desk triage stuff to make ends meet because the bait shop we own barely breaks even. After spending his entire day there, watching his dream deteriorate with each slow, customer-less day, he is also overworked and worrying about me. I try to only tell him what I absolutely need to most of the time, so that the palpable tension stays at a manageable level.

When the girls are settled in the back seat, June clicks on the pink heart reading light clipped to the seat pocket and shows Poppy a picture book called *Grumpy Monkey* she checked out for her reading homework and they giggle at the illustrations with mouthfuls of orange chicken, which I usually wouldn't let them eat in the car, but right now a quiet ride home is more important today.

"'Norman was slumped. His eyebrows were bunched,'" I hear June read, sounding out some of the words slowly, then some more giggling and wrappers crunching.

"Good job, Pops," Clay says, making a right on Ivy Street.

"That was June," I say, a common correction.

"Great skills, Juju," he says instead, and they laugh.

Poppy's voice begins to read. "'I told you what would happen if you went p-p-public. I won't kill you, I'll make everyone around you pay, remember?'" Clay tenses, and I whip around in my seat and look at her.

"What are you reading? What the hell is she reading?" Clay slows the car down and looks in the rearview mirror, adjusting it to see the girls.

"What does it mean?" Poppy asks, holding out the folded note with an outstretched hand.

"Where did you get this?" I ask her, trying to stay calm, but I can hear the bite in my voice. She shrinks a little in her seat.

"It was on the floor," she says, pointing down. Jesus, it fell out of my pocket into the back.

"It's a play," I say quickly. "It's just the page from a play that Mort is working on, you know Mort. It's just lines a character is saying. But it's not for kids," I take the note from her and she shrugs and opens a fortune cookie. I stare at the note with a sticky orange chicken fingerprint on it now, and then fold it back up and shove it in my pocket.

Clay's knuckles whiten around the steering wheel and his neck blooms red blotches, but he doesn't say anything with the girls in the car.

After they're dressed in Dora jammies and sitting at the coffee table on the living room floor coloring next to the fireplace, I walk into the kitchen where Clay stands at the counter storing away Chinese leftovers. He's slamming lids on Tupperware and whipping chopsticks into the trash. When he sees me, he carefully places both hands on the counter, an attempt to stay calm, and simply looks at me.

"Can we sit down?" I say.

"No, tell me what the hell is going on. I'm not an idiot. I saw your face when you heard the words being read, so something has happened. What?" I don't respond right away. He opens the fridge and almost pulls out a beer, but he is headed off to a shift at the hospital, so he just slams the fridge with a sigh and stares up at the ceiling for a moment. I sit at the table.

"It showed up on my car yesterday. I was trying to find a time to tell you." He sits, as calmly as he can manage. It's the first time I've seen someone's face drained of color yet look like their head could explode simultaneously, and I understand it. It's the way I feel when I think about the girls being hurt—the utter helplessness and rage it evokes.

"Where? Here?"

"No, at the Oleander's. After my shift. It was just on my car." He stands, then sits and clenches his fists, and he takes a slow breath, then he stands again, walking over to the alarm system we put in after the incident last year, fuming. He punches in the code and arms it.

"This stays on when you're home. It's not just for nighttime anymore. Anytime you're in the house, this is on," he says, and I don't try to explain what a nightmare that is with the girls running in and out and forgetting to disarm it and the crushing noise it makes and the police calling just for me to say, "oops sorry. False alarm." I just nod in agreement.

Before he can say anything else, I hear the girls' video end and the local news begin. I head in to turn it off when I stop cold, and I turn to see Clay in the frame of the kitchen door with his eyes fixed on the TV, also frozen in place.

There is a video playing as the top story.

"Authorities have obtained a video that might lead to clues from the frightening events that took place last October when a Rivers Crossing resident was assaulted at Firefly Cafe on 6th Street. The video has never been seen before, and it seems the bar owner across the street had security footage which is just now surfacing.

"It shows a figure walking into frame, pulling a hood over his face and then moving around to the back of the building. There is no footage of the man leaving the cafe which leads police to believe he fled out the back and into the woods behind it. The following images are of the police finding the victim just in the nick of time." The newscaster with a blond bob and tight lips disappears from the screen and I see my car parked there, police surrounding it. Then I see myself being wheeled out on a stretcher like a corpse.

"Go brush your teeth," I snap at the girls who just blink back at me, confused by my sudden mood change.

"Now, please!" I say and they scramble to their feet, looking crestfallen as they run down the hallway to their bathroom. The newscaster finishes up her short segment with...

"The owner of the cafe went missing on the same night and was never found, which has left local authorities baffled."

This is why now. This is why he's left a note and he's back, because first the criminal profiler on the news yesterday stirred the whole thing back up—maybe said something that hit close to home although who knows what that would be, it's all so generic—probably a white male, probably local, likely committed sexual crimes in the past. Useless information if you ask me.

And then, the next day, there is the first trace of actual evidence, and even if you can't make out the person in the image, he knows it's him, and maybe it could start to lead to something. Shit.

"Shit!" Clay hisses, echoing my thoughts. I see his clenched fists as he shakes his head at the ceiling, speechless. Then he pulls his coat on and hands me mine.

"Girls, stay inside. We'll be right back."

"What are you doing?"

"Come on," he says, pulling on my sleeve and I follow him reluctantly, shouting "Clay! What?" behind him, all the way out to the back shed. I stand shivering in the doorway as he pulls boxes off a wooden shelf. He tosses an empty gas can out of his way and mumbles his frustrations under his breath the whole while. I know what he's doing.

"I don't want to touch it," I say as he takes the handgun out of the lockbox. He knows this because I said I would take a few lessons and learn how to use it for his peace of mind when he started night shifts, and I did that, with protective gear and an instructor. I'm not shooting cans off tree stumps in the woods behind the house. That's what this is, and it's not happening.

"Did you even know where the key to the lockbox is?" he asks.

"Clay, I remember how to use it."

"How do I know that? How would you even get it if something happened? You insist on it not being in the house, but that doesn't work. Starting now, it's staying in our room."

"Clay," I start to protest, but he's right. I hate guns; I hated learning how to shoot it. This stranger who took so much from me that night forced me to learn to use it, and now I get to feel

so unsafe I keep a loaded gun in my bedroom. He sees my re-
solve weaken as my eyes flit from the gun to him, imagining
how I'll ever sleep again with this in the house.

"We'll still keep it in the lockbox. And I need you to refresh
your lessons," he says. I know he's trying to do something in
this moment to make him feel like he has some control, rather
than punching walls and going down to the Trout to drink.

"Fine," I say softly.

"Let's make sure you remember how to…" he starts to say
as he takes it out of the box.

"No! I'm not fucking shooting that thing out here. The girls
are inside. *Goddamn it!*" I scream which startles him. My voice
shakes, my whole body trembles with cold, then the tears come
and I start to panic again. He lays it down and wraps his arms
around me and we just stand there in the silence—the distinct,
eerie silence only the snow can create when it's killed off every
living, buzzing creature, and the night air rings in your ears.

"Okay," he whispers, and I cry into his coat sleeve, thinking that if someone wants to kill me, I'm glad at least to have
him by my side protecting me.

Inside, after I read the girls the whole *Grumpy Monkey* book
twice and they've fallen asleep, I go into the bedroom and look
inside the top drawer of the dresser where we decided the gun
would stay. The key is taped to the top of the second drawer,
and Clay has left for his night shift, so this should make me feel
better, in theory. I have an alarm and a gun—two things you
shouldn't need living in rural Minnesota. It's why we stayed
when we found out about the twins. There was a long stretch
of time when we thought kids wouldn't happen, and we had
begun making plans to start a new life in Milwaukee, but then
we stayed because it's so safe here. That's what we said. That's
what we thought.

Maybe we *should* move. Maybe that's the solution; except
Pops and Juju's grandparents are here. Their friends, our friends,

our business. Can I let him terrorize me out of my whole life? Maybe.

I go into the dim kitchen. I'm keeping the lights low so people can't see inside the windows, just in case. I pour a glass of Malbec and sit on the ottoman in front of the fireplace to warm my hands. After an hour of staring into the glowing embers and going down my mental list of every person in my entire life I've ever known, I still can't think of who I might have wronged to bring this all about. Who hated me this much, and why? But I've lived a pretty simple life in an equally simple town, and I can't come up with any names. I never do come up with anything but a splitting headache and an anxiety attack. So I ease into the old recliner next to the fire and open a copy of *Wuthering Heights* that Mort insisted I read because he was personally offended that I never had, and I top off my wine and cozy in, attempting to relax at least a little bit.

The story is, frankly, boring me to death, but I try to scribble down a few talking points so I don't disappoint him and hopefully make it seem like I'd read the whole thing. By half past eleven, I'm about to click off the lamp and head to bed when I hear a flicker, a pop, and then all of the lights in the house go dark. My heart pounds and I immediately look for my phone to turn the flashlight on, but I can't find it. And now that I think about it, I haven't used it since I ran back into the Oleander's to call Clay. Did I leave it there? Drop it?

I run down the dark hallway, fumbling and feeling for walls, to check on the girls. I don't want to start freaking out and wake them up. They're still asleep. I take the pink heart reading light clipped to Juju's bedside table and click it on, making my way back down the hall to search my purse and coat pockets for my phone. It's not there.

There's no way to call for help and my car is at the Oleander's. I'm…trapped. Oh my God. My heart is beating wildly, and a cold sweat climbs my spine. And then there is a tap at the front door and I freeze, paralyzed in fear as I stare toward the door with my mouth agape, holding nothing but a child's reading light for protection. I clutch my heart in the darkness and choke down a sob as I scream "Who's there!" into the silence. There is no answer.

I hear footsteps crunching over snow, and another tap-tap at the kitchen window, and I'm shaking so violently I drop the light I'm holding and crouch to the floor, covering my mouth with both hands and trying to breathe.

"Who's there?" I say again, but it comes out as a whimper. There is a hard knock at the front door, but nobody answers. "Who's there?" I bark again, my voice cracking. Then I run to the bedroom for the gun.

7

Mack

"Who the fuck *is* that?" The words reverberate in my mind still, later that night.

I pause the video at 10:31 p.m. and try to zoom in for the hundredth time, thinking something will spontaneously change, but it only shows a pixelated blur.

When Billy decided we needed a couple of Bloody Marys instead of coffee this morning upon seeing me suppress a panic attack while watching the surprise footage in his father's office, he sat with me and showed me how to email myself the large video file in Dropbox. And now I sit at home in my bed, wrapped in an electric blanket with Linus and Nugget burrowed under with me, their little Chihuahua noses pressed against my legs as I rewind and replay the short clip over and over.

I called Shelby nine times trying to warn her that the footage exists and that Billy's mother couldn't hand it over to the news fast enough, relishing being part of the mystery and spreading the drama of it all. And now I'm not only obsessing over this useless clip, I'm worried about her and why she's not answering.

I pick up my glass of wine from the nightstand and sip it, staring at the blur some more. I want to find something, anything in this footage, and when I do, I want it to make me certain it wasn't Leo in that frozen frame. God, just give me that. Just give me peace that he wasn't the monster I know people whisper about in this town. But I don't get to have peace because it's fuzzy and distant, and utterly stupid and pointless. And I can't tell. It could be a woman, for all this footage gives me. Lou was right when he said he had nothing. There's no value here. It could be anyone in the entire world. Then, when I replay again, I see the movement of something—the knitted end of a scarf it looks like—flitting into the edge of the frame. I was so focused on the figure, I hadn't paid attention to the foreground.

Chills run up my arms as I wonder…is that just a passerby? Or at that time of night, with a storm raging and with the place closed, is this a second person involved?

Suddenly I leap out of bed, startled by the dogs clawing their way out from under the covers and barking wildly, flying down the hallway, going nuts over something. I pull on a robe and slip my feet into slippers because it's freezing in here even though I keep inching up the thermostat. I assume they're losing their mind over an Amazon delivery guy, but they stop at the door to the basement instead. They scratch and howl at the gap between the floor and the bottom of the door. I try to pick up Linus, but he wiggles out of my arm and scratches at the door frame.

"What's down there, guys?" I say mindlessly as I move to the kitchen for a wine refill, because they bark at everything that moves, and it's always nothing more than the wind blowing usually, but then I stop in my tracks. Because shit…what *is* down there?

I stay frozen when I hear a rattling noise. I put my glass down and pluck a knife from the drawer and stand behind my dogs, looking at the basement door. The door itself is rattling slightly, not like someone is jiggling it because it's not locked, but like the wind is shaking it. *Wind*. In the basement.

"Shit, shit, shit." I keep the knife in hand and cover my head with the hood of my robe.

"Stay here," I tell Linus and Nugget as they jump at me in excitement. I walk out into the darkness and trudge through the deep, powdery snow around the side of the house. Snow is falling into the opening of my slippers and wind is cutting through my flimsy fleece robe.

"Fuckedy fuck," I mutter until I reach the back and see what I expected to see. The cellar door that opens from the back of the house with stairs leading down to the basement is wide-open. Okay, I didn't exactly expect to see that since it's been padlocked closed for a decade, but nothing else can explain wind coming up the basement stairs.

I lumber through the deep snow until I reach the open doors, thinking maybe the lock rusted and these winds finally broke it off, but when I see the lock up close, it's clear it was cut clean through. These doors must have been open all day, which explains why it's so cold in the house. Someone was here when I was at work. I feel my heart thump and the cold makes me shake, and I'm too afraid to shut the doors now, because what if I'm locking someone into my house? I'll stay out here and freeze to death while I call the police first—have them clear the place, I think. But shit, my phone is inside. I consider walking the quarter mile to the next house, but I'd probably die from frostbite in this robe. Why didn't I put on the boots by the front door? There's no way. I have to go back in.

Then I hear something. A tiny sound—like a whimper, or crying. I try to look down into the basement with only the small bit of moonlight behind me and the pilot light from the water heater down there to see anything by. I see movement. I'm frozen in fear for a moment, but before I can run, or think, or anything, the light catches two small eyes and I scream so bloodcurdlingly loud that I wonder if the neighbors might have heard and might come to help.

Then to my shock, I realize it's not a psychopath waiting to murder me. It's an animal. It cries again, and my instinct to help a hurt animal—an instinct that overrides almost all else in life— takes over, and I rush down the stairs to see what's happened.

It backs up and hides under the stairs, and I pull the cord for the basement light on and follow it. Once I see it cowering in the corner of the staircase I hold out my hand, and it doesn't come to me. It backs up into the concrete wall to the side of the stairs and presses its little forehead into it, but there is a *Braveheart* poster hanging there from a million years ago when Leo was gonna make this area a man cave until he gave up on the idea. The poster tears with the weight of the dog backing into it. The poor, sweet dog stands wet and shivering as I move toward it, and I realize the tear in the poster leads to an opening behind it. I rip the poster off the wall and see something that shocks me to my core.

It's a crawl space or hidey-hole or whatever you want to call it that's been chiseled out of concrete and covered with a Mel fucking Gibson poster. To hide…what?

I see only a couple of cardboard boxes inside. Holy shit. Leo went to a lot of trouble to hide something to the extent that even police detectives couldn't find it. Not that they looked very hard. "He left of his own accord" is the consensus, so they're not searching my basement for hiding spots to solve the mystery, that's for sure. First, I approach the dog, and it doesn't run now that I have it gently cornered and I'm speaking to him in the obnoxious baby voice I speak to my other dogs in, telling it to "come to mama."

"Oh, sweetheart," I say, reaching out and stroking its head.

"Poor baby." It lets me pick it up and wrap it in my robe, so I climb the stairs on the opposite side of the basement that leads to the door off the kitchen, and I'm greeted by Linus and Nugget growling and barking at the bundle in my arms.

"Oh, calm down guys," I grunt as I bring the dog into my bedroom and wrap him in blankets by the fireplace. When I go back downstairs, I carry a flashlight and an old padlock. I close the cellar doors and lock them again, this time from the inside so the lock can't be cut. Then I pull the boxes out of the crawl space and balance them one on top of the other, teeth chattering as I get the hell out of this awful dungeon and run up the stairs, back to the warmth of my kitchen as fast as I can manage.

Now that I know there's nobody in the basement and my adrenaline is pumping, I clear the rest of the house myself. My gut tells me whoever was in here came when I was away and is long gone. The dogs would have been losing their minds barking all night if there was still someone here, and this realization makes me feel a whole lot calmer.

Still I go room by room, whipping open closet doors and shower curtains, even kitchen cabinets as if some psychopath would contort themselves to lie in wait in my cereal cupboard, but you never know, so I check everything. Once I am confident it's all clear, I check all the door locks one more time and double-check the basement door off the kitchen too.

If somebody got through the cellar locks, they had to have been inside my house, and the thought sends waves of nausea through me. What did they want? What the hell were they looking for? *This?* I stare at the boxes. They are both filled with stacks of paper. That's it. Paper. Not body parts or gold bars, or a secret key to some safe-deposit box with a billion dollars in it. So what the hell was he hiding all this for?

Before I wrap my head around starting to sift through it all, I pour a bowl of food for the stray pup and grab some towels to dry off this little guy. Once he settles, I put down bowls for

Nugget and Linus and after they sniff the new guy for a minute, they calm down and eat. All of us sit on the floor in front of the fireplace and I begin sifting through the boxes I found.

"Where did you come from?" I ask as he leans into me, shivering. I tuck the blanket around him and hold him close to me. Of course he was looking for a warm place if he was out in this weather. He's probably a Lab mix, and I'm guessing wandered over from the Millers' farm because they always seem to have a dozen dogs they can't take care of.

"You look like a Gus," I tell him, and I keep him in my arms as we all warm up together, and I stare again at the boxes in front of me. My instinct should be to tear them open so I know what the hell could possibly be so important, but there's a bigger part of me that doesn't really want to know. Because right now there is still… I don't know, hope, I guess. But something in there might change everything. Did he have a mistress? Is he on the dark web as some sort of pedophile? A serial rapist? My mind is reeling. There was a moment I thought that maybe that crawl space was from the previous owner, but I can see Leonard Connolly written on every visible file poking out, so it's his, and my stomach lurches again.

The first files I look through are a few debts I didn't know about, and high interest loans he took out to pay them back. His work bag went missing when he did, and I've always found that hard to understand because he was out for drinks before he disappeared, so why would his work bag be gone? And I have always wondered if he kept all of his financial papers in his work bag to hide this shit from me…once I discovered all his debt the hard way, long after he was gone. I still wonder what's with his missing bag, but there are a lot of documents that he went to great trouble to make sure I never saw, so I guess most of this I probably already figured out by other means and online accounts I discovered. What else is there that *hasn't* already blown up in my face?

Then I see a file about the Oleander Terrace. I try to put Gus on the floor, but he presses his head into my chest again and I can't bear to put him down, poor baby, so I open the file with one hand, patting Gus's little back with the other, and page through the papers on the floor. I don't really understand what I'm looking at. I know Leo bought the Oleander's when his mother moved in there as some grand gesture, back when all his investments were doing well. His mother passed soon after that, but he kept the business, and as far as I know, it's still afloat. Even though Shelby, who had been there years before Leo and a partner bought it up, complains about it barely staying in business.

Leo always said most facilities like that are privately owned. Most are struggling or understaffed already, and he was gonna turn that around—a labor of love for his mother because he was thriving and thought he could do anything in business in those days. After his other investments went under and the Oleander's started to struggle, he blamed it on COVID like he did everything else, citing ninety percent of facilities were grappling with devastating losses, etcetera, etcetera, and I'm sure he planned to unload the place like every other one of his investments until…he vanished.

But what doesn't make sense is that it looks like the residents' personal checks to fund their stay, and the Medicare and Medicaid checks, are filtered through a bank account at Northview Bank. The deposit amounts don't match funds paid out to the Oleander's and Leo did all of his business banking through Affinity Plus. So what is all this? I truly cannot make sense of it, but it's something. And I know who might be able to make sense of it.

Miles Kessler was his business partner when they bought the place, but Miles didn't last more than six months, and now that I see this, I need to know why he left. Leo said it was because of Miles's problem with alcohol—that Leo needed to buy him out because it was affecting the business. Fair enough. I bet that if I call down to the Trout right now and ask for Miles Kessler, I'll be told he's hunched over an old-fashioned at the end of the bar next to the scratch-off booth, coat still on, by himself, and intermittently crying, like almost every night. He's a permanent fixture.

"Okay," I say to Gus. "You stay here and I'll be back," but he whimpers when I try to put him down and my heart breaks. I try again. "Come on, bubs, you can stay by the fire. Look, I have a puppy cookie," I say, taking out one of the boys' biscuits from my robe pocket. Linus sits up and gives me a look. Gus just leans his head into my chest.

"Oh, sweetheart," I say. And I know I won't leave him alone. He's still a puppy—a pretty big puppy, but still young, and scared after what he must have been through in the cold to wander all the way over here. So I find my big parka with the fuzzy hood, and I tuck him inside and he sits on my lap in the car as we drive through the snowy streets over to the Trout to find Miles at the end of the bar.

When I arrive, the place is busting at the seams with body heat and everyone's big coats and drunk voices. Strings of Christmas lights and garland still hang from neon beer signs and decorate the sides of the pool table. A woman sings a Pat Benatar song on the karaoke stage and it's warm and inviting as ever. I spot Miles immediately, as I knew I would.

Then I spot Billy behind the bar with a martini shaker in hand.

"Looks the same to me," I say, bellying up to the bar top as he serves cosmos to a couple of twentysomethings who look ridiculous in their light leather jackets and heels the way only young women can get away with when it's subzero outside, but attracting male attention is still more important than pneumonia.

"Thought I would wait until things thawed out in the spring before bothering to do any updates," he says smiling. And it's nice that he doesn't make my appearance here awkward since he did apologize a dozen times for his father this morning and I still sort of just ran out of the place without saying anything to him after I got the footage I needed, leaving him two Bloody Marys to himself. He doesn't mention it.

Then, to my horror, I notice I'm still wearing my house slippers and I don't have a stitch of makeup on and I'm suddenly very conscious of how disheveled I must look. I can feel myself blushing in front of him and simultaneously questioning why I care so much.

"You have a dog," he says without a note of judgment and I become a bit less self-conscious and remember that's really part of the reason I stay here. A woman in fuzzy slippers and a man's parka with a dog hidden inside doesn't really turn heads in these parts.

"This is Gus. He has no owner, apparently. It's a long story. Can I buy some jerky from you?" I ask, pointing to the jar on the counter.

"On the house," he says. "May I?" he asks, and I nod. He opens the jerky and feeds it to Gus.

"He likes you." I smile, because the gesture warms my heart a little bit, and I notice the tiny moments like this ever since my life became like living in the pits of hell most days.

"If I had to guess your drink…" he says.

"It's whatever Miles is having," I say, and Billy raises his eyebrows, looks down to Miles and then back at me with a nod.

"Okey doke."

"Thanks," I say, and I move down the bar and sit next to Miles. He doesn't acknowledge me. Now there's a man belting out a Neil Young song on the mic, and it makes Miles look even smaller and sadder, if that's possible. I tap him on the arm, and he looks up at me with swollen, bloodshot eyes, but he smiles broadly.

"Heya, Mackie Mack! Whatcha doin' here? Let me buy you

a drink. I won ten bucks on the scratch-offs," he says proudly, showing me his win.

"Heya, Miles," I say back. "I just came to ask you a question actually, so how about I buy *you* one and maybe you can help me out."

He looks around and then points to himself. "You came lookin' for me?" he says, and before he gets the wrong idea or I gag, I just jump right in.

"Yeah, listen. Can I ask you about when you and Leo went in on buying up the care home—the Ole?" I say, and his head drops.

"Oh" is all he mutters.

"Oh what?"

"I didn't have nothin' to do with all that and I can prove it," he says, and my heart speeds up a little bit.

"With what?" I ask.

"I left as soon as I found out what Leo was doin'."

"Wait, he said he bought you out because…" I don't mention the alcoholic part. "Because you weren't pulling your weight," I say instead.

"That's so fucking typical. That's what he said, huh? Me. After everything, he coulda come up with a story that didn't make me the bad guy. Well, ain't that some bullshit. I shoulda turned him in, shit."

"Miles. Turned him in for what?"

"Oh, come on. You gotta know all the shit he was into by now. He was skimming part of all the residents checks into his own account before they went through to the Oleander's system. You'd think stealing from your own business would be an idiot thing to do, but he realized there was no money to be made with the place and I don't know how he was planning to unload the whole thing, but I'm sure he had something in mind," he says, and Billy comes over and places two Manhattans in front of us.

He aims a concerned look my way when he sees the expression on my face, but I shake my head with a tight smile to indicate it's fine and he doesn't have to toss Miles out or anything, which he looks like he'd be happy to do. I feel sick to my stomach. I'm also a bit surprised at how easily Miles is offering up this information, but I guess he's hammered, and also probably keen to defend himself if trouble around Leo or money is being stirred up with his name attached.

Everything I've learned about the family man that I loved—that everyone adored and looked up to—has changed me, chipped away at who I thought I was bit by bit, but this is vile. Stealing from the elderly who already have little enough to be living at the Ole? My God. Who was he? How could I have not known any of this?

I'm not some idiot who turned her head to all her husband's indiscretions or pretended shit wasn't happening to keep a marriage together. We talked about everything. *Everything*, I thought. He was my best friend.

After almost a year and half, I have been able to absorb some of the shock, but this… Was he really this person?

"So you never told anybody? You just let him steal from vulnerable people?" I say, and it comes out just as accusatory as it sounded in my head.

"Look, Mack, he paid me out, plus a nice bonus. I walked away. It was his mess, and I wasn't gonna ruin his life," he says, slurring his words but trying to mask it. "If he let the place go under and lost his investment, nothing new. Nobody was gonna die. The residents would be bussed off to different homes on the outskirts, and that's shitty, but I didn't make it my problem. Couldn't afford to," he says.

I blink at him. There is a lull in the karaoke, and I hear the rise and fall of the conversations around me. One of the high-heel girls barks out a high-pitched laugh. Billy's voice asking people what they're having and placing napkins on the bar, bottle tops popping, a karaoke host trying to fill the void with awkward forced enthusiasm for the next singer. It all swirls around me while it sets in that Leo was a terrible fucking person. The love of my life was a thief and a really good liar.

"Thanks," I say to Miles, sliding my Manhattan next to his half-empty glass for him to have and leaving a twenty on the bar. There's nothing else to say to him. That's exactly what those checks and that paperwork I looked through mean. It's all clear. I just want to go home and somehow try to make sense of it all.

Is this what got him killed? Does someone know what he did?

Shelby can't possibly know or she would have told me. I know she would have. I need to find out, though. Because what happened to her that night is clearly connected, and what if there are things she knows about this that she's not telling me?

As I get up to leave, I see Billy out of the corner of my eye wave the lowball glass in his hand at me and call my name. For the second time today I'm just walking away without a word, and I don't have the energy to care that he probably thinks I'm as unstable and broken as everyone whispers about. I just carry little Gus to the car and I wait for it to heat up before I pull away.

I see the orange glow of the bar windows and hear the music spilling out into the parking lot. The warmth and the friends and the laughter—the happiness I can't imagine ever truly feeling again—my whole body aches with a longing to go back in time and remember what it's like before I lost myself.

I look over at the box of files I brought just in case Miles acted like he didn't know what I was talking about so I could show him. I dig around inside one more time, waiting for the damn heat to start blowing through the frozen car vents and the window to deice.

I look at the Oleander file again with such a feeling of shame, even though it wasn't me who took their money. Then I see one more manila envelope in the box. I pull it out and see paperwork for an account at Northview Bank. There's a password written on the back.

Holy shit, it has all of his routing and account numbers. With trembling fingers I pull out my phone and find the bank's website, and go to the log-in page. I use the account number and the scribbled password, and the account opens. All of his activity is right there in front of me.

Blood swooshes between my ears and my head feels light as I try to catch my breath. Tears begin to well behind my eyes when I see it.

"Oh my God, oh my God, oh my God," I mumble as I shakily scroll through the page. Gus cries upon feeling me panic. I try to catch my breath. The screen blurs through my tears as I take in what I'm seeing.

This is Leo's secret account. The last withdrawal was yesterday. That son of a bitch is still alive.

8

Florence

I scream bloody murder when Shelby finally opens the door because she has a gun pointed at us. A gun, of all things! I explained that when she didn't answer the door, Herb went around the side to see if she was in the kitchen, and then we thought we'd try the door once more because she must be home this far past the girls' bedtime.

"What the hell are you doing here?" Shelby asks breathlessly, holding her heart and sitting herself down on the nearest armchair to breathe.

"The power is out at the Oleander and Heather didn't know who to call."

"Well, why didn't you call me?" she says, and she still seems quite sour with us. She places the gun in a box and locks it, then blows out a long slow breath and tries to be gentler with us. "She should have fucking called me. A first course of action before giving me an actual heart attack."

"We did, dear," I tell her. "Call you. Eight times."

"Oh. Shit."

"Where's your phone?"

"I don't know, it literally vanished. Okay, wait, what about the generator? You're telling me the backup generator didn't come on either?"

"I don't know much about generators, but it appears not."

"Louis Gomez in room nine is a wizard with that sort of thing—well, you know that, but he's still at his daughter's for the holidays," Herb adds.

"Okay," Shelby says. "Damn. Everyone's okay?" she asks and we nod. "So, we need to get someone over there. Did Heather call anyone else to help?"

"Well, after she couldn't reach you, Mort suggested trying Evan or maybe Clay to come take a look, but then she just started crying saying everyone was gonna die, so we thought we'd take over. Plus Evan was off shift and lives across town and you mentioned Clay was at work, so we figured this was best," I say.

"Right," Shelby says. "Shit. Okay. Wait here a minute and just…make yourselves at home while I set up the portable generator heater in the girls' room and try to find my damn phone."

We pull quilts from a pile by the stack of firewood and bundle up as the house gets colder. Everyone around these parts has generator-powered heaters and firewood. We just wait out a power outage in bad storms as a way of life. Shelby pokes her head back around the hall corner and adds…

"In the meantime, please call Willard's HVAC, will you Florence? Tell them it's an emergency." And I do. At least nobody is connected to any medical equipment or anything. It's not that sort of place. There are a few gas heaters and fireplaces at the

Oleander's too, so the worst of it will be missing a *Great British Bake Off* marathon and a lot of complaining, but they'll live.

Herb's the only resident who still has a driver's license. Bernie has an old Firebird he stores in the back lot and spends summer days trying to restore it, but I've never actually seen him drive, so I can only assume Herb is the only one who still does, but that's not the reason I keep him as a friend, mind you; don't get the wrong idea about that. He smokes cigars in the car so I earn my rides each time putting up with that filth. I told him it smelled barnyardy and he said actually some cigars are supposed to smell barnyardy and musky but that I was incorrect and his smelled like wood and leather. I told him I just bought a new cherry blossom–scented shampoo and I preferred not to waste my nine dollars on cherry blossom shampoo only to smell like a barnyard or an old book, and could he wait ten minutes until we arrived and smoke it outdoors. The saga is never ending.

"I think she meant sit here and don't touch anything when she told you to make yourself at home," I tell Millie as she plucks through the bottles on the rolling bar and holds one up. The flames from the fire are too dim for me to make it out. "Chocolate vodka," she explains. I didn't know they made such a thing.

"I think we could all go for a drink," Herb says, warming his hands in front of the fire. It's no use telling them that maybe now's not the time, and let's deal with getting heat to thirty-five seniors before they freeze to death, but I let them have their fun because I guess there's not much we can do except get the right people over there to help.

After Shelby sets the girls up in one bed with extra blankets and a heater, and after Willard's is on the way to the Oleander's, she joins us by the fire and we huddle in—Shelby on the floor in front of the ottoman, and Herb sitting on the hearth. Me and Millie in armchairs with blankets across our legs. We're used to whiteouts and power outages up here—we're built sturdy for it—but right now, knowing there's some psychopath out there on the loose, it takes a different shape, and I can tell everyone is on edge.

"I gave her a list for emergencies," Shelby says, taking the Baileys away from Herb who tried to take a swig straight from the bottle, placing it back down on the coffee table.

"I mean what if it were a fire? Would she call me and send you all over town before calling the fire department?" Shelby seethes, and she has every reason to be worked up.

"She said she didn't want to get the bill from Willard's if it was something Clay or someone could fix," Millie says and I see the expression on Shelby's face shift when she hears this. We aren't supposed to know there are money troubles. I don't know much, really. I wish I did—just that things are tight, so I think Heather was trying to help, bless her.

"Herb wanted an egg foo young anyway, so we were headed to the Super Jumbo on the way," I say, patting Shelby's back.

"If Willard's can't get it back up and running, we'll call Helping Hands—that transport service—in case we need to bus everyone over to the Y for the night. God, I hope not," Shelby says.

"Willard's is heading there and will call back in thirty. Heather's a basket case, but they're all fine," I say, placing my phone on the coffee table so we all hear the call when it comes. Then I take a sip of the warming martini that's really just vodka and Baileys in a mug, but Millie can call it what she likes, it's hitting the spot.

We're all quiet for a few minutes and I look around Shelby's house in the flickering light. A cozy, one-hundred-year-old farmhouse, creaky floors, drafty windows. It's tidy but small, slightly dated with its wood paneling and kitchen wallpaper patterned with small fruit baskets, but it's like every other house in this neck of the woods, and people seem to like the nostalgia of it; the cabin feel. There aren't a lot of HGTV-style renos up here and I like it that way. Maybe it's because it's something to rely on—that it all stays the same here and feels like it's suspended in time, dated as it may be. It's a comfort.

"I didn't hear about blackouts or any lines down," Shelby says. She stands, goes to the counter and checks the gun box is locked for the third time and brings a few more candles over, which she sets on the coffee table to help light the room. It feels like we're sitting around a campfire in the woods, and it's not so far off from that. Herb didn't get his egg foo young, so he's chomping on a sleeve of butter crackers he found when he was "making himself at home" and Millie's already downed a couple of shots of Baileys, which I wasn't aware was meant to be consumed that way, so she's smiling inappropriately considering the situation. The old fool is of no help whatsoever.

I, however, am not here to eat at Super Jumbo or get tipsy off expired Baileys. I am here on a fact-finding mission for my new podcast, even though I haven't told anyone that. I looked it up on my laptop yesterday, and I have a plan. "Shelby, dear. While we're waiting for Willard's I wanted to say I saw the news, and I know you must be anxious about seeing that footage."

Shelby seems to freeze at this, her eyes wide and slightly shocked. Nobody talks about what happened to her, like a silent pact we've all made, but it's time. Something's happening. Herb puts the packet of butter crackers down and Millie stops midsip and stares at me.

"Is it okay if I ask you a couple of questions?" I ask, taking out a notepad and pen.

"Now?" Herb says, more loudly than necessary.

"We can't go anywhere at the moment, nobody has much to say, so I thought maybe we can talk about what the hell's *really* going on around here."

"Flor, I'm not sure what you mean. The footage didn't show anything useful," Shelby says. "Nothing I didn't already

know—we all know a guy got in. It didn't help anything seeing a blur on a camera. So...".

"Well," I say. "It's just that I know your car battery isn't dead,
because I was with you just a few weeks ago when I tagged
along while you ran errands, and you got a bunch of those
candy cane things filled with M&M's because Jensen's was out
of the Santa Pez you wanted, and we stopped for peppermint
mochas and an oil change. And they said your battery needed
changing, so you got a new one."

"Holy crap, Nancy Drew?" Millie adds, and I notice she's
starting to slur a bit.

"Oh" is all Shelby says. The wind outside howls and the
windows rattle in their frames slightly. The house squeaks and
sighs. Her face is pale and her eyes look lost.

"I know you think we're all self-absorbed, but that's mostly
just Herb."

"Hey," Herb says half-heartedly, picking up his crackers and
squirting a blob of Easy Cheese I hadn't yet noticed he'd pil-
fered from the refrigerator.

"But you were white as a sheet when you came back inside,
so if it wasn't your battery, what was it? Also, I might add that
I think someone murdered Otis Thorgard, and I think it's related to you, dear."

There is an audible scoff or maybe a stifled gasp from everyone. Then, complete silence.

"May I have some more of that Bailey-tini thing, Millie?"
I ask, and she hands me the shaker with her mouth hanging
open, which I find a little melodramatic.

"Jesus, Flor" is all Herb manages.

"Otis was sick in the hospital," Shelby begins, but I interrupt.

"Yes, and you have every reason to have episodes of panic—
you don't need to explain that. And yes, Otis was sick in the
hospital, but I have reason to believe there was foul play and I

worry that whoever this—this *psycho* is, he's back. To be fair, probably never left, but is targeting people again."

"She's lost the plot," Millie says, shaking her head and pulling the sleeve of crackers across the table and plucking out a few.

"Foul play?" Herb echoes.

"It means she thinks he was murdered, Herb."

"I know what it means, Millie!"

"Look," I say and then I lay out the torn-up note Winny let me keep and tell them her story, how Otis was afraid and thought someone was out to hurt him, and the warning to Mack and Shelby. When I finish, the only sound is the heavy moan of the wind outside and the cracking fire. Shelby holds one of the scraps of paper to her chest—the one with her name written on it in Otis's handwriting.

"What?" she says in a whisper to herself.

Suddenly my phone rings, buzzing across the coffee table, and we all jump. It's Willard's so I hand it to Shelby, who is holding her heart and catching her breath at the shock the sudden sound gave us all. She stands and walks to the kitchen to take the call.

Millie and Herb stare at me, but I'm watching Shelby's reaction to the phone call and I can tell it's not good news.

"You're full of surprises, ain't ya?" Herb says.

"Yes, and I'm going to need your help with a few things," I say. I hear Shelby make a couple more calls and we stay quiet and sip our drinks, and when she returns, she hands me my phone. She looks small and scared, standing there in Christmas elf socks with a blanket wrapped around her shoulders.

"The electricity isn't…repairable at the moment," she says.

"Not even the generator?" Herb asks.

"No," she says, a bewildered look across her face. "So we're going to arrange bussing everyone over to the Y. Heather is calling and they'll set up cots, the same as when we had that tornado damage a few years back. That's nice of them…" She's starting to babble. There's something she's not telling us.

"It's okay, sweetheart," I say. She smiles weakly and takes my hand.

"Uh, you all can stay here if you like. We have a guest bed and another portable generator heater…"

"We'll let you rest, Shel."

"Yeah," Herb says as we all stand and start to gather our things. "We should be with Mort and Bern anyway. Mort gets scared when this sort of thing happens, even though he won't admit it, and Bernie is depressed, so this won't help."

"Depressed? Bernie? Why do you think that?" Shelby asks.

"He's different. I can just tell, and then one day I said, Bernie, are you okay, because you seem a little depressed lately, and he said why would you think that, and I said I don't know, look at you. You're kinda pale and slouchy, and he said, I'm eighty-seven you dick. And I said fine, you're not depressed, and we dropped it and made some peanut butter sandwiches and watched *MacGyver*, but I think he really *is* depressed. He didn't eat his sandwich and he didn't really watch the show. That's how he's been lately. I don't want them to feel scared, so we'll head over," he says, and it sort of touches me—his care for his friend, and I remember why I hang out with the old goat, but I don't tell him that.

"Give her your phone, Herb," I say instead. "She can't be here without a phone.

"You wanna come with us?" I ask.

Shelby shakes her head. "No, I called Clay. He's on his way back, but I'll see you tomorrow. I'll be talking to the Y and make sure everyone gets there safe, though. Call if there are any problems."

I nod, squeeze her hand, and we all wrap our scarves tight and pull on hats and gloves, filing to the door.

"Hey," Shelby says, stopping us a moment. "Thank you for telling me all this. Please, though. Promise me something."

"'Course," I say without thinking.

"Don't get involved. Please don't tell anyone else—don't let this stuff get out there. Someone will get hurt. Please," she says, desperation in her eyes.

"Of course, dear, if that's what you want," Millie says, but I don't say anything. I kiss her on the cheek and wave from under my bound scarf as I exit, because I plan to get very involved and nail this son of a bitch to the wall.

Back at the YMCA, there are cots set up around the gym floor and each of the Oleander residents has their own spot. "It's lights-out," the assistant manager who came in to "handle the crisis" says, like we are children at a lock-in. Most folks are asleep or chatting with flashlights, like we used to do back in my Girl Scout days. Eddie Wallington brought his cap and nose plugs and decided to take a swim in the lap pool, but that guy's always had a screw loose, and Bob and Heath are shooting hoops in the courts down the hall, but other than that, all the normal folks are exhausted between the ordeal and the late hour. Mort and Bernie join me and Millie and Herb in our own little circle next to the Kidz Korner. So naturally Herb is sitting in a tiny plastic chair at a kids' table with his knees up to his chin, coloring a Strawberry Shortcake page and chewing on the end of an unlit cigar, and Mort is trying to tell a "classic" ghost story with the flashlight under his chin, but nobody is paying attention.

"Excuse me," I say, clanging a banana-scented marker onto my water bottle until I have the gang's attention. When everyone is looking at me and Mort has taken the godforsaken flashlight out from under his chin and gives up on his campfire story, I decide to just say it.

"I think I'd like to find out who killed Otis and who tried to kill Shelby, and I think I should start a podcast," I say.

"A what now?" Millie says.

"I read about a few crime podcasts that helped catch the killer by getting information out and hunting down clues, and I think I'd be quite good at that. I don't think we can just sit around and not try to help. I could investigate."

"Mort has a podcast," Bernie says.

"Mort does not have a podcast," I reply with confidence.

"Sure he does, it's called *Mort's Literary Musings*," Bernie says, and I look to Mort for confirmation I'm certain won't come, but then it does.

"Right now I'm focusing on classical Greece to the Hellenistic kingdoms, but I cover everything—not to brag," he says.

"Jesus," Herb says, pushing away his Strawberry Shortcake coloring book. "What are we even talking about? You wanna talk about Shelby in public? On the air? I'm sure she'll love that. Way to not get involved." Herb grabs at a half-colored Snoopy lying on a doghouse and glares at it disapprovingly, then finds another that has not been touched—a Bart Simpson he seems happy enough with.

"Have you ever even listened to a podcast before?" Millie asks.

"It can't be too different from news casting," I say.

"Right, Florence was in news. She *could* do a podcast," Mort says.

"Stop saying podcast," Herb grunts.

"You gotta listen to this one," Bernie says in an uncharacteristic burst of enthusiasm as he takes out his phone and looks for something on it. "It's called *Dr. Death* and it's about a surgeon who paralyzed or killed almost all of his patients."

"I listened to that one. Yeah. You don't know if he's evil and did it on purpose or just totally off his nut," Herb says, rejoining our little huddle as Bernie pushes Play on the *Dr. Death* podcast for us all to hear. Then a few people tell us to hush, so he plugs in headphones and we take turns passing them around in the darkness, perched at the edge of our cots, listening to sections of it and whispering to one another.

When we get to the part where the doctor paralyzes his best friend and the best friend still sticks up for him, Mort takes the headphones out and hangs his head. All of us do.

"Poor Jerry Summers, Jesus," Herb says. Then, after a few solemn minutes, Herb is crunching on a package of Chex Mix that seems to have materialized out of nowhere and shakes his head some more.

"I don't think you know what you're getting yourself into, Flor. I think we should butt out like Shel said." He tries to pass around the mix, but nobody wants any.

"I could help," Mort says. "I don't really do it seriously. I just like to chat and reply to the comments, really. Right now I'm analyzing Euripides, and do you know…" He starts to chuckle to himself. "Someone thought he wrote *Antigone* and we got into quite a heated discussion until he realized he was referring to Sophocles, and not Euripides at all. We had a good laugh about it."

"Oh my God," Herb says, continuing to hem and haw over Mort's nerdiness, rolling his eyes and trying to make baskets in the trash across the room with pieces of Chex Mix to show his disinterest. Mort is unperturbed.

"We could all help," Bernie says. "Mort could show us the ropes."

"I think it sounds fun. I could do everyone's hair," Millie says.

"It won't be on camera," Bernie says.

"But you still want to look nice," she defends.

"Everyone who thinks we should stay out of it, raise your hand," Herb says, raising his hand and looking around to see he has no allies.

"Oh Lord," he mutters.

"It needs to be on video from now on," Millie says. "You

wanna reach a wider audience. I was watching *The Rich Roll Podcast* on YouTube. I mean the guy just sits there with a talking head for two hours, but it's still on video. Plus he's hot, so it's fine."

"I think that's a good idea," I say. "And we'll need rides to places, so you have to be in."

"Are you sure you know what a podcast is, Flor?"

"Vodcast," Millie corrects.

"I mean to investigate," I say.

"You've all gone mental," Herb says, then lies down on his cot and covers himself with his sleeping bag. "You're all fruit loops," he adds and then puts his sleeping mask over his eyes and turns over.

"We'll start tomorrow," I whisper to Mort as I pat him on the arm.

As everyone else gets settled into sleep, I slip out of the room and outside the front door where the wind is merciless and icy flurries sting my skin. I quickly dial back the number for Willard's.

"Willard's 24 Hour HVAC Service," a man's voice answers.

"Uh, hello," I say. "I think we spoke to you earlier. I run the night shift at the Oleander Terrace and you guys came out to look at the breakers earlier. I just wonder if you'll be sending over an email or anything outlining the damage and when it can be repaired, cost, all of that."

"Oh, well, I told the lady earlier we can't fix it."

"But you're the HVAC experts," I say, incredulously.

"Whole thing's gotta be replaced. Someone burned it—it's melted. The whole breaker box, wires, all of it."

"Burned?" I ask, finding that my heart is beginning to speed up and my mouth is suddenly very dry.

"Yeah, like someone took a freakin' blow torch to it or something. Never seen anything like it in all my thirty-two years.

The owner filed a police report, but I won't have an estimate for the total rewiring for a day or so, sorry."

"Burned. Deliberately?" I ask.

"Oh yeah. Torched to a crisp."

"And the backup generators—why didn't they come on? Sorry if you already went through this. For our records I just wanted to…"

"Same thing with the generator. Someone was back there and destroyed all of it. Could have killed people in this cold, that's for sure. It seems like that's exactly what someone was trying to do, 'cause it sure ain't easy to melt metal. I'm sorry to bear the bad news, some people are just crazy. Like I told the other lady, I'll try to get it all back and running for you this weekend if we have all the parts in," he says.

"Thank you," I say, numbly, ending the call. I go back inside, taking in the warmth of the entryway for a moment, then sit on a heating vent and stare across at a poster of a kitten holding on to a branch by one paw. It says "hang in there." Something like rage begins to bubble up inside me—fury for my dear friends, for Shelby, for poor Otis.

Someone did this on purpose; my God. Someone wanted at least one of us dead.

9

Shelby

"It vanished into thin air," I tell Mack when she asks why I'm setting up a new iPhone when I just got an upgrade for Christmas a few weeks ago.

She brought a couple of day-old boxes of eclairs for the gang to have and we sit together in the front office, rocking in the old leather chairs and eating custard out of the middle of the pastries with our fingers. She feeds broken-off ends to the dog wrapped inside her coat.

"You had to have dropped it in the snow and it died, and that's why it can't be tracked. What else makes sense?" she says and I shrug, uninterested in talking about it any further. I've been on calls with the phone company and in the damn AT&T store half the day already. She's also acting off. I know she tried to tell me about the security footage before it showed up on the news, and what else can either of us say about it except that it's creepy but not helpful? But it does bring up the question of whether or not there is a second person involved because of the scarf. A feminine scarf, she points out, but I don't know about that. It seems like a stretch. I'm not apathetic to the video—of course it's horrifying to see, but it's seemingly worthless.

"Can I put him down?" she asks as Gus wiggles off her lap and shakes out his ears. Before I even answer he's marched out to the common area, and I can hear a symphony of squeals and kissy noises as the residents delight over him.

"Do you have a gun?" I ask her out of nowhere, and her face changes, tenses, she puts down her eclair.

"Somewhere" is all she says, and we both stare out at the skeletons of trees and the frozen parking lot outside the front windows. We were both lovingly forced by our husbands to learn how to use one in case of a self-protection emergency, and just like me, she probably forgot how, and where it even is.

I told her about Winny and the note and how it named us—how it was some sort of warning to us. We've both been quietly paralyzed in fear that this could happen—that since Leo's disappearance is a mystery and nobody was ever caught for my attempted murder, whatever insane, evil, freak thing that happened that night isn't over. She was quiet when I told her—just petted Gus's head and stared. We've exhausted every possible suspect, angle, theory, and fear over the last months. And all the tears and the rage too, so what's left to say? We've always felt someone lurking in the shadows.

"I'll find it," she says.

Herb appears in the doorway, holding Gus in his arms.

"This little guy took a big ole Stanley Steamer right in Bernie's slipper."

"Oh, sorry about that," Mack stands. Gus wriggles from Herb's arms and runs over to Bernie who's laughing and slapping his knee at the ordeal.

"Who knew all Bern needed was a pile of dog shit to cheer

him up," Herb says. Mack and I stand in the door frame and look out to see Gus hopping around, getting pets from everyone and then taking off with one of Millie's half-knitted pot holders, which makes Bernie hoot even louder.

"I thought he wouldn't leave your side," I say, smirking at Mack. She shrugs and watches Herb play tug-of-war with him over the pot holder.

"Well, that's just rude," she says, hands on hips, both of us thrilled to be changing the subject. "You could take him overnight if you…"

"Yes," I answer before she finishes. "I think everyone could use that right now," I say, and I can still see the techs through the side window—the guys from Willard's finishing up some final wiring that was damaged. It's been a handful of days since the electricity was purposefully cut, and even though that was fixed, now they are repairing the generator. And although everyone is back in their routine, there is a quiet pensiveness around the place, and it's clear the residents are still frightened to some extent. Back inside the office, Mack shrugs on her coat and picks at the rest of her eclair.

"You wanna tell me what Evan Carmichael is doing hanging out at the Ole? I thought I was having a high school flashback."

"You think I'm setting you up with him," I say flatly, but a smirk plays at my lips.

"I mean, I was there the other day with Billy. Your subtlety was Oscar-worthy."

"Well, for your information, I got him to work here part-time while he fixes up his dad's place."

"Well, they all seem to be getting along," she says, pulling on her hat and nudging her chin in the direction of Herb, Evan, and Florence, who are huddled around the old computer at an ancient particle board desk in the corner of the room.

"Yes, Evan is showing them how to use Instagram, I think."

Mack laughs at this then calls Gus over and kisses his face a few times.

"I'll be back, buddy. You have fun, sweetheart. If it doesn't work, I'll pick him back up anytime," she says to me and then hollers at the gang, who wave and thank her for the treats.

After a lazy attempt at some paperwork, I give up and go over to nose in on what the gang is cooking up over at the computer. I try to eavesdrop as I make a cup of tea in the kitchenette and then flop on the couch next to Millie. Gus is curled up in Bernie's lap on the recliner and the rest are still hunched over the computer.

"What's going on with them?" I ask as she knits a new pot holder.

"Mort has a podcast."

"No he does not," I say.

"Oh, Shelby, I'm glad you're here, there's something I'd like to…run past you," Florence says, but she's interrupted by Evan, who gasps as he points at the computer screen.

"Mort! You have over a hundred thousand subscribers," he says, pushing his chair back from the keyboard and shaking his head in desbelief. Florence and Mort have kitchen chairs pulled up next to him and they look at one another.

"Is that a lot?" he asks.

"Oh my God. Are you…? Yes! You could be making a lot of money. Do you even—" he stutters, stops, and looks utterly bewildered. But Mort just shrugs.

"Right now we're discussing the works of Edgar Allan Poe. I guess people like Poe. He married his thirteen-year-old cousin. Most people don't know that. And he died of 'brain congestion' but that was just a nice way of saying alcoholism."

"Nobody even knows who you're talking about," Herb says, busy tossing plastic darts at the dartboard on the wall and drinking a Pabst, but still can't contain himself.

"Poe? Are you serious?" Mort takes off his glasses, giving his attention to Herb.

"The mascot for the Ravens?" Herb asks.

"The mascot is literally a raven taken from a Poe story," Mort says, flustered.

"This guy's a nut," Herb says, looking around for passive agreement.

"Okay," Evan laughs. "Listen. Mort. You could be selling ads. You could be getting sponsors. This is amazing," he says.

"I just like talking about literature," Mort says flatly and Evan blinks at him, clicking away at the keyboard some more and poking around in Mort's apparently fascinating YouTube account.

"Whoa. Okay. So what happened in the last day that gave you half a million views? Holy crap," Evan says, and Mort takes over the keyboard and clicks about for a moment. He plays a recent video podcast he recorded. It's him in the frame with a tweed suit on, and he's standing in front of the corkboard in the craft room holding a pointer and giving a lecture. We all watch for a moment to see what amazing content there could be to explain all this, but all we hear is Mort's monotone voice on camera.

"Edgar continued his studies in Richmond. He entered the University of Virginia in 1826 at the age of seventeen. During the year he attended the university, Edgar excelled in his studies of Latin and French…" Evan clicks Pause.

"Kill me," Herb says, tossing another dart.

"I think I know what happened. Shelby, dear, this is what we'd like to discuss with you."

"Mort's podcast recounting the young life of Edgar Allan Poe…? Is that what you want to talk to me about?" I ask.

"No. Mort let us guest host his podcast yesterday, and I imagine that's what the fuss is about," Florence says.

"You didn't tell me it went up online. I didn't even get to

see it yet," Herb says, coming over and sitting on the arm of the couch, peering between Evan's and Mort's heads to see the screen.

"Oh Lord. What did you do?" I ask, partly in jest, but getting increasingly concerned for some reason.

"Will you keep an open mind?" Florence asks.

"Tell me what's going on," I demand, and Mort presses Play. The video shows the whole gang sitting around the fireplace in this very room. Herb in his armchair, pulling apart Oreos, Mort with his tweed and pointer standing near the hearth, and the rest on the couch sharing a bottle of wine and picking at Christmas chocolates.

The video starts out with Mort announcing that Florence will be guest hosting, and he will allow her to lead the discussion about the very ominous goings-on in Rivers Crossing. He thinks the tone of the story is in line with his Poe series, and so it's an appropriate adjunct to his series.

Then on-screen Florence nervously smiles at the camera and lays out the facts of Leo's disappearance and the night of my assault, and then starts talking about Otis and Winny. There is a tightening in my chest that starts out as a fist of pain, morphing into full-blown anger very quickly.

"Are you fucking kidding me?" I snap. I stand up and Mort pushes Pause on the video. Evan looks horrified.

"Well, it's not the best quality video 'cause the lighting in here sucks, but Mort says posting the video on YouTube will help grow the audience, so we thought people would look past the lighting," Herb says, cluelessly.

"Herb, please," Florence says, then places a hand on Evan's shoulder. "He didn't know anything about this until just now."

"Why would you do this? I told you not to get involved. For your own safety," I say, vibrating with frustration…and fear, if I'm honest, about the possible implications.

"Well, dear. I know that's what you did say, but it looks like a lot of people watched this, and what better way to catch the son of a bitch than blast this all over to Timbuktu and back? It could help. We can't do *nothing*."

"I gotta agree with Flor on this one, as much as it pains me to do so. Cops came out when the HVAC and generator were destroyed. But what can they really do? I guess it's not exactly their fault, even though the detective has a head full of chipped beef still. They can file a report, whoopee. We have security now, fine, but there's a slim chance anyone will be caught. This could actually help in a big way, not a report in some drawer Chipped Beef scribbled up," Herb says, and I must say I'm surprised at his conviction. And it's not that he doesn't have a point, it's that they have no idea how much danger they could really be in.

"I'm trying to protect you," I say.

"We made it this long, we can take care of ourselves, Shel," Millie pipes in.

I run my hands through my hair and blow out a deep breath. "Well, what the hell else is on the video?" I ask, and Mort presses Play. Herb passes around an oversized container of Cheese Balls as we all watch. Heather comes in and doesn't know what's going on but sits and watches anyway, taking her share of Cheese Balls in her palm when they come her way.

The video continues. The gang is still having what seems like a cozy fireside chat with drinks and wooly sweaters, only they're talking about me.

"Someone in this small town of ours knows who's doing this. Someone you probably know—a friend, a neighbor—is responsible and yet, no leads, no clues. And now Otis has been murdered in his own hospital bed, and it's time we take justice into our own hands if the police can't get to the bottom of it, and that's all I have to say." Florence ends her speech, a bit over-the-top if you ask me, but then it turns into a free-for-all with the whole gang piping in.

"Oooh, we have a serial killer. How exciting," Millie says.

"We don't have a serial killer. Leo is missing, no one has said he's dead, and let's be honest because we are all thinking it, he's probably involved," Mort says to my utter surprise, and they all turn and look at me apologetically at this comment before turning back to the screen.

"So he probably doesn't want to be called dead is all I'm saying. We only have Otis dead and that comes with a lot of question marks, so let's take a pill and not say serial killer just yet."

"Take a pill yourself, Mort," Herb says.

"Yeah, up yours, Mort," Millie echoes, and Mort tries to keep control of things. They go on to argue about whether there is a woman's scarf in the frame the news showed of the security footage, and what motives Otis's killer might have—how all the cases have to be connected. Once Mort finally pushes Stop on the video, they all turn to me.

"We learned that most people only watched about a third of the video, so Evan is gonna help us learn how to edit," Florence says and Evan holds up his hands in a gesture that says, "I didn't know you didn't know."

"I mean, only if that's like, okay with you," he says with wide eyes that look a little bit terrified of what my reaction might be. "I just—it's gone viral, apparently, so…"

"Oh, that's terrible," Millie says.

"Mill, join us in the twenty-first century, will you? That's a good thing," Herb says, wiping orange cheese crumbs from his fingers onto his pant leg.

"He said viral, Herb! Do you have your listening ears on? Viral… Like the pink eye you probably carry around. That's not a good thing," she says.

"Oh my God," Herb mutters, shaking his head.

"It's not okay with me," I say. "None of this is okay, Florence. What the hell?"

Florence stays very calm and speaks in a soft voice.

"I know, dear, but I read about some podcasts that helped bring someone to justice—don't you think the best way to protect your girls is to make the details public? There's a much better chance of finding him or at least maybe scaring the person into not making themselves susceptible to getting caught if they continue to do more terrible things?" she says with conviction in her voice, and I sit back down and take it in. *My girls*, I think. Could this really be the way to make a difference?

"I don't know," I say quietly to my lap.

"Evan says people must have liked how candid we were. Not a rehearsed single host like they're used to, but us silly antiques sitting around just chatting, I guess," she says.

"It's refreshing," Evan says, staring at the screen and scrolling. "The comments are saying that, I mean. I'm not saying that. There are a lot of comments. Wow, this is nuts." He keeps looking through them all with a bewildered look on his face.

"Mort says he was going to take a break from English literature and move on to bread making and nobody wants to hear about that," Florence says.

"Hey." Mort pushes up his glasses and glares at her.

"The real mystery to solve is how Mort has so many followers," Millie says.

"He's very charming," Evan defends. Millie and Herb look at him. "No, really, Mort, I looked at some of your stuff today. I watched your talk titled 'Holden Caulfield Was the First Karen.' Brilliant, I can see why people watch you."

Mort blushes. "Want me to tell you what a Karen is, Millie?"

"Karen Wallington? Who works at the Dickie's dry cleaning? Which other Karen do we know?" Millie asks.

"That's it," Herb says in an exasperated tone, picking up his cigar and a lighter and walking out the front doors.

"Of course we won't continue if you don't want us to, right, Florence?" Evan asks, and even though he's just showing them how to edit and get sponsors, I appreciate him taking the lead on this. They won't care if I say no, though. He may think he's being noble by asking, but if the five of them have their minds set, they would film this in the middle of the night in Mort's room on their smartphones and block me from accessing it… or something like that. I need to think about it.

"I don't know yet," I say.

"I could see a woman wanting Leo dead for—you know, being involved," Heather says out of absolutely nowhere. Everyone turns to look at her.

"I'm just saying I agree with the thing in the video—a woman's scarf. I mean, I don't know about that, it looked like a plastic bag flapping to me, but before I worked at the hospital—like when I was younger—I worked at Pipers Pizza that Leo owned and all the girls hated him. He never paid us on time, never gave us enough shifts. Erin Wylie had a kid to support and there were like three customers a day. I guess that's not enough to kill a guy, but sometimes I wanted to… Making us split our tips with him. I mean, I hope nobody killed him. He's probably alive stealing tips from someone else, just on a beach in Mexico, like everyone says."

"You worked at the hospital?" is all Florence responds, after all that. Then… "When Otis was there?" Heather nods, and suddenly I hear the front doors fly open and the sounds of giggles and yelps only six-year-olds can make as Poppy and June skip into the rec room with Clay following behind, holding Happy Meals in one hand and purple glitter backpacks hanging from the other.

"Hi, Mom," Juju says, and then they're both on their knees at the coffee table screaming over Gus and asking if they can have him.

"He's Bernie's," I say, and Bernie looks up with a surprised expression and a suppressed smile. They go and sit by Herb the way they usually do because he sneaks them Fruit Roll-Ups or rock candy or some other garbage, and don't ask me why a grown man has any of those things. Today it's peppermint bark. He slides it to them under the table so I don't see it, and I pretend not to.

June hugs Florence and asks her if she wants to see the drawing she did in school, and Florence kindly makes a big to-do about how she should be an artist, then Poppy bounces over to sit next to Millie.

"Can you knit me red mittens?" she asks and she's asked Millie this every time she's seen her since before Christmas and is still trying to eke a late gift out of her that will never come.

"She only knows how to make a square. Maybe one day, years from now, she'll figure out how to put all of her squares together to make a scarf instead of forcing pot holders on everyone," Herb says, and before Millie can say "Up yours," I shrug my coat on and announce I'm leaving early.

I pull Clay away from Herb's box of Cubans he's trying to sell to him, and explain that we are taking the girls ice fishing this afternoon. Mort and Florence have moved away from the computer and she is putting a pot of tea on the stovetop in the kitchenette, and he is looking at his feet, and I know they are ready to defy every word I just said and jump back into this podcast armchair detective thing the minute I walk out.

On the car ride to the bait shop, I think about what they said. I think Mack would lose her mind if she found out this was being discussed publicly. But it also feels like something. Something more than anyone else is doing to unravel all this— give me my life back, my family's safety back. Still, I have to put a stop to it. It's my fight, not theirs.

It's dusk when we arrive at the bait shop. The girls sit on milk crates by the minnow tank while they eat their French fries and name the fish until they lose track of who's who. Clay sits in his oversized red flannel on the stool behind the counter that's covered in kitschy trinkets—a miniature Paul Bunyan statue, a plastic football, a piggy bank, a talking fish, a handful of Smurf figurines, a vase filled with beer bottle tops. He brushes the nugget crumbs from his fingers, takes a beer from the mini-fridge under the counter, and adds the bottle top to his vase.

The place looks more like it could be on an episode of *Hoarders* than it does a profitable bait shop, but he stands by people loving the cozy nostalgia of the place. The girls sure do at least. They're always unearthing new crap from the piles of boxes and collectables he tells them are not toys, but still lets them play with whatever they come across—a 1970s Hot Wheels or one of Mr. Potato Head's feet. I once made the mistake of telling him the place would make a better secondhand shop than bait store, but I won't make that mistake twice. Breaking about even each month was not what I imagined when we opened the shop six years ago, but now I try to enjoy the cozy kitsch and not dwell on how much money it's not making us, at least for a little bit longer.

The girls don't like ice fishing, but they do love the hot chocolate and playing in the ice hut that resembles one of those ever popular tiny homes equipped with a fireplace, card table, and board games, and even mounted fish on the wooden walls. The hut, which Clay's named Salmon Slayer and loves more than anything, is everything you'd expect from a northern Minnesotan fisherman—a man cave on ice.

The girls bring electric blankets we plug into a portable battery pack and curl up with hot chocolate and a movie on their tablet, and I drink a mug of wine and chat to Clay about the new contestants on *Survivor* or how the pawnshop on 1st Street is rumored to close. Anything but the news, or that note on my car, or Otis, or anything having to do with real life, and we are both happy to pretend nothing is wrong when we're with the girls.

On the weekend, the lake is peppered with a handful of other ice fishers, and their trucks are lined up near the snowbanks by the bait shop where they tailgate and drink beer half the day. But on weeknights, most of the other ice huts are empty and the extreme temperature has folks waiting until the promised warm-up coming next week. And by warm-up, I mean single digit temps instead of subzero.

The girls ask if they can skate on the ice after the thrill of cocoa and time in the hut has worn off, and I remind them they didn't bring skates, and it's dark.

"We just wanna go ice shoeing," June says, the clever name they made up for sliding around the ice in their boots without skates.

"Five minutes, and I'm watching you from the door, so don't go out of my sight."

"Take the lantern, Pops," Clay says, and she brings the lantern with her and sets it on the ice. I watch them hold hands and set out, giggling and squealing with each almost fall. They charge and slide across the ice and then back again. I smile at their simple joy and feel lifted that they seem happier as time passes—adjusting well.

And then I hear something. Something that stops my heart.

There is a loud crack in the darkness that echoes, and then a guttural, terrified scream.

"Poppy!" I scream so roughly my throat feels like it fills with blood. Clay jumps up and follows behind as I run, screaming wildly, across the ice to where June stands weeping and shaking, watching Poppy grip onto the edge of the broken ice with her tiny pale hand as she starts slipping under. The ice is broken wide open even though the lake has been frozen solid enough to drive on for weeks. It's impossible. What's happening?

"Poppy," I scream again, Clay is behind me with the lantern so I can see her, but she's not there. Her gripping fingers let go and all I can see are wisps of blond hair being pulled under the icy black water.

"Baby, no!"

10

Mack

At 4:00 a.m. I trudge into the bakery to begin making the cinnamon roll dough and get the coffee started. I haven't slept and my mind is still reeling, but I go through my morning ritual: start the fire in the fireplace, turn on the lamps on the end tables, plug in the fairy lights, then once I quickly get the first batch of dough proofing and a few muffin batches in the oven, I pour myself a cup of coffee and sit by the fire for a little while, usually to relax before the busy day ahead. Today, just to pull my shit together so I can function even a little bit.

I almost told Shelby yesterday about Leo—the account, its activity—but then she was telling me about someone trying to kill the residents or her, and the note from Otis, and I just couldn't. Deep down I know she thinks Leo is behind this. I just can't believe that. I'm not ready to let myself believe that until every other possibility is exhausted.

The bank was less than helpful. Of course they wouldn't give me any information, even though I had all the account and routing information. My name is not Leonard, and they don't give out information without a secret PIN, so what I can tell from the online information is that money is being transferred to a prepaid debit card so it's not traceable. There is no withdrawal location, no ATM, no point-of-sale data. Just another smart move by Leo to hide the money we *did* have left…which he hid in a secret account that he can pull from anonymously and I can't access. I hate him.

I think of Rowan and her college money, and the stability of our house, and her future… I wonder if I should keep all this from her forever or tell her one day who he really was, and it makes me sick, and I hate him even more.

This is usually the time of the day where I handle the mess of my life the best. The smell of cinnamon muffins in the ovens, coffee brewing, the dark stillness outside and the Bublé song playing softly as I sit in the moody light by the fire and have a few moments to myself. It's been healing, opening the bakery… even though I have no choice because he left me broke. I try to put that out of my mind most mornings. But now I want to scream and tear my fucking hair out at the thought of it all— what he's done to me.

I wish I didn't know. I think I mean that. Because the thought that he owed some very scary person money and that got him killed had really seemed like the most logical explanation…until now. Now I have no idea what the hell that absolute son of a bitch has done. One day I mourn for him and what might have happened because he got himself too deep into some dark shit and I forgive him, and the next, I find out he's alive and still stealing from people and hiding.

The tap on the locked front door startles me, and I jump to my feet. I see through the glass that it's Billy Curran, rubbing his hands together and blowing on them as he visibly shivers in his inappropriately light coat. What in the world? I go and unlock the door to let him in.

"Hi," he says. "I know you don't open until five, but I saw the lights on…"

"'Course, come on in," I say, and he follows me to the counter where I pour him a cup of coffee. "Are you just closing up?" I ask.

"Yeah. We're in different worlds, you and I. Not sure if I'm cut out for the 3:00 a.m. bar closing anymore. Last time I did it I didn't have back pain…or need readers to see the checks." He follows me back to the couch and sits in the leather chair nearest the fire, and it's nice, I realize. Having him here. He has a calming presence, and even though I've known him since middle school, I don't really know him at all, but the familiarity is still so comforting.

"Hmmm" is all I reply, smiling at his remark.

"It's so much more peaceful on this side of the street," he says, looking around at the serene ambience. *Yeah, sure*, I think.

"I had a crazy thought that I know is totally out of the blue," he says, a little shyly.

"Okay?" I say, glancing toward the kitchen when I hear my oven timer go off.

"Do you wanna maybe get dinner with me later?"

"Dinner?"

"Yes?"

"Tonight?" I add, because I don't know what else to say.

"Uh. I thought maybe, yes."

"Why?" I ask, stupidly.

"Well…" he stutters and I know I've made him uncomfortable, but I'm just so taken aback by the invitation.

"I should make it up to you—my dad giving you a heart attack, the fact that he had this footage all this time. Maybe just a mental break from all that's been going on."

"Oh. A mental break for you?" I say, not knowing why I am unable to just face what he's asking.

"Well, you're the one who came to the bar in slippers, so I was thinking you," he says, and I burst out laughing, to my surprise.

"Right," I say.

"I mean, God, no pressure. I just thought it might be nice to catch up. We were friends once, and I guess—I heard you've been through a lot...not that you have to talk about any of it," he says. I think about this for a moment.

"Everyone in town would talk," I say, and although that seems petty, they would...and I can't deal with anything else right now.

"We'll go to Brainerd. They have a new Thai place," he says, and I can tell he's sensing my rejection.

"Okay," I agree, surprising even myself. I haven't slept, he is just coming off an all-night shift, we haven't spoken more than ten words to each other since college, and I'm still mourning being abandoned by my husband, but hell, somehow it is suddenly the only thing I want right now. To be in another town, not thinking about my problems, sipping red wine, and eating pad thai with a handsome, long-lost friend. Hell yes to this.

"I can pick you up at six-ish if that's okay,"

"Uh, yeah," I say. "Yes." He offers to pay for the coffee, but I decline and he puts money on the counter anyway and then disappears back out into the icy morning that still feels like the dead of night.

I don't have time to think about what I just did or what it means, because I'll burn the first batch of bakes if I don't run to the kitchen immediately, so I try to put it aside for the day.

When I arrive home in the late afternoon, the snow is blowing again and it's already getting dark. I practically tiptoe down the drive to gather the mail from the mailbox with my arms out on either side for balance so I don't slip on the ice and end up in a snowbank. When I make my way back inside the pups yelp and turn themselves in circles. They run outside for the seconds it takes them to pee and run back in. God, why do I live here? Why do I stay in this miserable frozen tundra anymore?

I toss the mail on the counter and light the fire so Linus and Nugget can curl up and chew on their bully sticks. Then my mind turns to what I will wear tonight. God. I'm immediately embarrassed by my own thoughts. It's not a date. I'm married, first of all, it's just an old friend, second of all, and maybe most importantly, it doesn't matter what I wear, because it will be covered up by a parka in this bullshit weather anyway.

I make a cup of tea and turn on the television—a home renovation show plays, and I passively wonder what these young couples buying seven-figure houses do for a living. Then I grab the stack of mail and flop on the couch. I open a depressing bank statement—our joint account of twenty years, and the low number still shocks me. The private account I discovered isn't impressive either, it's under ten thousand dollars. I wonder how much it was over a year ago when he disappeared, and if he's just been living off of our stolen savings, gambling it all away. And now it's getting low, and what does that mean? I guess he keeps trying to win a jackpot until he ends up on the street, sleeping behind a dumpster somewhere. Or maybe he tries to come back at that point? I mean, who could he go to after all this? He's burned every bridge.

Then I open the phone bill and glance at it. What I see steals my breath. I gasp and the dogs lift their heads and look at me before laying them back down. I apologize to them for some reason, and then stare at the bill again. How is this possible?

Leo's phone shows activity. After all this time. How? I kept the line because of course I would, he was missing and so was his phone, and just in case anyone ever found it or something, I don't know. I *had* to keep it, and since the night he vanished, it has been off—no way of tracing it, no activity.

He's fucking with me. He has to know I would see this. Was he banking on the fact that the phone bill is on auto draft and

I probably don't look at it much? No. No, because he still has money. He doesn't need to use this line. Between bad business deals, loans, and gambling, he lost almost half a million dollars in our personal accounts over the last few years while lying to me, moving money around, pretending things were okay, hiding it all. He left with money, and there is still some money there, and any sane person trying to stay gone and undetectable would be using a disposable phone. He turned this one back on for a reason.

But what earthly reason could there possibly be? He hasn't hurt me and betrayed me enough, so now we're playing games? I'm so enraged that my hands shake and red blotches dot my chest. I do think about this being someone else. Of course. Some teenager found his phone and is using it, but don't they make that very difficult these days? The phone is locked and dead and you can't just get it turned on for a new user. Or maybe it's all easier than I think. But that bank account proves he's withdrawing money.

Or maybe…he was killed and the person who did it has his ID and all the information they need to be making withdrawals from his account. Oh my God. I was so angry I hadn't thought of that when I saw the bank account. But why, then, would they be stupid enough to use his phone? None of this makes sense!

I call the phone company, and I can already tell from the way the woman answers the phone that she's not going to be helpful. "Uh, yes. Hi. I… We have three lines on this account. I wonder if you can look up something for me. My line, my daughter's, and my husbands," I say and then give each phone number. "My husband is the one ending in 7862 and it's been shut off for over a year. We locked it, so it couldn't get stolen… used by anyone else, but kept active. So, I see that it has been reactivated as of a couple weeks ago. Twelve days, it looks like, to be exact. Uhhh. Do you know how that happened?" I say, holding my breath, hoping she has some miracle answer that breaks a hole in this mystery.

"Well, someone would have to call in and use your PIN and reactivate."

"Right," I say. "So someone called you and you turned it back on. So they had to have the PIN?"

"Well, of course they didn't call me directly, but whoever helped them would just ask some basic security questions and yeah, turn it back on."

"Okay, so I'm correct that this phone was totally off until twelve days ago, right?" I ask, and there is a pause because I probably sound desperate and I'm asking odd questions about my own phone line, but it is mine and she went through security measures with me, so she sort of has to answer.

"That's correct. Anything else I can assist you with?"

"Yes, who called in? This is the phone of a missing person and I need to know who called and reactivated it!" I say, practically yelling, even though it's not her fault she's useless.

"I don't know. I would assume you. Someone with your PIN and…"

"It obviously wasn't me. Was it a woman? Are you saying a woman called and turned the phone back on?" I say, because somewhere in the back of my mind that damn scarf in the video that looks feminine is starting to niggle at me and I know she doesn't know, but my frustration is mounting.

"I couldn't know that," she says.

"Don't you record calls…for training purposes or something?" I ask, and I hear her take a patient breath, and my breath hitches.

"We MAY record calls, but that's not my department and I don't know that they can track a call if you don't know who called or when they called. I can transfer you to my supervisor," she says.

"Yes," I say, and I talk to the supervisor who is equally as useless and tells me I can file a report and they will investigate if I think my information was stolen or is being misused. I hang up.

I decide I should call Detective Riley. But then I hesitate. I mean, I really sit on it for a moment, because I should have called him when I found the bank files yesterday. I should tell him about the note Otis wrote. And when the cops were out at the Oleander's taking reports about the vandalizing of the HVAC, Shelby should have told them about the note on her car and the note from Otis, and how this is all surfacing right about the time the news is finally covering the first clue about that fateful night, but we didn't for a reason.

If you listen to the folks around town, it's because Riley is Shelby's ex-fiancé and he hates Clay, and there have been petty disagreements over the years. Some would say Shelby has been overheard calling him a sexist good ole boy and an incompetent small-town detective who got his credentials from a Cracker Jack box. Oh, the talk. Apparently, Riley is still in love with Shelby, which is why his wife, Belinda, and her brother opened a bait shop over on Rice Lake to put Clay out of business, and it's also why Clay got drunk off Christmas punch one year at the annual holiday parade and threw up on Riley's car. But this is what happens when you have known everyone in your life since elementary school. It gets messy. But I don't believe he has it out for her.

I think the simple fact is, nobody blames the force for having zero clues about what happened to Shelby that night because they believe Leo went mad and he is responsible, because nothing else makes sense. They did their investigation. The coincidence is too much, so he must be involved. He appears to have left of his own accord, and his evidence of financial ruin and how he hid it from me gives reason for him to run from his crumbling life.

And after all this time, there's also the scribbling from Otis, a very ill man, about someone trying to kill him. Sure. Give that to Riley and see how seriously he takes it. *Let's put all our force back into finding Leo Connolly because Otis Thorgard, practically in a diabetic coma, warned of danger.* The vandalism at the Oleander's was kids, they say, but *"they'll make a report and she should get cameras around the place"* is what they told me and Shelby.

It's exactly like Riley said: if all leads are exhausted and there's no reasonable hope that new information will come to light, that's when you consider no longer actively investigating. Fair. So what will he do with this bank and phone information? Probably very little. Because Leo is not being actively pursued as the suspect in what happened to Shelby. There is zero proof, just a hunch and assumption by everyone including the police, and this evidence actually strengthens the argument that he left with all our money and doesn't want to be found.

Well, guess what. I'm not calling Riley. I'm going to find that son of a bitch myself.

"Holy shit!" I yell out loud and leap from the sofa, spilling tea down the front of my sweater and all over the floor. "Oh my God," I say, standing frozen for a moment, feeling a brief brush of disbelief. I can find him.

I'm shocked it took me the thirtysomething minutes since I found the bill until this second to remember I can look at our tracking app. Unless he turned it off himself, we all have tracker apps. I used to use it to keep tabs on Rowan when she was out as a teen, and it's useful if you can't find your phone, but spying is an additional perk I've never used it for. It should allow me to see where he is. I sit back down, and then I stand back up and shake out my hands. I'm trembling with nerves. I sit back down and take a breath and then wipe a few splashes of spilled tea off my phone screen and click the app...and there it is.

"Shut the fuck up," I whisper to myself, cupping my hand over my mouth. His phone is moving southbound on highway 10, headed toward Fargo, North Dakota.

The doorbell rings. Shit. Billy.

I go and open the door, and I know the color has drained from my face and my eyes are wild and confused, and I'm covered in tea and my nerves are frayed. He doesn't look me up and down or comment on how I don't look remotely ready for dinner out. He just smiles, holding a bouquet of flowers to my surprise, and I feel terrible, but I don't have time to feel terrible or worry about anyone's feelings. I'm quaking with adrenaline and rage, and a little bit of terror at what I might find if I pursue this, so much so that I just blurt it out as I pull a coat on and practically push past him.

"Sorry. Shit. I'm so sorry, but I think my missing husband is alive and driving down the interstate as we speak and I have to go to Fargo. Sorry."

"Oh. Right…now?"

"Yes. Right this second."

"I'll go with you," he says.

"What? No. Why?"

"Because you should have someone with you. It could be dangerous," he says, and I just stare at him and blink for a second. But I'm not thinking about danger or about him dropping everything to drive on slippery roads to goddamn North Dakota for someone he scarcely knows anymore, or how exhausted I am, or what I'll say or do when I find Leo. I am just going. Right this second, before I lose him again.

"Let's go," I say, and within minutes we are driving through the inky blackness, fat snowflakes tapping the windshield, snow squeaking under the tires on the snow-packed roads as we drive into the night.

11

Florence

"Just tell us where it is!"

"Oh, don't shout, for God's sake, Millie," I say, realizing I'm also shouting. Millie decided she was tired of the winter so she made a pitcher of sangria and brought her lawn chair out into the common area. She's been sitting there in a swimsuit and snow boots listening to bachata music all evening while we have been chatting over the next topic for the podcast and how to reach more people...and now we've received a call that Poppy has been in some sort of accident, and I need Millie to sober up. We are all awaiting Evan, who we've talked into taking us to the hospital in the resident van to see her. While he warms the van up, I don't think it's too much to ask of Heather, who used to work at the hospital, to tell us where they keep the visitor sign-in log.

"You're all behaving very badly," she says with crossed arms.

"That would be unethical, and I think you're getting too vain-glorious for your own good. This podcast is going to your heads." We all look at Mort.

"It means fame-seeking," he says.

Then we all look back to Heather, and I must say, I have to mask my astonishment at her knowledge of that word. Maybe we've pegged our dim-witted caretaker a little bit unfairly.

"You're obstructing justice," I reply back, but she holds firm.

"Does Evan know he's driving you to commit a crime or does he just think you're visiting Poppy?" she asks.

"We *are* visiting Poppy," Herb says, and then Evan comes in the front doors, banging snow off of his boots.

"All ready," he says, and I can see through the glass that the Mystery Machine is warmed up and coughing out puffs of smoke from the tailpipe into the icy air.

"Aren't you on till ten?" Heather asks Evan, not for any noble reason, but because she likes to flop on any furniture nearest to him in the common area and pick at her Coke can and twirl her hair as often as she gets a chance. His helping with the podcast is taking away from that.

"Shelby said if he ever needed to take off early for something that came up, he could. What more important thing could there be than to show our support for her now? Right, Evan?" I say, turning to him. He shrugs.

"I mean…" he says with an expression that reads "she has a point" but he doesn't say anything else.

Heather chews on her lip and turns on her heel with a "Humph!"

Mort, Herb, Bernie, and I all file out the doors and Evan helps us into the van one by one. We sit and wait for Millie to change into something appropriate, and then we head to the hospital.

The drive to the hospital is solemn until Millie decides to use it as an opportunity to get to know Evan a little bit more because she wants to set him up with her daughter, Faye, which I think is a dreadful idea for many reasons, not the least of which is that she has a terribly uneven temper and was once arrested for punching in the drive-through window at a Wendy's when they ran out of breakfast Baconators. But in all fairness, that could just be a rumor.

"What's going on with your hair?" Herb asks, his attempt at an icebreaker. Evan touches the side of his head where it's newly shaved on one side but long and floppy on the top.

"What do you mean?" he asks.

"It's all smashed to one side."

"Yeah," Evan agrees with a chuckle.

"It's neat," Herb says. "I was a barber in the navy."

"Oh yeah?" In the rearview mirror, I can see Evan smile, taking interest.

"My father was a barber too...till the Japs blew off his head."

"Oh... I'm...sorry," Evan says, looking horrified.

"Not your fault," Herb says, biting the head off of his Keebler elf cookie and handing the package around to share. "Anyway... it was pretty much all the same haircut. Bzzzz. Nothing cool like that."

"I can do yours like this if you want. I cut mine myself."

Herb beams from ear to ear and then Millie takes her turn to chat up Evan but from the back seat of the van, so she's practically shouting.

"Ya got a girlfriend, Ev? A buncha bastard kids running around somewhere or anything like that?"

"Millie," I snap.

"What?" she takes the cookies from Herb, and Evan responds before I can interject.

"Fair question, Millie. No to both. I was engaged for a couple of years, and then after my accident happened, she took a job in Toronto. We tried the long distance thing, but it was tough and she met someone else..."

"Kind of a late bloomer, what are ya, forties, and you were just engaged the last few years?"

"Yep, same age as Shelby. We almost went to prom together, but don't tell Clay that," he says with a smirk.

"I could see that," I say.

"Why?" Millie asks. "Shelby doesn't like cops?"

"Because they're both nice, I meant, and Shelby doesn't not like cops, she doesn't like Riley because his head is full of beef tips," I say.

"Chipped beef," Herb corrects.

"That's just because she broke his heart," Bernie says, and I resist the urge to turn around to look at him, because it's not often he pipes in, and I don't know how in the world he knew that.

"God, did she date the whole town?" Millie asks. "You know someone who's not a tramp? My daughter, Faye. Do you know my birth canal was narrow, and having her almost killed me?"

"We all know that," Mort says, shaking his head and rolling his eyes.

"She looked like a sea creature, and I had to get her a special helmet for her long head."

"Okay, Millie. Thank you," Herb says.

"I'm just saying. She's a good girl, been through a lot."

"You're not exactly selling her, are you?" Herb says, abruptly changing the subject. "So that's what happened to your face huh? That accident. Heard you got shot. Thank you for your service by the way." He does some weird salute and I can't help but look at the ceiling and shake my head at this conversation. He shouldn't be asking about someone's deformed eye.

"Thank you for *your* service, Herb," Evan says back. "Yep, I sure did. But I got through it. I mean I can't see out of an eye of course…and there's some hearing loss and dizzy spells—can't serve on the force anymore. I'm sure you saw your share of things like that in the service," he says, kindly obliging Herb.

"Well, I mean I already told ya my dad got his head blown off, so…"

"You sure did," Evan says, because what else *can* he say? And then, mercifully, we are pulling into the hospital parking lot and Evan drops us right at the front emergency exit and tells us he'll wait right here and play *Forge of Empires* on his phone until we're through…whatever that means.

We all buy a gift for Poppy from the gift shop, and everyone hands them to me when it's decided that I'll go up while they wait in the lobby waiting room so it's not too much. As I wait in the elevator, I look down to see that the gift Millie handed me was a pair of red mittens she must have been working on for a very long time to learn how to make for little Poppy and my heart warms and I feel a tear threatening to fall, but instead I smile at the beautiful gesture and stay strong as I walk down the hall to her room.

When I see Shelby, she's pacing outside Poppy's room on the phone, dabbing her eyes with a paper towel, then she ends the call and notices me. I hand her a tissue from my purse and she seems quite surprised I'm there, but hugs me tightly anyway.

"What are you doing here?"

"We're all here. The gang is down in the waiting room. We don't want to bother Poppy, we just wanted to come and sit with you if you need us," I say, and she hugs me again and sits on the little vinyl bench in the hallway. I sit next to her.

"What happened? Is she okay?"

"She'll be okay. We pulled her out right away and the fishing hut was really warm, we had heated blankets while we waited for the ambulance. God!" She starts to cry again. "I have been on the phone with the police, and they're saying someone did this."

"What do you mean? How could someone…"

"They found…someone cut holes all over the ice near our spot. Someone was probably trying to weaken the ice so maybe the ice hut would fall through and kill us. It's a miracle nobody else fell into one of these when we walked across from the car to the ice hut. Someone wants me dead, Flor. And he almost got Poppy instead," she sobs into my shoulder.

"But she's okay, love, she's okay." I pat her back and make a soothing noise with my lips, but I can't believe what I'm hearing. I mean, I know the threats are real and something terrible is going on, but there are little girls involved, and for someone to go to such lengths...my God.

"How could someone do that and not be seen?" I ask, because that's the first question in my head.

"Nobody else has been out on the ice in days because it's too cold. They would have had every opportunity, probably hoping the weather warmed maybe—so by the next time we were there, the ice would be weakened even more. It could have been so much worse," she says, and then blows her nose and wipes the mascara from under her eyes.

"I'm so sorry, love," I say.

"Thanks. She's asleep, but I wanna be there if she wakes up. Tell the gang thanks for coming, but I'm gonna stay with her."

"Of course. Here," I say handing her some coloring books and a stuffed elephant and the lovely red mittens. I point to them. "From Millie," I say, and she squeezes them and smiles.

"We just wanted to be here if you needed us."

Shelby stands to go, then she sits back down suddenly, holding the gifts on her lap, looking left and right to make sure nobody is within earshot.

"That podcast. I've thought about it, and I wanna help. Let's get this motherfucker," she says. Then she stands again, moving to Poppy's door, and turns to me one more time. "Don't tell Mack. She'll freak, but maybe we can get enough info out there to make a difference until she finds out about it on her own. It's my girls involved now. I can't worry about that." I nod and she disappears back into the hospital room.

I'm glad to hear this because I planned to do it anyway, but it's very pleasant news that I won't have to deceive my friend in order to help her. Before I go and find the rest of the gang, I look to see if Karla Laurier, the nurse who tended to Otis much of the time, is working. Winny told me she'd be a good person to chat with if I wanted to suss out some information that might help us, and she doesn't have the stomach to come back to this hospital. I can't blame her for that.

I ask after Karla at one of the nurse's stations and a distracted woman in tight scrubs and a side ponytail tells me she's in Critical Care on the third floor. As I walk down the sad, gray hallway and smell the antiseptic and bleach wafting from hospital bedding and the microwaved food sitting untouched in room trays, I feel a pang of sadness for Otis who had to spend his last moments here, but I take a deep breath and try to keep my head in the right space. I am here for information.

The receptionist points me to room 302 when I ask again for Karla on the hub on floor three, and moments later I find her in an empty room, wrapping a vomit-soaked sheet up into a bundle and throwing it into a linen bin.

"Oh, Mrs. Hopkins was brought down to imaging, I'm afraid," says the stout nurse with rosy cheeks, her hair pulled back so tightly into a bun it looks like her hair follicles might be torn from the roots.

"Oh, no, dear, I came to talk to you, if that's alright." Karla stops what she's doing and turns to look at me.

"Oh. Um, what can I help you with? Are you a family member?"

"Actually, I'm here about Otis Thorgard. I was told that you cared for him often."

"I did. Oh, sweet Otis. I'm so sorry. He was your…"

"Friend," I say. "Winny tells me you were a great comfort to him." And when I look at Karla I'm certainly not getting murderer vibes, but I guess that's probably the case with all of these sorts of awful situations. Amelia Dyer notoriously murdered four hundred people and she looked like the organ player at my church. But it really could be anyone with access to Otis. The hospital staff are all listed on the website and I plan to go through each name, but the list is so big it's beginning to seem like a futile task. The visitor log coupled with the hospital staff site might at least give us a short list of suspects.

"Did Otis have many other caregivers or visitors?" I ask, and the look on her face is hesitant, like she might not answer or might begin to question my question, but it's innocent enough and I put a pearl headband with a rose on it in my hair earlier for extra effect, so she just sits down on the edge of the bare bed and sighs.

"He had a million visitors. Everyone loved Otis, and he's lived in town his whole life. Why do you ask?"

"I'm writing a story about dear Otis," I say. "Just interviewing folks close to him in his final days so I can paint a nice picture."

"Oh," she says, perking up. Maybe happy I'm not going to put her in an uncomfortable position, or just happy to be named someone "close to Otis." "Buddy from the cafeteria would come and do crosswords with him, Clay Dawson would bring him waffles from the IHOP sometimes when he'd come in for shift, Nancy from the gift shop would bring him balloons sometimes—the ones that were losing their helium and would go to waste. He always got a kick out of that, even though the Elmo's and Dora's faces looked droopy. Gosh, all the nurses doted on him. He had lots of friends and family visit. Hard to keep track. I guess you can put down that he was surrounded by love and support by those who knew him best," she says.

Thanks for the cliché, I think to myself, but leave the writing to me, but of course I don't say that. This was a fool's errand, it seems, but I dare to ask one last question.

"Do you remember anything about a ripped-up note—something Otis seemed upset about at all?"

"Um… I don't know about a note, but I do remember him tearing up something—some paper the night before he passed, because I swept up the scrap he dropped and asked if I could throw the rest away for him. He shoved the scraps in his sweater pocket, which I thought was odd…which is why I remember, but patients like him have a lot of strange behaviors, so I didn't think much of it," she says, and then she's paged from the little radio thing she wears on her waistband and quickly excuses herself.

I stand, brush the folds in my slacks with my palms, and pick up my handbag. Well, at least Winny hasn't lost the plot. Otis did put that torn note in his pocket. Of course I believed her, but I did wonder a little bit about the validity of her story. What if someone planted it there, what if she herself had gone off her nut and done something terrible? I mean, when things become this strange all around you, you really can't trust anyone. But he certainly did write those warning words and try to hide them from someone. I shudder as I walk out of the vomit stench of the room and back down the bleak hallway. At least that was something. A small piece of the ever-expanding puzzle. Poor Otis.

When I arrive back downstairs, I clutch my chest and rush to the front desk when I see Bernie lying on the ground in front of it, staff circled around him.

"Oh God! What's happened?" I cry and see Herb behind the desk shoving a file folder into his coat. Millie and Mort stand over Bernie with the nurses, and Millie leans into me and whispers. "Don't worry, he's fine. He's creating a diversion."

I look at Millie with my mouth agape and then down to Bernie, who gives me a very subtle thumbs-up as he lies there with his eyes closed and his tongue hanging out. I cannot believe what I'm witnessing.

"Don't look at me like that, it was Bernie's idea," Millie says, and then I see Bernie open one eye and see Herb with a thumbs-up, and he suddenly begins to push himself to a seated position.

"I'm okay, just low blood pressure," he says, and the nurses help him to sit in a wheelchair that someone brought over.

"Are you kidding me?" I whisper. Then there is some back and forth when Bernie tries to stand and say he's fine and is going home and they insist he stay for a while for observation.

"Okay, alright," he finally acquiesces. He winks our way and then makes a waving gesture to us to make a run for it. Before I even fully register what is happening, Millie has me by the hand and the four of us are scurrying out the front door and into Evan's waiting van. As soon as the doors are closed, Millie hollers, "Go, go, go!"

Evan flashes a confused look into the rearview mirror. "Um...okay."

"Before they catch us!" she adds dramatically, and Evan presses the gas to our getaway car and we pull away from the hospital full of adrenaline and pride. Herb hands me the file covertly, pleased with himself for his accomplishment, and I take it and quickly begin looking through it with the light on my phone on the ride back.

"Anything I should know about?" Evan asks.

"Nothing!" Herb says and pulls out his Keeblers at some feeble attempt to appear normal. I scan through the visitor log of people who signed on the date of Otis's death and the surrounding days. There are dozens, of course, but it's not a huge hospital, so not so many I can't get a quick assessment, and it's a lot of names I know because I've lived here so long, and some I don't, and then one name stops me cold. I suck in a sharp breath when I see it there in black-and-white. It's so shocking I can barely believe I'm looking at it.

Leo Connolly was there, signing his name into the visitor log at 10:18 p.m. the night before Otis died.

12

Mack

"It stopped again!" I shout, startling Billy and he swerves slightly at the jolt before regaining control of the car. "Sorry, but he stopped."

"Where?" he asks, rubbing his sleepy eyes. We have been driving for a couple of hours and haven't said much because my mind has been reeling and he's trying to be respectful and supportive, I can tell, but I'm sure he doesn't know how the hell he's supposed to act…so the hum of the heater and the low volume of a country station coming in and out on the radio has filled the silence for most of the ride.

On the tracker app it shows the phone is no longer moving down highway 10. My heart is beating frantically. The phone was stopped for over an hour when we first got on the road which allowed us to practically catch up to it, but then, when we were somewhere outside of Winnipeg Junction, it started again, and I was worried we'd be driving all night to God knows where. The stop it made was in the middle of nowhere it looked like from the location—just a roadside pit stop exit with a bar, strip club, and a gas station.

"It's just this side of Fargo," I say, practically shouting. "It looks like it's in the parking lot of a diner called Toasty's. We're only twenty minutes away. Oh my God." I take a deep breath and tap my nails on the back of my phone nervously, willing the location not to change.

"So what's your plan when you see him..." Billy asks. "If I'm allowed to pry."

"I mean, you *are* driving me across the state to help, so I suppose you're allowed to pry," I say. And then I don't elaborate because I don't know. "Am I supposed to have a plan?" I ask. "I've never tracked down a runaway husband before, so I'm not exactly sure how this goes."

"Oh," he says, flatly.

"Yeah."

"Huh."

"I know. But I just want answers. I guess... I'll know what to say when I see him. I think. Or maybe I'll just kill him if the opportunity presents itself," I say, and he shifts his eyes over to me, then back to the road. I don't say that I'm kidding. My blood is boiling at the thought of him living a secret life somewhere and making a mockery of the years and years we spent together, of Rowan, our families, our whole lives. Maybe I could just run him down in the Toasty's parking lot once I see him.

Suddenly, I feel Billy's hand on top of mine on the console. He squeezes it.

"You have me for backup if you need me," he says, returning his hand to the steering wheel. Of course it's crossed my mind why he's going so very far out of his way to help me. I'm not a fool. Most people pity me, which is something that I detest, of course, but it's something I have grown accustomed to. That could be it. Also, he wanted to catch up over dinner. We were friends once. I don't know if Shelby's assessment of his feelings for me are true or not, but that was many years ago, and time and grief have utterly deteriorated me now. I know how pale and bone thin I've become—I'm not blind—and preoccupied with Leo, and depressed, and unfriendly, and exhausted. Who in their right mind would turn their head for me now? Nobody, which is why I think pity is likely his motivation for being so helpful. And right now, I guess I'll take it…as pathetic as that feels to say. I just want answers, and I need somebody's help.

Toasty's is right off exit 42 and sits across from a gas station and Norma's Pie Palace. A series of lampposts light up the icy parking lot where a couple of big rigs are parked sideways along the side of the lot closest to the freeway, and only a handful of other cars are parked in front of the orange glowing windows of the diner. Billy parks and I stare at the app. I turn behind me and point.

"It's…there," I say, looking toward a parked tow truck. "Holy crap. It says it's right there."

I leap out of the car and run across the slippery lot and when I reach the place the dot on the app shows, I bang my knuckles against the truck's passenger window and then swing the door open and step up into the rig.

"Jesus!" The man in the driver's seat yells, gripping his seat and looking around in fear, probably to see if he's about to be carjacked or something. He was watching a video on his phone and laughing with his feet up on the dash before I terrified him. The heat from the cab of the truck billows out along with the smell of Arby's smokehouse brisket and sweet tobacco. I slide into the empty seat next to him and point at his phone. My mouth opens, but no words come at first and he just sits there frozen, his eyes bulging for a couple of moments.

"What the fuck?" he yells as I grab the phone from his grip in one fell swoop.

"Where did you get this?" I demand. "Is Leo with you? Is he inside?" I look to the diner doors, making sure he won't escape me no matter what.

"Who?" he asks, shaking his head and trying to grab the phone back.

"Where is he?" I scream at the man, and he looks frightened now. "Where did you get this?" I yell, and I know it's Leo's because I bought him the stupid phone case with the purple Vikings logo on the back.

"Jesus, lady. I found it, okay? All's I did was find it, and then I turned it on, but it died pretty quick and then I went and got a charger at Dollar General 'cause it had Netflix on it and I thought why not?"

"When?" I ask.

"Couple weeks ago."

"You thought, why not steal a phone?"

"Yeah, I did. I thought why the fuck not because you know why? Because I ate a piece of peanut brittle my aunt Rhonda made for Christmas that I left in my glove box too long so it was kinda frozen and when I took a bite, I broke my tooth. And when I called the dentist, he said it will cost six hundred bucks that I don't have, and now I got an exposed nerve that hurts like a motherfucker and I don't even get back to Brainerd for four more days anyway. And I have to ask my sister, Linda, to borrow money, and she's gonna give me a lot of shit about it before she'll give it to me *and* she'll make me babysit her fucking kids…and they're repulsive, and I can't even enjoy the rest of the damn Christmas freakin' peanut brittle. So, yeah. I saw it sitting there and thought I would watch some free Netflix so my ninety-minute break wouldn't be so fucking miserable. Sue me!"

"You found the phone in Brainerd?" I ask, ignoring the rest of everything he said.

"No. It was in a motel room I was staying in outside Riv-

ers Crossing. In a nightstand drawer, so I didn't really steal it
then, did I?"

"What's the motel?" I asked, stunned, unable to think
straight, trying to make sense of how he has Leo's phone.

"Lumberjack's over by the Waffle House and that new brew-
ery," he says and I shove the phone in my pocket, then climb
down from the cab of his truck and slam the door behind me.
I walk numbly back to Billy, who stands nearby, hugging himself against the cold wind and watching me without interfer-
ing, which I appreciate because most men would have tried to
play hero or attempted not to let me get in this guy's truck or
interfered in one way or another.

"Not Leo?" he asks as I approach, and I shake my head and
walk past him toward the warmth inside the front doors of
Toasty's. He follows, jogging ahead a few steps and opening
the door for me.

Inside, we sit at an old weathered booth and I don't speak
yet. I think the shock is still settling in. I was sure it would lead
to him. I saw it all unfolding. The details are fuzzy; the whys
elude me, but I clearly envisioned him in front of me again:
not dead, not on the arm of some secret girlfriend, not high
on drugs. Not any of the other explanations I have come up
with over the months about why he would have vanished like
this, but just there, alone, and so, so sorry. He got in way over
his head with the money and the lies, and thought it would be
better for me if he disappeared, and then he'd beg my forgive-
ness. But all I got was a tow truck driver watching *Love Island*
on Leo's phone in a diner parking lot. How is this my life?

I look at the giant plastic menu on the table in front of me.
The walls are papered forest green with a pine tree pattern and
the floors are old, chipped linoleum. A cat rubs itself against
one of the vinyl stools at the dessert counter and then disappears into the back. There are only two other customers, an
elderly man smoking a cigarette, hunched over a cup of coffee

at a two-topper and another man sits at the bar, pouring co-
pious amounts of syrup onto a stack of hotcakes. The waitress
finally puts her phone in her apron and notices us.

"A double bourbon on the rocks," I say as she approaches,
before she even asks.

"Uh. It's a diner, sweetheart" is all she says, and I'm supposed
to know what that means, I guess.

"What?"

"It's 24/7 breakfast. Ain't no booze here, sorry," she says,
placing a pot of coffee in front of us instead, and my skin prick-
les with annoyance.

"Scooter's across the highway is your only option. There's a
polka band tonight though, so go at your own risk."

"I, for one, love polka," Billy says, trying to make it okay
if I want to drag him around the middle of nowhere for even
longer and drink myself to oblivion, so just to make sure he
doesn't think I'm completely unstable or some kind of alcoholic
who needs to run to the polka bar to numb myself when we
could both use a cup of coffee or better yet, some sleep, I just
sigh and look at the menu again.

"I'll have the big country breakfast with the fried eggs, hash
browns, and the strawberry pancake slam."

"Whipped cream?" she asks.

"Absolutely," I say.

"It comes with pecan or blueberry pie?"

"The three-thousand-calorie country breakfast with a strawberry pancake slam comes with pie as a side?" I ask. She just
stands there waiting for my answer, tapping her foot with her
pen in hand.

"Pecan," I say, then look to Billy.

"I'll have the same." He smiles, closing his menu and handing
it to her. We both glance at the phone sitting in the middle of
the table. I nervously peel open a bunch of Splendas and pour
them into my coffee. I flick the empty paper squares around the

table mindlessly, the way we used to do as teenagers when we took over the corner booth of a Perkins late at night and only had enough pocket change for pots of coffee to earn our right to hang out there to escape our parents and the cold nights.

"That guy found it in a motel room near Rivers Crossing."

"What? Wait. It's been... When did he find it? That doesn't add up," Billy asks.

"Couple weeks, he says."

"Why was his phone there? How could it have not been noticed for over a year, almost a year and a half?" he asks.

"It makes no sense," I say. "I mean, did someone plant it there in a motel drawer? Why? If someone killed him, they wouldn't leave his phone behind. If he's running, he doesn't leave his phone behind. I mean, what the actual fuck?"

"What if he stayed there and whatever happened, he didn't mean to leave it behind? You said it was in a drawer. I mean, what if it was stuck in the back and really did get missed all this time, turned off, wedged behind a motel Bible or something?" he says, and I think about it a minute.

"Well, *Love Island* Tow Truck Guy said it was in a drawer, and assuming he's not lying, then, I don't know. Maybe. But what the hell was Leo doing there between drinks with the guys that night and disappearing? Was he there doing some dirty business with a scuzzy loan shark, or what we're all thinking— having an affair, because why not throw *that* into the mix of all the unthinkable things this man I thought I knew was actually capable of?"

Billy is quiet, but gives me a sympathetic look. The food comes, and the waitress, who has plates balanced all the way up both arms like a circus performer, somehow makes room for them all on our table. As I stare at enough food to feed a family of eight, I want to start sobbing into my pancake slam. It's so stupid and out of place to think about this right now, but every year for Thanksgiving we used to drive to Grand Forks, me and Leo and Rowan, and we'd always stop at Applejack's Diner for Rowan's favorite French silk pie, and the place had the same dusty curtains and old records on the walls, just like this place. Leo would stuff himself with bananas Foster and sausage biscuits so he didn't have to eat my aunt Minnie's turkey hotdish or fruit Jell-O mold. He could probably eat all of this. Even the pecan pie. Or he'd save some and feed it to her dog, Harold, when she wasn't looking.

I try not to cry. I look at Billy, of all the people in the world, sitting across from me in this moment, and it's so surreal. I am getting accustomed to surreal, I suppose, but this life I find myself in—this complete one-eighty is so crippling some days it doesn't feel real at all. I question what I'm even doing here, why I don't just let Leo go if he wants to be gone so badly. Billy watches me stare down at the greasy plate with a blank look on my face.

"Are you gonna...see what's in it?" he asks, nodding to Leo's phone.

"Well, it's almost dead and needs a charger, and I could probably use a drink first," I say, and then he asks the waitress for some take-out containers and pays the bill, and before I know it we are both drinking bourbon on the rocks at Scooter's across the highway.

I picked up an iPhone charger at a Wally's Gas 'N' Go because for some reason Billy has an old Samsung, and I didn't bring one. So now the phone is charging on the floor under the bar and I am in no rush to look at it because right now there is a flicker of hope that something important could surface, but when I look, if nothing is there, I don't think my heart can take anymore.

We watch a few truckers bustle in in big coats, rubbing their hands together from the cold and sharing a round wooden table in the middle of the dark, drafty dive bar. They order tap beer and talk quietly to one another. I wonder about the young woman bartending—where she must live and what life circumstance landed her this particular job in this middle-of-nowhere frozen tundra. She wears a hoodie with a hole in the elbow and leans against the end of the bar, plucking away at her phone with her press-on nails and a sort of scowl. Can't say that I blame her. Do they still call them press-on nails? Probably not.

"I'm sorry you're going through this," he says, tracing the rim of his lowball glass with his finger. I offer a tight smile and nod, then I look down at my drink and take a sip. What is there to even say anymore?

"You have a really great support system in a place like Rivers Crossing at least. Everyone seems to be rallying behind you," he says, and a small, sharp laugh escapes my lips, making his eyebrows rise.

"No, sorry. I do."

"What?" he says with a tilted head, a genuine question.

"No, I just—I think most people enjoy gossiping about it. I mean…I see it. I hear the stories. You knew him…once upon a time. What do you think happened?" I ask, and I see some color drain from his face. I don't usually ask people point-blank "what do you think happened?"

"Uhhh. I mean, I don't really know him anymore. After college, I went in with him on that first pizza place for a summer until I met Nora on a trip to Milwaukee, and the rest is history… I think the last time I talked to him was a few years ago, when he was trying to buy the Trout from my parents."

"Yeah," I laugh. "I told him Lou would laugh in his face at that offer which is exactly what happened."

"I guess I shoulda stayed in the pizza business, considering how you two made out on it in the end," he says, and has no idea how I really made out in the end. I'm sure most people think we built a little empire on all of his business investments. I mean, we did, of course, but they don't know how it ended. I don't tell Billy that Leo probably only wanted the Trout because it was an established, rock-solid business in town, and he'd fucked up everything else by then.

"Sorry to hear about Nora" is all I say instead.

"Thanks," he says, and picks at a bowl of pretzels on the bar. I don't ask what happened. I heard about her running off with an anesthesiologist. I mean, if that's true, but it's probably a variation of that—an affair of some sort. I've come to learn the rumors in Rivers Crossing are usually rooted in some reality and then liberties are taken. I should know.

"You like being back?" I ask.

"Hmm," he says, looking at the ceiling and thinking a moment. "I haven't really figured that out yet."

"Well, it should feel like home, not like a punishment," I say with some weird sense of authority. And I suppose I mean the words, but living here feels more like a punishment than home to me these days, so I guess I'm just reciting something I'm conditioned to say.

"Yeah. Good point. I've known you since middle school, so spending time with you definitely feels...more like home than like a punishment," he says and his eyes meet mine. I feel myself blush against my will and I look away.

"Well then, you're a real nut, because you're drinking bottom shelf bourbon at a roadside bar after a wild-goose chase with the biggest pity case the town has ever seen...and you should think I'm crazy and should *absolutely* feel like you're being punished right now."

"Don't say that. You're not a pity case. People just care...but in weird ways, because we're all hardwired to be really bad at handling this sort of...trauma. It makes people uncomfortable, but that's on them, not you," he says.

"Thank you," I say, feeling my heart lift just a tiny bit.

"Plus, I wouldn't be here if I didn't want to be," he adds.

"Well, I did get you through ninth grade math, so you owe me." I smile, and he chuckles at this.

"It was a dumb class. Why are we discussing Bobby buying forty watermelons and eating six of them and trading twenty of them for two coconuts each... I mean."

"It was practical problem solving," I laugh.

"What's practical about buying that many watermelons? And why would Bobby be trading them with anyone? What sort of currency is that?" he asks.

"And how could he have managed any of that after eating six of them," I say, realizing I've had a few too many sips of bourbon to the one Billy has been nursing. I feel suddenly a little bit woozy and lightheaded. "Okay," I say, pushing the glass away and taking a deep breath. "I think I've amply prepared myself to open the phone." I try to slide off the stool to crouch down and pick the phone up from where it's propped by an outlet on the floor, but I lose my footing and stumble. He grabs my arm before I topple over.

"Yeah," I say. "Okay then. I think I might be a little... buzzed," I say, and he keeps hold of me until I safely sit back down. I turn on the phone and wait for it to come to life.

When it does, my hands shakily scroll through, clicking on contacts, texts, call history. I don't see anything that stands out. I immediately wonder if he had a second phone for all these dirty dealings of his. He must have.

"No activity since it was turned on two weeks ago except the Netflix the tow truck driver was watching," I mumble out loud. His last call was to me three hours before I got home that night to find him gone. Just calls to the guys, local businesses... then I see a number that he's called a few times in the week before he disappeared—a number that's not saved, but is local. I stare at it for a moment, then put a finger up to Billy to tell him "hold on a sec here" and I push the call button.

It rings twice before the upbeat voice of a young woman answers.

"Pop's!"

"I'm sorry, what?" I ask confused.

"Pop's Grill. Can I help you?" she asks, Billy looks at my perplexed expression and gives me a quizzical look back.

"Uhhh. I'm…sorry. Grill? No… I was looking for Leo Connolly. I must have…"

"Oh okay, hold on," she says.

"What? He's there?" I gasp.

"Well, he works here." And I'm so stunned by her words that my grip loosens and the phone drops from my hand.

13

Shelby

I sit on a wooden pew in the dark hospital chapel. The room is small and a candle burns on a wooden altar in the front. I'm the only one here, my soft crying piercing the eerie silence. I watch the red light flicker against the stained glass images, making Jesus and a white dove look lifelike on the window above me.

She's okay. She's fine. She was only in the water for a few seconds and could probably go home tonight if we wanted, but will stay just one night to be safe. Thank God, yes...but this does little to lessen the rage burning inside of me. And then, somewhere in the chaos of nurses and visitors I hear that word again. "Grateful." We should be so grateful it wasn't worse. I don't know who said it, and whoever it was I know they only meant well, of course they did, but I still feel the urge to punch them in the throat. So I do a couple of Hail Marys and whisper a short prayer and on my way out, I pick up the Styrofoam cup of stale hospital coffee I left on the ledge by the door and flick away the tears that are starting to form in the corner of my eyes.

I asked Clay to bring Juju to my mother's house for the night so we could stay with Poppy without traumatizing her any further, and I'm surprised when he's not back after an hour. I call and it rings through, and so I call again and he answers in a hoarse whisper.

"Sorry," he says. "June is upset. She doesn't want me to go. She keeps asking if Poppy is gonna die."

"Jesus," I say. "She seemed okay when you left. She talked to Poppy. She knows she's okay," I say, confused.

"I know. She's just tired, and it was a lot."

"My poor baby," I say. "Well, just stay, then. I'm sure Mom won't care if you crash in the downstairs guest room."

"Well, we'll be back at the hospital to get you both first thing," he says and we say our goodbyes and everything just feels dreamlike and off, and it's more than just the trauma of it all. I can't really put my finger on it, but my spine tingles and I don't know if it's the ghostly halls of this prehistoric hospital or something else.

I forgot I promised Poppy her Little Mermaid blanket because Christmas is over so she doesn't want her reindeer one, and how can I say no to that right now?...and her Yoda doll, damn. I need to get home and back here, and I could really use a toothbrush and something that's not tight jeans to sleep in at the hospital, so I guess I'll have to call a cab.

Even though I know Poppy is in a deep sleep, I go up and check on her one more time before I run over to the house. Inside the room it breaks my heart to see her hooked up to a heart rate monitor and blood pressure cuff. Of course I've been sitting here all night in this environment, but walking in with fresh eyes and seeing my sweet baby surrounded by tubes and plastic and metal and beeping sounds is still jarring.

She's so warm now, the rise and fall of her chest rhythmic

and peaceful. I kiss the damp curls on her forehead and quietly close the door, making a mental list in my head of the things I need to pick up at home and I'm so lost in my thoughts I almost miss it, and then I stop, back up a few steps and peer into room 309.

"Bernie?" I say, tapping my knuckle against the door in a courtesy knock. He's sitting in a hospital bed, eating a plate of rice and beans and watching an old episode of *Matlock*.

"Oh! Hey, Shelby," he says with a wide smile.

"What the hell?" is all I manage to spit out.

"I'm just fine. Just some palpitations." And he must register the concerned look on my face because he adds, "Promise."

"Okay," I say. "Good."

"Coleslaw?" he offers, holding out a paper cup covered in a thin plastic cover. I sit in the chair next to him and take it.

"Sure," I say, unwrapping a plastic fork and eating the waxy slaw.

"I'm glad she's okay," he says. "You gave us all a fright."

"Thanks, Bern," I say, and he turns down the volume on the TV.

"Did you know Andy Griffith used to get upset on the set of this show because the crew would always steal his apples and peanut butter and it was his favorite food? All the greats are gone. It's a shame."

"Yeah," I agree, and we watch the episode in silence for a few minutes. A scene unfolds—it zooms in on a swimmer in an indoor lap pool with goggles and a swim cap. He is swimming laps alone when the back of a man in a suit appears. We only see the suited man's back and arms as he catches the swimmer before he can push off the wall to swim back the other way—he holds the swimmer's head under water forcefully until his body goes limp. Bernie scrambles for the remote and switches it off as quickly as he can. I don't react.

"So tell me, what do you think about this podcast? I was surprised to see you involved."

"Me?" he asks.

"Yes, you."

"I'm not used to getting asked what I think," he says with a smirk.

"Well, you're around a lot of strong personalities, I suppose," I say.

"I suppose I am." He chuckles. "'When a man is denied the right to live the life he believes in, he has no choice but to become an outlaw,'" he says and I stare at him.

"Uh-huh," I say, wondering if he hit his head.

"Nelson Mandela," he says, and I understand now that it's a quote.

"I see," I say, but I don't really see. I put the coleslaw on his dinner tray and pick at the fork prongs.

"Maybe Florence isn't an outlaw exactly, but taking the pursuit of justice into our own hands when nobody else is working to do so to protect you…it's something along those lines. You're being forced to live in fear. I can't say we're cracking the case, but it's getting people's attention," he says. He pats the corners of his mouth with his napkin and sets it down.

"I don't know if that's a good or bad thing yet," I say.

"Me either," he agrees.

"How exactly the hell did it go viral? Who's listening to this? I mean—these listeners have to be all over, not really local… I thought about it, but it doesn't really make sense that it could do any good—do anything but stir shit up."

"Well, as you know, Mort has a podcast," he says, and I grunt in hesitant agreement, because as it turns out, he really does.

"And for some reason, people like listening to him make literary references nobody gets and talk about his bunions, I guess. Evan says he's actually charming, but I didn't take the time to actually listen, so what do I know? I guess we just piggybacked off of his popularity and folks liked listening to five old goats sitting around arguing with one another about the facts of the case, and people also like true crime," he says, and I wince. I've just never thought of it that way—heard anyone call my life and Mack's life "true crime."

"Sorry," Bernie says.

"No, it's okay…"

"So, I think an unsolved case got everyone worked up and probably nobody in this little frozen town listens to *Mort's Literary Musings*, but it only took one person at Frannie's Cut & Curl or the Trout to hear about the whole viral thing, and now everyone in town knows about it. Florence is opening a tip line."

I think about this for a moment—about how the police are probably still at the lake examining the ice that somebody purposefully drilled into to try to hurt my family. And I think about how that's what it took to get them remotely invested in this again—in the constant, looming threat I've been fearing since it all happened over a year ago. Maybe getting people whispering about it a little louder than they usually do will actually prove helpful. Maybe a person who knows something will slip up, maybe the more facts that leak to the public, the more it could unearth some information somebody doesn't even know they are holding on to. What do I have to lose at this point?

I don't respond out loud. I just nod, because I don't really know what else to say and I'm so very exhausted. So I change the subject.

"You still seeing your daughter this weekend?" I ask.

"Yes, ma'am. The church is having a potluck and she made spicy cornbread," he says, and I notice him twisting some sort of necklace or locket chain hanging around his neck—one I hadn't noticed before, but I guess he's always in a turtleneck and scarf and not a hospital gown.

"That looks fancy," I say, and he looks down at it and smiles. He rests the pendant in his palm and leans over for me to get a closer look. It's the image of a border collie etched into the metal.

"My Cynthia gave this to me over twenty years ago when our sweet Roxy went over the rainbow bridge. It opens up and there's a little clipping of her fur in there," he says, a look of pride across his face as he shows me. Just the very thought of this makes me instantly tearful, but I hold back. Bernie talks about that dog to this day like it was the greatest loss of his life. Not more than Cynthia of course, but a close second. I touch the little tuft of white hair and then my hand flutters to my heart.

"Oh, Bernie, that's lovely. I didn't even know you had this."

"Haven't taken it off in a few decades...except for an MRI once. I tried to fight them on that, but they said the magnetic force would pull the chain so hard it would tear my head off."

"Nobody wants that," I say.

"Well, it was Lucy Singletary working that day and I think she exaggerated, but still. Haven't parted with it except those thirty-five minutes," he says and slips it back under his gown.

"Say hi to Ginny for me," I say, standing to go. "And I'll see you back at the Ole on Monday. Gus will be very excited." He smiles at the mention of Gus.

"I'll save a couple of cornbreads in a Tupperware for ya," he says.

"Can't wait," I say, moving to the door.

"Shelby." He stops me and his face has changed. A shadow flashes across it and he pauses as if he's about to say something important. "Please be careful out there. I wanna see you Monday," he says, and I know he means it with fatherly concern, but it scares me—the words from someone else's lips articulating that I have to be extra careful just existing in order to make it to Monday. That the threat of not making it is real.

I pull a woolen hat over my ears and shrug on my parka. "I will, Bern. Tell 'em to get ya outta here." I smile and hold my palm up to wave goodbye, checking in on Poppy one more time before I head out to run to the house.

Minutes later I'm in the lobby waiting for Cecil's Taxi Service to pick me up. I recognize Howard Lutsen behind the wheel when the car pulls up, so I sit in the front seat. He turns up the heat for me and offers me a stick of spearmint gum, and then we pull away and I watch the hospital building shrink in my rearview mirror. The shapeless brick building against the backdrop of wispy falling snow swirling in around the lampposts in front of the building. I've always thought it looks like an abandoned insane asylum you'd see on a ghost hunter show. I think about all of the pain that has been felt inside of those walls, all of the wailing after the loss of a loved one, all of the death, and it makes me ill to leave my baby there even though it's just for a quick run to the house. I almost tell him to stop. I don't know why, but something just feels wrong.

I tell myself I'm letting it all get to me and I need to stay calm. Howard plays a Queen song and smokes a cigarette out the window, and between the cold air and the loud music he's singing along to, I feel like I've entered some sort of temporary hell and I just want this day to be over.

When we pull up to my house, I hoist my bag onto my shoulder and let myself out the passenger's door.

"So you can wait like ten minutes, right?" I ask because I was told that my ride would wait when I called.

"Oh, you're going back? They didn't tell me. I got a pickup at O'Leary's Pub. It's just Brenda Levinson, but she mixed some of her meds with shots of Jäger at the bar and I guess she's puked all over the snow in front of the building. Dave don't want her back inside puking up on the customers and stuff, so I gotta get back over there before she freezes to death outside. I can be back here to get you in twenty, though," he says.

"Twenty is fine, How, but please no longer. I need to get back," I say and he gives me a salute.

"I will do you one better and make it nineteen minutes. You can time me," he says looking at his watch and pushing some stopwatch feature. I don't indulge him, I just give him a thumbs-up as he pulls away and screeches down the snow-covered dirt road.

I put my bag on the front step and fish around for my keys and then open my front door, but before I can punch in the code to turn off the alarm, I realize it wasn't armed. The blue light isn't flashing on the console. I freeze for just a moment before closing the door behind me because what if someone broke in and I'm walking into danger. The door was locked though, and in these few seconds I take to decide what I should do, there is a sound behind me—the shuffling of feet in the snow approaching me, and it's so fast and out of nowhere that I'm just paralyzed in fear and can't register what's happening.

And then I'm suddenly very aware as a plastic bag is forced over my head from behind and someone is pulling it tight across my face. I don't even have time to take in a sharp breath to hold, there is just suddenly no air, the plastic sucking into my mouth with each desperate gasp. I can't scream. I just flail my arms to try hit or punch whoever it is, but they're behind me and I...can't breathe. I bang at the buttons on the security system next to me wildly, trying to hit the emergency alarm, but nothing happens. I start to feel my head float and I see colors like firecrackers behind my eyes. My fingers are starting to tingle and I can't even scream. I can't *scream*.

I'm going to die like this.

And then I think about the Phillips screwdriver I left on the console table next to the front door when I was installing more security cameras around the house yesterday, and I silently beg God to let it still be there. I have seconds before I collapse to the ground, so I swing my hand and feel for the table, my fingers touching yesterday's junk mail and a glass jar for keys, which I feel break as I slam the items on the table around blindly. I feel a shard of glass slice the side of my hand and I panic more, but then I feel it. By the grace of God, I feel the handle of a screwdriver I've had for years, and I grip it as tightly as I can and reach behind me with all the force I have which is quite weak, but it's enough. My surging adrenaline and rage is enough to swing and...not miss. The long metal end sinks into flesh.

I hear a gasp and a moan, and the grip around my neck loosens. I faintly hear footsteps crunching over icy snow, running in the direction of the woods far behind the row of houses. It takes me a few moments to pull the plastic off and gulp in air between shaky sobs. I'm on my hands and knees just trying to get my breath back, but my whole body is trembling violently and my heart is beating in my throat. I try to take in a few steady breaths, and I will myself to stand so I can catch who it is before they're gone.

I run only as far as the edge of the house and look out across snowdrifts and boney trees. All I can see is a dark figure, too far away to make out anything, just a moving shadow. Then I look down to see a drop of blood. And another. They've left a trail of blood like breadcrumbs on top of the freshly fallen snow.

I run back inside my front door and lock it behind me. I slide down the back of the door and let the hysterical cries escape me. "Why?" I scream over and over again until my throat is hoarse and raw and I can barely speak. I stand and push everything off of the console table in one violent swoop, screaming as loud as I can one more time.

And when I'm done, I reluctantly call Detective Riley, because now we have DNA.

14

Florence

The police are here, and it's got everyone quite excited. Poppy is on the sofa wrapped in a Little Mermaid blanket with Gus who she is giving licks of her jumbo candy cane stick, and everyone is doting on her while June sits on the floor in front of the rec room TV and watches a *Teletubbies* episode with Herb.

Mack is in the front office asking Detective Riley a lot of questions in an annoyed tone of voice. Apparently, she was in Fargo or some such place, heading to a roadside diner or something, I don't really know all the details, but she raced back after she heard what happened to Shelby, and after the police left Shelby's house, she stayed the night at the hospital with them. Rumor has it Billy Curran dropped her off and that has everyone talking, but it's none of my business.

"This is outlandish," Herb says, perched on the edge of an ottoman and pointing at the television. "These Teletubbies are totally inappropriate looking. I thought this was a children's show."

"Herb," Millie warns from her spot at the puzzle table where she is quickly knitting a green pot holder to give to Detective Riley before he can leave.

"There's no plot. Zero conflict. I mean, what the hell? They just jump around and make irritating noises."

"Herb," Mort says from his spot in front of the computer where he and Evan are working on selling ads on the podcast.

"Come on, June. You gotta be bored to shit. Curious George doesn't even talk and he's more interesting than this, right?" She nods in agreement. He switches it to *Peppa Pig*.

"Oh, see now. This is good. This is quality stuff," he says, handing June a tube of ranch Pringles, which she takes and happily watches *Peppa*.

I try to listen to what Shelby and the police are talking about in the front office, but I can't be too obvious, so I only walk over to the coffee station three times during their conversation and take my time stirring in the powdered creamer so I can strain my ears to hear. All I really understand is that they dismissed the electricity and generator being destroyed as teenagers, but now that Shelby has been attacked yet again and told them about the threat left on her car, they have now gone full swing on opening her case back up.

I suppose it's a good thing, but they have come up with diddly-squat in all these months since the first attack, so I still think talking directly to people will be more effective than the police taking down a report, and then what? Someone out there knows something, and Detective Chipped Beef has a slim to zero chance of being the one to crack the case with the way they've handled it so far.

I take my time shuffling back over to my spot on the sofa. It's a comfort having Gus and the girls here. Bernie came in with Shelby this morning when they released him, and he works on his crosswords while Millie knits and the TV murmurs in the background. The smell of tuna hotdish baking in the oven warms up the room, and it's dark and overcast outside. Inside, a string of colored Christmas lights still hang limply over the board game bookcase and blinks. It's a cozy, lovely moment with everyone here…except that there is a murderer on the loose ruining everyone's good time.

After a little while I hear Mack say her goodbyes, and the detectives leave. Shelby comes out with a gray look on her face. Who can blame her? She was almost suffocated, and I'm not really sure why she even came in to the Oleander's today except I guess I wouldn't want to be alone at the house either if it were me, and sometimes distraction is the best medicine.

"Who wants to finger paint?" Shelby says, forcing an upbeat voice when she comes into the rec room. Herb raises his hand. "Not you, Herb. Come on, girls. Irene is gonna show you her watercolors and then we'll finger paint in the craft room. What do you say?"

"Yeah!" Poppy says, kissing Gus on the forehead and popping up from her spot as if nothing at all has happened. Children are incredible that way. June follows close behind and they all disappear down the hall.

"Okay," Mort says, startling me. "When we record tonight's episode we want to lead with finding Leo's name on the sign-in at the hospital. This will really rattle folks." I might be mistaken but I think I see dollar signs in his eyes. He's becoming uncharacteristically enthusiastic about the new income the podcast is generating and *Mort's Literary Musings* is receiving more views by the hour.

"Bring it in, guys, bring it in," Herb says as he pulls up a chair next to the computer desk, and I do so, but not without a roll of my eyes and a shake of my head at being told to "bring it in" like we're in a locker room. I sit next to Millie at the puzzle table so we can all chat relatively privately.

"Of course it wasn't Leo," Millie says.

"Of course not," Mort agrees. "Unless he was in some wild disguise and snuck in to kill Otis, but that seems far-fetched."

"Or someone used his name," I say. "To throw a monkey wrench in things if it were ever looked into—someone who had a reason to have Otis dead. Who in the world would want to hurt Otis Thorgard?"

"It makes more sense that it wasn't Leo in disguise…because what if the person who killed Otis also killed Leo? They were in business together for years—what if this is money related?" Evan says.

"Oh, this is good," Mort says, jotting down notes for the recording later.

"Otis and Leo were in business together—a few restaurants, but Leo was in business with damn near everyone at one point or another," Bernie chimes in, his afghan on his legs and cross-word still in hand.

"That's true," Evan says. "I even partnered with him for that first Pipers Pizza he opened the summer after high school. I mean, okay, he had a dozen other partners after that, and maybe a dozen people to have bad blood with him, so it might be money related, but where to even start?"

"God, I even got sucked into an Amway sales position he pitched me a few years ago," Herb says and we all turn and stare at him. "I was looking to make a few bucks and it sounded good."

"It's a pyramid scheme," I say, matter-of-factly.

"Well, I know that now, don't I, Florence?" He stomps over to the kitchenette where he pulls the tuna hotdish from the small oven and scoops himself a large bowl before returning to his chair with a pout.

"Well, listen," I say. "I don't think we're talking about small, transient things like Evan and half the class of '94 going in on a pizza place twenty-five years ago for a summer…or a pyramid scheme," I look to Herb shoveling hotdish into his mouth. "Who has real skin in the game—who lost something?" I think about how Leo always was a sucker for a get rich quick scheme—and it worked out for him...until it didn't. Now it's so much clearer, and I can see why that propensity turned into gambling when COVID hit and things started a downward turn and snowballed.

"Evan says he played pizza entrepreneur for a couple months way back when, and we all know how many other guys he tried to rope in before it all crumbled and didn't work out, but eventually...he did well," Herb says. "Everyone thought he was an arrogant nut, but he made a ton of money in the end. Otis was the only long-term partner besides that drunk guy that's always at the Trout, what's his name?"

"Miles," Bernie says. "Poor soul."

"Otis is a generation older than Leo's school friends—he's not one of the school friends he tried to use to turn a buck," Mort adds. "Not a kid he paid in free beer and a pipe dream. Otis actually stayed and built up the business with him until Otis and his wife sold their half to Leo so they could retire and buy some campground on Lake Superior or wherever."

"No bad blood," Herb says. "So we're back to where we started. Super. This is going nowhere. You want this episode to suck, Mort? We got nothin'. You know what we should do?"

"Oh God," Millie mutters.

"We oughta get Riley to let us interview him."

"For what?" Mort asks.

"He said he had three calls from random people just this week saying they thought they spotted Leo, and then Shelby told him it was probably because of our podcast."

"Told you we should have a tip line—they'd be calling us instead," I add. Herb ignores me and keeps on.

"Well, you saw Riley's look when she explained how popular the podcast was. That guy will do anything for attention.

NOTHING EVER HAPPENS HERE

He'd be all sweaty pits and stutters if he thought he was important enough to be interviewed for a viral show." Herb cracks a
Bud Light from the minifridge, takes a sip and then crosses his
arms across his chest as if to say he's now open to our response.

"I think you're tooting our horn a bit hard, Herb," I say.

"He *does* always seem to have a lot to prove," Mort says
thoughtfully.

"You know," Evan swirls his wheely chair around and turns
away from the computer. "I might be able to get some inside
info—off the record, really see if they know anything. I mean,
one cop to another. Former cop, but still…"

"Yeah," Herb says, excitedly. "He always shakes Evan's hand
all firm and respectful and calls him 'officer' and ignores the
rest of us. If anyone can gather intel, it's probably Evan."

"I didn't get to give him his special gift," Millie says out of
nowhere.

"So?" Herb says,

"So I got the good yarn at Threaded Treasures. It's Danish.
So, yourself!"

"What's the point, Millie?"

"The point is that I'm going too. Evan's new here, why does
he get to have all the fun? I say we all go."

"I also think we should all go. It *is* called *Mort's* Literary
Musings," Mort says.

"How could we forget." Herb shakes his head and sips his
beer.

"I think we all have to go too," Evan says. "We gotta make
him feel important. Bring the recording equipment, make a
whole thing of it."

"We don't even know if he'll agree to it, so we're getting
ahead of ourselves," I say.

"If Evan asks him, he'll agree. He respects him. Thinks it's
a badge of honor that he got part of the side of his head blown

off in the line of duty," Herb says. "Sorry," he adds, looking to Evan. "Chicks like scars and shit. It's cool, if you ask me."

Christ, I think. Herb just assumes Evan also thinks his injuries are a badge of honor and a chick magnet, but he is so indiscreet and baboon-like that he really doesn't know if it's a painful topic still or not…and good luck shutting him up before he puts his foot in his mouth.

Poor Evan doesn't even have a whole ear anymore on his left side and has significant eye damage, but he always wears a cap, so you can't really see the full impact. You forget after a while and get used to it. I quickly change the subject before Herb embarrasses us all more than usual.

"Evan, you *should* be the one to call and ask him, I think. It's our best shot." Everyone nods in agreement, and Herb scrolls through his phone for Riley's number and mumbles something about having saved it for fifteen years and so he hopes it's still the same number. And it is, and then he puts it on speaker mode and lets it ring and it's all very dramatic as we hover around Herb's phone shushing one another when he answers. Herb gives Evan a dramatic gesture to start speaking, and Evan appears put on the spot.

"Detective, it's Evan Carmichael… Officer Carmichael." They say their hellos and small talk before Herb gets impatient and gives him another "move it along" gesture.

"Say, you heard about the podcast we're doing? We thought it would be good for people to hear directly from law enforcement—kind of like a press conference, in a way. Of course, only public, on-record type information, but a goodwill gesture that shows the police are handling whoever seems to be…" He pauses and Herb mouths "terrorizing." Evan ignores this. "Whoever seems to be responsible for the recent attacks and threats."

To my surprise, Riley tells us that he's off duty tonight and his wife is going to the meat raffle at the VFW, so we can come over for a drink and he'd be happy to chat with us on our very popular podcast.

Before I know it we're piled into the van, the whole gang of us singing along to Billy Joel and driving the black, icy roads over to Riley's two-story near downtown Rivers Crossing.

"Whoa...ohh, ohh, ooh..." Millie starts, singing over everyone else. Herb took an hour trying to figure out which shareable snack would be appropriate for the occasion and somehow landed on caramel corn and spicy cashews. He holds them in his lap proudly and Mort pokes and taps at all of the audio equipment he carries in a Bartlett pear box from Aldi. Bernie sits quietly with his favorite afghan spread over his legs, the way I always see him in my mind. If someone said to me, "picture Bernie this second," it would be what I'm looking at right now, a peaceful, meditative look across his face and the afghan his wife crocheted for him across his lap. He notices me staring and looks at me. I give him a wink and he winks back.

When we arrive and all of us old bats make our way over the icy drive with Evan's help and without any fractured hips, we find ourselves in Riley's basement where a roaring fire burns in the brick fireplace. He holds a lowball glass of whiskey and wears a thick woolen sweater. He welcomes us in, looking a bit surprised as one after another of us round the corner of the narrow staircase, and now there are six of us standing in his finished basement with its red carpet, shabby pool table, and plaid couches looking like everything you'd expect in a northern Minnesota lake town. Dated, endearingly tacky, full of warmth and wood paneling.

He offers us all drinks and we linger around the fireplace sipping on whiskey sours...except Evan, who's driving and technically working still, holding a Diet Coke.

"This is for you," Millie says proudly as she hands the detective a pot holder made of the good yarn from Threaded Treasures.

"Oh. For me?" he says, with the same confused look everyone has when she thrusts a square of knitted yarn at them.

"It's a pot holder," Herb says.

"It's a prayer square," Millie corrects.

"What the hell is a prayer square?" Herb asks.

"It's blessed with a prayer and given as a symbol of love and goodwill," she says.

"Oh, lovely, Millie. Thank you so much. Belinda will love it too."

"I thought it was a pot holder."

"Up yours, Herb," she says with a dismissive wave, directing her attention back to Detective Riley and giving him googly eyes.

"I got a pan of Hamburger Helper sitting on the one you knit for me back home as we speak," Herb adds, genuinely confused.

"Why don't we all sit," Mort suggests, and everyone finds a spot on the plaid couches except for Riley, who sits on the brick hearth of the fireplace.

"Nice place ya got here, Dennis," Herb says. I see he's pulling out the first name. I wonder if that's a premeditated tactic to take him down a notch, but knowing Herb, probably not. He opens the canister of spicy cashews, takes a handful, and passes it around the room.

Dennis Riley is young enough to be Millie's son, but apparently she can't help herself and she has her chin resting in both palms, gazing at him. He's a tall, heavy guy with ruddy cheeks and disproportionately small hands, and I just don't see the appeal.

After a few minutes of small talk about how great the fried walleye is at the new sandwich grill in Duluth and how it's been snowing for days and how Riley's wife called and won six pork chops at the meat raffle tonight and how she's his good luck charm, Mort finally gets impatient and moves to plug in the audio equipment and Evan helps him set up, making it look extra official.

The wind outside howls and rattles the drafty basement windows. Millie helps herself to a second drink and Herb gives Evan the nod that he should start. Evan nods back. He taps a cocktail spoon against the side of his raised Diet Coke can and we all quiet down and look in their direction, on the other side of the fireplace where the microphone is plugged in. Evan nervously sits down and taps it twice to make sure it's on. Mort then places the mic and stand in the middle of us all to pick up everyone's voice.

Evan begins reading the lines we gave him. I must admit, I thought he'd memorize some of the talking points and speak a bit more extemporaneously—he's not exactly a natural.

"What we know," he begins. "We're here with Detective Riley of the Rivers Crossing Police Department to get some more information about the recent attacks that have occurred in our town. Detective, can you tell us a little bit about what you know so far?" he asks. The point of having Evan lead was that all of us are virtually invisible and Riley is a guy's guy and would take things more seriously if this was Evan's thing too and not just a bunch of nosy geezers playing armchair detective, but Riley looks flushed.

"Is this live?" he asks.

"No," Mort says. "No, no. We will add all of the intro material and thank our sponsors and everything…then we will edit this down and polish it up so only the stuff you want to keep will air." I think Mort about exploded with delight at saying the words "our sponsors." He really is getting a big head about that.

"Well," Riley starts. "We are doing our best to follow up on all leads. We are aware that people are anxious and concerned that they or their families could be in danger, but…"

"I'll tell ya what we know so far," I say, and Mort looks horrified that things are happening out of sequence, but who wants ten minutes of vague nonsense and filler words, really? This is all crap he already said on the news, and that's not what we're here for.

"We know that Shelby was threatened with a note and later attacked at the lake ice fishing, and again at her home. And so it's implied in a roundabout way that there is no public threat and this is maybe a personal vendetta. But we *also* know that Otis Thorgard died under suspicious conditions—perhaps foul play—and might be connected to Shelby and the disappearance of Leo Connolly. Are you opening a search for Connolly again, since he should be a suspect in both the case of Otis and Shelby right now? Do you have any other suspects?"

"Ugh…" Riley takes a handkerchief from his pocket and dots the sweat on his forehead. "We're looking at all potential suspects at this stage. All of this only just happened, and we are still dusting for prints and running DNA, so we'll have more to announce on that soon," he says, trying hard to recover and not spoil his moment in the spotlight. The whole gang is looking at me railroading Riley and going off plan, but I don't slow down.

"I'm certain that when Winny Thorgard told you she suspected foul play in Otis's death you did a full investigation, so you probably already saw this," I continue, thrusting the hospital clipboard toward him. "So I'm wondering if you have any thoughts on Leo Connolly's name on the visitor log for the night before Otis passed." I see Riley's Adam's apple bob as he swallows down a sip of his drink, pressing his lips together in a tight smile.

"Well, as you know, some things are confidential. But we are looking into all leads," he says. And of course I know he's never seen this, and I also can't blame him for not taking Winny seriously when she announced out of nowhere that she suspected something was very wrong surrounding the circumstances of her husband's death. Otis was quite ill, and who would think anyone on planet earth would have a beef with the dear man?

I don't hate Riley, and I don't fault him entirely, because every clue does seem to lead to a dead end. But that doesn't stop me from wanting to back his ass firmly into a corner on a viral podcast so the whole world is watching how he handles things, and what he does next. My intent is to force him into action, but I hope it doesn't backfire.

"If you'll excuse me for just a moment," Riley says. "I hear Mr. Ruffins whining. I'll just pop upstairs and let him out." We all watch Riley turn the corner and disappear up the stairs.

"I didn't hear Mr. Ruffins," Millie says, and it's clear she's getting tipsy. "That's a cute name, though," she giggles. "Ruffins." Everyone else is staring squarely at me.

"What?" I say, hand to heart.

"What the hell?" Herb yells, and I put my finger over my lips to shush him. Millie tugs on his sleeve and he sits back down.

"Don't worry," I whisper.

"So it was never your intention to get his actual perspective. You just wanted to…" Herb says, and then stops to come up with a word.

"Screw him!" Millie says, and we all shush her.

"I wouldn't say that. Winny brought her suspicions to the police. He ignored her. Now it's our turn…"

"This is not a good interview," Herb interrupts.

"Well," Mort says.

"Well what?" Herb says. "You're railroading him. He's not giving us anything."

"Except perhaps soaring ratings when we edit this," Bernie says, quietly plucking a stray thread from his afghan and eating a handful of the caramel corn Herb passed around, and understanding exactly what I'm doing.

"Well, let the man talk at least," Herb grumbles.

"Of course," I agree. Another statement from Riley saying that he is "looking into all leads" for the thousandth time on the record is all we'll get out of this, but sure.

When Riley returns he pours himself another drink and asks if there is anything else we'd like to ask about, so Evan nicely asks him a few roundabout questions, making him feel important, which is all he really wants out of this. How many years have you been on the force? How are you handling tips that are coming in? And Riley gets to brag and talk about himself a bit even though he's giving equally roundabout answers, but I already got what I came here for, so I'm ready to go anyway.

And then a very strange expression spreads across Herb's face, and his eyes widen. For a moment I think he's passing gas and trying to do so discreetly, but then he stands and says, "We gotta go!" so abruptly, and I still think that might be the reason. But then the look on his face morphs into something like fear, or panic if I'm reading him correctly, and we all begin standing and gathering our things.

"*Matlock* starts at nine," Millie says, and Riley says he understands completely and that it was a pleasure and genuinely thinks he came off well, which is fine by me. Evan helps Mort with his pear box of audio equipment and takes Bernie's arm, carrying his afghan to the van.

We all sit in the freezing van and wait for it to warm up as it puffs smoke out of the tailpipe while Evan searches for a radio station to land on that will make everyone happy. I turn around in my seat and look at Herb, but before I can ask him why he wanted to run out of there so quickly I catch the deer in headlights look that's still plastered across his face.

"You okay, Herb?" I ask gently, and Evan turns the radio down and looks back at us in the rearview mirror.

"Everyone okay?" he asks.

"What if he's lying?" Herb asks.

"Who? Riley?" Mort says.

"About what?" Evan adds.

"What if he's lying about all the supposed leads they're tracking down and evidence they are looking at and…"

"Why? What the hell are you talking about?" I ask.

"Yeah, why would he do that?" Mort asks.

"Because…maybe he's involved," Herb says pulling a familiar-looking object from his coat pocket.

"What the hell is that?" Millie asks, squinting at it.

"I found it down the side of Riley's couch," Herb says, and before he even explains what it is, I recognize the telltale pink daffodil case.

"It's Shelby's missing phone."

15

Mack

When the girl said Leo worked there, I was stunned into silence, but then I stuttered out a response and asked if he was
there now. She told me to hold on and I heard her ask someone. Her voice came back on the line and she said she guesses
he's not there now.

"I don't ever see him, so call back on the day shift," she said.
I was ready to tell Billy to go on home—and that I would sit
at Pop's Grill all night and wait. From what the GPS read, the
place was back toward Rivers Crossing anyway—just thirty
minutes outside of town, and he could drop me there, but then
the call from Clay came and we rushed to Shelby's. Clay was
asleep at her mother's and not answering, so I had Billy drop
me off at her house. After the police finally left her place it was
close to midnight, but she insisted on sleeping at the hospital
so we both went. I slept sitting up in a padded window seat

with Shelby's head in my lap, stroking her hair and thanking God, again, that she's okay, and angry as hell that this could happen again.

Now I'm two nights sleep-deprived, and I can't think clearly. I called my neighbor, Sandy, and asked if she could take Nugget and Linus last night. I'm home after leaving the Oleander's, and more police questions, and Leo finally turning up, and the pups aren't here, and it all feels so surreal. There are no clicking nails on the hardwood, no relentless barking, and the silence echoes. My heart aches. I turn on the TV to fill the void. Dr. Phil is telling some poor old man that he's being catfished and has given his life savings to some scammer in Nigeria and I don't have the energy to walk over and change it to the news, so I listen to the man denying it's true. He promises Dr. Phil that Jenny Smith loves him and when she can access her million-dollar bank account, she'll pay him back and they'll finally be together, and it's so brutally sad and also annoyingly exploitative, and then I think: that's me. How am I any different? I'm a fool. Imagine what he'd be saying to me if I were sitting there on that stage—how did you not see the warning signs? There must have been something!

I start a pot of coffee and listen to the machine gurgle to life, sitting on the window seat in the kitchen nook as I wait for it to brew, and the tears begin to fall.

"Stop," I say out loud to myself. No, I'm done doing this. It would be so easy to pick up the dogs next door, order a pho soup from The Wok, and curl up in front of the bedroom fireplace for the next forty-eight hours with a couple of bottles of wine and a marathon of *The Great British Bake Off*, but I can't. That would signal the beginning of a downward spiral for me, and a depressive episode will not be helpful right now. So instead I take a scalding hot shower, dress, pour my coffee into a travel mug, and head to Pop's Grill…where my once-millionaire entrepreneur husband apparently works flipping hamburgers next to a truck stop and a discount liquor depot.

When I pull up to Pop's it's afternoon, and the sky is low and overcast. It's dark enough for the streetlamp to be illuminated in the snowy parking lot where there are only a few cars parked. The Pop's sign blinks in red neon above the building and a Hamm's Beer sign buzzes electric in the diner window. I sit in the car and look at it for a few minutes, trying to understand what double life he could have been living that would bring him here. How would he even find this place? What possible reason could there be for him working here? I mean, I would be certain it was all a mistake, but Leo Connolly isn't the most common name, and this number is in his phone. What if he's really in there?

Steeling myself, I open the car door. The blast of frigid wind forces me to pull my parka tighter around me and run across the lot to the front doors. Inside, I scan the room for Leo. It's a big place—the sort of truck stop where truckers can shower and use pay-by-the-minute massage chairs tucked back in a nook where there is a TV mounted to the wall. On the other side is a convenience store with fountain sodas and Minnesota memorabilia; shot glasses with walleye pike on them, or Great Lakes ball caps. In the very back is a cafe. I walk through and see a handful of truckers sharing pitchers of beer at vinyl tables in the middle of the room, a few folks on bar stools at the counter eating plates of beige food. And then, I see a couple of slot machines on the wall. One guy is playing the Luck Of The Irish quarter slots, and it beeps and trills like an old '80s video game.

I think about Leo's gambling habit that I didn't know about, and my stomach lurches. I walk up to the counter and ask a woman whose name tag reads "Tawny" if she knows if Leo Connolly is working. She curls her lip in confusion.

"Uh… Hey, Chad, is some guy named Leo working?" she

calls to the back, and a young man with a pimply face and a Pop's apron appears in the doorway to the kitchen.

"Leo? Old guy?" he asks, but my attention has flipped, and I strain to see what I think I just fucking saw when Chad opened the kitchen door. I walk to the side of the counter with wide eyes and my mouth hanging open as I push the kitchen door open and see it.

"Him," I say, pointing to his photo on the wall alongside a half dozen others that say "Employee of the Month" above them.

"Oh, Connolly! He hasn't worked here in forever," Chad says.

"I called and asked for him yesterday and the woman on night shift said he worked here."

"I mean, he *did*. Maybe she assumed he still does 'cause the employee photos are there forever. We stopped doing employee of the month, but Randy hasn't bothered to take those down yet."

I feel again like I've been punched in the side of the head. Another dead end. Another trick.

"How long did he...work here for?" the words are hard to even say, but I quickly jump into getting as much info as I can out of this kid instead of starting to throw the blueberry waffles on the counter at everyone's face and pulling my goddamn hair out, which was my first thought.

"Uhhh, a few months, but that was over a year ago. Hey, if you know him, can you tell him to pick up his stuff? He left his bag in one of the lockers. I would have tossed it, but it's not bothering anyone, and he's a nice dude, so I just left it there. He never returned my messages to come get it."

"He has a bag here?" My heart skips a beat.

"Yeah, he just sort of stopped showing up one day," he says.

"Last October," I ask, and the kid nods. "I can take the bag. I'm his wife," I say, and both Chad and Tawny give me a sideways glance. What kind of wife doesn't know their husband makes Pop's bacon burgers behind her back?

Chad finally shrugs. "Sure. There's lockers between the shower rooms. It's number 23." He hands me a small key attached to a rubber spiral keychain, and tells me to just leave it in the lock when I'm done. He disappears into the kitchen again, where I get one last brief glimpse of Leo's face on the wall. Leo, wearing a name tag and a Pop's apron, and the whole world feels a little less real…hazy around the edges.

I sit heavily on the bar stool behind me and stare at the key for a long moment before looking around the room. I feel like I might be ill.

"Good guy, that Leo. You're the wife, huh?" I snap my head to the right and see a man in a purple Vikings cap and matching parka. He's holding a mug of draft beer and dabbing his mustache with a napkin.

"Sorry?" I say.

"I've been comin' here every day for years. I live in the RV park back behind the place there. Not a lot of dining options," he laughs. "The chicken fried steak's not bad. I've had better, though."

"You know him?"

"Sure, we used to go over to Lady Luck after he got off shift most nights."

"What the hell is Lady Luck?"

"The…casino? Down the road." And some of it starts to make sense. Not the "him working here" part, but secretly gambling outside of town? That tracks.

"You were…friends with him?" I ask, only able to speak in short, stunned sentences, apparently.

"Well, I mean we played blackjack and drank Summit together. Not exactly close." I can see the glossy yellowing in this man's eyes that tells me he's had a long relationship with alcohol, and rough skin that's seen its share of cold and wind.

No wedding ring, a pile of ones on the bar for more cheap beer to keep-a-coming. So, does he live in an RV behind the truck stop because he gambles? Or does he gamble out of boredom because he lives alone in an RV behind the truck stop? A question that is none of my business, but I see a life that easily could have been Leo's reflected in this man's eyes, and it makes me very curious how he got here.

"Name's Ron," he says, holding his hand out to shake.

"Mack," I say, taking his outstretched hand in mine and shaking it once.

"Buy you a beer?" he asks.

"Yeah," I say without thinking, then figure I might be glad I had one before I open that locker. He pushes a few bucks across the bar and Tawny pours a foamy Summit from the tap and places it on a cardboard St. Pauli Girl coaster in front of me.

"Sorry, uh… Ron, did Leo, by any chance, tell you why he was working here? Did you know he has a family in Rivers Crossing—he ever mention that?" I ask as the thought starts to press down on my chest—one I have suppressed before—that maybe he has an actual second family somewhere. Like in that Lifetime movie where the stepfather murders his whole family, shaves his beard, changes his clothes, and drives to his other wife and kids like nothing ever happened. I mean, how can I *not* think that? It's all so bizarre.

"Sure," he says, and I feel my heart flutter, speed up.

"Oh," I reply. That's not what I'd expected to hear.

"Yeah, I mean. He talked about you and Rowan," he says, and I feel something rise up in my stomach. Why does this man, with trembling hands and slurry speech at Pop's Grill in the middle of nowhere, have my daughter's name on his lips?

"I'm sorry. What exactly did he tell you?" I ask, sipping the foam off the top of my beer, trying to remain calm and conversational.

"Well, just that he loved his family and really screwed up, but he was determined to get it all back—I don't know, get his shit together," he says. I swallow back the teary lump climbing up my throat. He was actually trying to make it right? I want that to be true. I can see a scenario where he just got so deep into debt he felt forced to lie to me as he scrambled behind my back to fix his financial mistakes, and it just kept spiraling down. But I can also see the scenario everyone else sees—that he's a maniac that got so greedy he screwed everyone in his life over and was just a thief and liar, and probably ran away with some college girl to a beach with my life savings. This is new information, though, and why would this guy lie to me?

"I don't want to betray the guy," he continues. "You should ask him yourself. You seemed surprised to know he hung around here, so maybe talk to him about it."

"He's missing. He's been missing for over a year," I say as calmly as I'm able.

"No shit? I wasn't sure what happened. I figured he got his shit together like he said—decided to stay away from the casino or somethin'."

"No, it appears he did not get his shit together, so if there is anything that you can tell me it might help find him. Please? Anything he might have said at all."

Ron scratches at his chin, looking thoughtful. "Well, we chitchatted all the time. I don't remember everything the man said. Alls I know is that he liked Lady Luck, you know? His whole thing was he said he had a master plan. He told me he usually drove out here to the casino in the middle of the night after you were asleep, and then he lost a bunch more money over time. He took a job here for cash that he kept using at the casino to make back his money—but I guess he never did."

"He told you that he snuck to the casino in the middle of the night? Jesus," I say, absolutely baffled at how I didn't know this. He would get up and say he was going down to the den to watch TV 'cause he couldn't sleep, and I would find him in the recliner in the morning. I never thought twice.

"Well, yeah, for a while. But then he said he told his wife—well, you—that he started a new investment opportunity, didn't say what—and then he could leave most afternoons and come here and work for cash, gamble for a little bit, and be back home by dinner," Ron says, taking a careful sip of beer from the glass in his shaking hand.

How did it come to this? He was so desperate to make some money back that he worked for measly cash at an hourly job to just suck that little more out of a slot machine and keep losing and keep trying. For the first time I feel a pang of empathy for what he must have felt—must have been going through alone.

"God, missing. I'm so sorry," he adds.

"Was he…do you know if he mentioned owing anyone money? Like I mean of course he owed money, but like, a loan shark? Or did he get caught up in anything like that—drug running, I don't know. A reason that would explain where he went, or if someone…had a reason to want him dead," I ask, pushing my drink away from me and feeling a confusing blend of emotions.

"No, he never said nothin' like that to me, sorry. I wish I could think of anything else that might help. God. Missing, huh? Wow." He repeats.

"Thanks, Ron," I say quietly, feeling a bit defeated and more perplexed than ever. I push my stool away from the bar and walk over to where the lockers stand outside a shower room. A hairy trucker walks past me in a towel, holding a Big Gulp and giving me a nod hello as he passes. I stare down the short hallway at the stack of old gym lockers and say a silent prayer that something in here gives me an answer. I walk over to them and find number 23.

I swallow hard, holding my breath as I click open the lock, and what I see doesn't really surprise me. His missing work-bag. The bag I have been wondering about all of this time is crammed sideways into the narrow opening, and I pull it out and hold it to my chest for a moment before hoisting it over my shoulder and walking quickly out to my car before anyone decides to stop me. It's irrational, since I was given the key and permission, but everything is irrational lately. I just don't want anyone to question what I'm doing or why I have it, and I find myself sprinting to my car and driving away as fast as I can.

A few blocks down, I pull into the parking lot of a Take 'N' Bake Pizza and park. I grab the bag from the passenger's seat and unzip the top, peering in at folders stuffed full of papers. I dig around them to see if there is another phone maybe, money, drugs; I don't know what the hell I'm looking for, but there isn't anything else. I pull out the three file folders and begin to riffle through them.

At first, I'm confused by what I'm looking at, and then it hits me. They're printouts of "paperless" communication forms from our mortgage company, and I quickly realize Leo changed the statements so only he would get them electronically and hide them from me. I don't understand why though—the house was paid off years ago. I realize what he's done before I even find the document confirming it. There is a second mortgage he took out and defaulted on, and it's been delinquent all these months. All of the notices only in his name, going only to his email address. I look deeper and see unpaid taxes too. My God. I gasp when I finally see the words "foreclosure." I'm losing the house.

Before I can scream, my phone buzzes inside my pocket and makes me jump.

"Fuck!" I hold my chest and recover my breath and then fish my phone from my pocket and look at it. A text. From an unknown number. I stare at it in utter disbelief when I read what it says.

Stop looking for me.

16

Shelby

A howling wind rattles the windowpanes in their frames as I sit on the living room floor with my laptop perched on the coffee table, looking at new security systems online. Pops and June are eating waffles at the kitchen counter. Clay lets them make smiley faces on top with blueberries and M&M's because it's Sunday, and because Poppy can have whatever she wants after what she's been through, and that's fine by me.

Yesterday Clay said he'd take the day off and stay with me, but we really can't afford to close the bait shop for a day. And, more importantly, I refuse to let this monster make me feel afraid in my own home. Then he wins. At least that's what I keep repeating to myself and everyone else, but of course I'm terrified. Maybe you *do* let the monster win. Maybe that's why there are panic rooms and restraining orders and pepper spray self-defense classes, and keep-your-eyes-on-your-drink rules, and walk-home-with-a-buddy advice, and Tasers, and house alarms. We are always fighting against the fear, and maybe at this point I should just run to Mexico, buy a beach condo, change all of our names, and let him win.

But here I still am. After the attack, life went on, and we are pretending the best we can that life is not crumbling around us. Sometimes I do think more realistically about running. I think about actually taking the girls and driving south until I feel the sun on my face and we land somewhere warm and safe and far away. And sure, maybe I would commit to running if I could afford to—if the girls weren't in school and we didn't have a business to run and if we had any savings, maybe. But even if I did run, if someone is really after me, deeply and personally gunning for *me*, of all the damn people in the world, and for whatever insane reason, wouldn't they follow? Would I really be safe anywhere?

It's Sunday now, so we'll open the shop for half a day. But since Poppy is probably too traumatized to go back there, I don't know what to do with the hours in front of me when Clay is gone. The security cameras around the house were cut—the wires clipped in two, the cameras removed completely. The power to the house was shut off by the breaker in the garage just like at the Oleander's, but this wasn't torched. The garage was unlocked so the psychopath just got in and turned it off. I imagine so that there would be no security footage of them to recover.

I can still set the alarm to sound off without the cameras, but that does little to persuade me to stay here alone with the girls all day—not unless I can see what's outside. I'm looking at motion sensor–activated floodlights online and doubling the cameras and learning about tamper alarms and backup power devices and all sorts of things you don't imagine needing to know when you settle your life into the middle of safe, small-town nowheresville.

"Billy can install it," Clay says, wiping his hands on a kitchen towel and picking up his coffee mug from the side table next to his recliner.

"What?" I ask, wondering where Billy's name sprang from.

"He's been a contractor and does electrical and plumbing stuff. I'm just saying, to save money, we can see if he'll install whatever you get," he says, and there is something I don't like about the way he says "whatever you get," like it's my sole decision to waste our money on security equipment we can't afford, rather than a life and death necessity, even though I'm sure that's not how he meant it to come off.

"There are instructions," I say. "I can do it." He raises his eyebrows at this, but knows it's not the time to argue with me.

"You sure you don't want to come with to the bait shop? Maybe it'll be good for Poppy to have us not make a big thing about going back—just act like it's fine," he says, and he has a point. Maybe I'm the one who can't stand the thought of it right now, and maybe she won't associate the warm shop that holds half her childhood memories with what happened outside of it on that dark ice, but today is not the day to test that. My nerves are frayed and my heart pounds from the constant anxiety of it all as it is.

"Actually, can you just drop us at the Ole today? The girls want to play with Gus and I have some paperwork to catch up on," I say, because of course the girls will always say yes to a puppy and all the Sour Patch Kids Herb can stuff them with, and I'll feel safer with everyone around. Clay seems relieved at the idea of this too, because he kisses me on the top of the head and tells me he'll pack lunches for the girls before he goes.

By 10:00 a.m., Poppy and June are at the card table in the rec room where a new jigsaw has been started—it's *E.T.* and has Elliot bicycling in front of the moon, and they quietly push pieces together and eat from the plastic candy canes filled with Skittles that Herb gave them while Gus chews a bully stick under

Poppy's chair, but I don't see any sign of the regular gang this morning. Oliver from room 16 is mixing himself a Swiss Miss hot chocolate packet by the coffee station, and Wendy from room 11 is watching *Ancient Aliens* on the television and playing solitaire on the coffee table.

I ask if Heather has been in this morning and Wendy says "beats me," so I make my way down the hall and peer in to open residents' doors. I only see Ed in his Viking jersey watching pregame coverage and already arguing with the sportscasters on his TV, and Kitty, who hides her vape pen when she sees me, and who is talking very loudly on the phone to her sister about how Rodney's only using her for her pension, and does she want her to sign up on Match.com and try to catfish him to prove it?

I keep walking down to Herb's room and try to think of which Rodney she might be talking about. It must be Rodney Galindo, because I heard Rodney Moyer moved to Ann Arbor and nobody calls him Rodney, just Rod. I stop and take a long breath when I hear voices coming from inside Mort's room.

The door is cracked, so I tap on it with my knuckle and push it open. I'm taken aback to see not only Herb, Flor, and Millie there, but also Evan, who isn't even scheduled to work today, and Heather of all people, all huddled together, with low voices and concerned looks about their faces.

"Am I interrupting something?" I ask, and Millie yelps. Everyone else whips around, startled.

"It's Sunday," Florence says factually.

"The girls wanted to play with Gus," I say, but I know they can see through that. They exchange strange looks I can't decipher, and Heather says she was just about to go make the rounds, but before she can even stand, I point at the computer table next to Mort and gasp.

"That's my phone!"

"But it's Sunday, and you're not supposed to be here, so we

haven't figured out how to tell you about this yet," Herb says. I
pick up the phone and hold it to my chest, looking at everyone
defensively. They all look back at me with sympathy in their
eyes, and Flor pats the spot on Mort's bed next to her. I just
stand, hand on hip, not sure who to aim my glare at.

"What they hell, guys?" I say, and Mort motions again for
me to sit, so I do.

"We interviewed Detective Chipped Beef last night, and
Herb found this in the butt crack of the man's couch," Millie
says from her spot in Mort's window seat. She picks her teeth
with a toothpick and shrugs.

Herb explains the interview idea for the podcast and how
they recorded some generic statements from Riley and didn't
expect much until he found this.

"In his couch?" I ask again.

"I told them they should put it back," Millie says. "I've seen
one too many horror movies to know that if Riley's a murderer and he notices his trophy is missing...who knows which
one of us is next? Probably Herb, though."

"Trophy?" Evan asks.

"Serial killers keep trophies after they kill people."

"She's not dead, Millie! She's sitting right here," Herb yells,
gesturing to me. "So how can it be a trophy?"

"Anyway, we called Evan this morning to see if he could
bring the recordings in from last night so we didn't waste any
time," Mort says.

"How about calling me?" I say, holding up my phone with
a curled lip and "what the hell" look on my face.

"Well, you don't know how to sync the audio, do you?"
Mort asks, and I sigh. I can see from the computer screen behind him that these sneaks have already recorded a whole podcast episode about it this morning.

"What if someone turned this phone in? Found it somewhere and turned it into the police, and Riley is not, in fact, a murderer?" I ask.

"I did think of that," Mort says.

"Yeah, but then why didn't he return it to you?" Herb asks.

"I had it locked down when I called the phone company. Maybe he gets a turned-in phone that's shut down and it's not a priority to find the owner because he has a psychopath on the loose? I don't know!" I say and I'm raising my voice now, so I take a breath and try to keep it together.

"So Riley takes home lost and found items from the department and sticks them down his couch cushions?" Florence asks.

"Did you ask him why he has it?" I retort.

"Oh, God no," Herb says. "We're not crazy. This is evidence now. He would just deny it—say he doesn't know how it got there. We need to get to the bottom of it."

"So," I continue. "This phone is the most boring phone on earth. Pictures of the kids, calls to school, and Pizza Central. Maybe some Pinterest and Amazon. No porn, no scandal, no unknown numbers, no blackmail. What in the world would Riley want it for? What would *anyone* want with this?"

"Maybe he's still in love with you and was hoping for some nudies," Millie says, and Florence spits out her sip of tea. Evan blushes, and Heather finally speaks up.

"Or…what if it's his wife?" she asks. Everyone turns to look at her.

"Belinda?" Millie sits up and looks around to see if anyone else thinks this is preposterous.

"Well, think about it. Everyone knows Belinda hates Shelby, and she bought that bait shop with her brother out of spite. The stories of Clay throwing up on the Riley's car and Belinda retaliating by telling everyone at Cut & Curl that Shelby has an STD? I mean, she'd do anything to throw Shelby under the bus," she says. And everyone *does* know these rumors, but I am surprised Heather pays attention to anything besides her false eyelashes and hair extensions, not to mention absorbing these sorts of details.

"That still doesn't make her a murderer," Mort says.

"Just sayin'." She shrugs. "Women are cunning."

"You know, she's not totally off track," Evan says, picking up a steaming mug of coffee from the computer table he's sitting in front of. Heather beams.

"I don't know about Belinda, but…what if we're all going down the wrong track and it is a woman?"

"Women don't murder people, men do. Come on!" Millie says, exasperated.

"I mean, have you seen *Snapped*? If there are enough women murdering people to create a whole multiseason show about it, then it's not totally out of the question," he says. "It's something to consider. Does anyone know Belinda, like actually know her *well*?"

"We all do," Millie argues.

"Outside of church, kids' ball games, PTA, and fundraisers, has anyone spent one-on-one time with her? Enough to know if she's a psychopath?" Florence asks. "Because I know that we all know everyone, but besides knowing that the woman has bad taste in haircuts and brings mint chip cookies to the potluck every year, I can't tell you I know much about her at all, really.

"So she goes on our list," Florence says, scribbling something onto a legal pad. I take it from her.

"What list? You have a list? Of suspects?" I look at it and all that's written is "Riley" with a question mark that's scratched out, and now "Belinda." I shake my head and hand it back to her, mumbling "Jesus" under my breath.

"Okay, I'm gonna go catch up on some paperwork," I say, but before I can go, Florence shocks me when she blurts out "Or Mack!"

I stare at her from the door frame and take a few steps back in. "I'm sorry?"

"I just want us to at least be open to the fact that Leo's disappearance and what happened to you are more than a coincidence. And what if she is helping hide him? What if she knew they owe people all over town money, and…"

"No," I say firmly, ending the conversation, and everyone is quiet. I turn and walk away.

I sit with the girls and we eat peanut butter sandwiches at the card table at lunchtime while Herb watches the football game. Mort is still editing the podcast they recorded, and Millie is asleep with her mouth hanging open, an empty mini bottle of Baileys next to her coffee cup on the side table. I let Evan go for the day since he wasn't scheduled and told Heather to take the day off since I would be here anyway.

Once the girls are in the craft room gluing cotton balls onto paper plates, I sit in the front office, and my blood boils at the thought of them pointing the finger at Mack. It's preposterous. I stare at my lost phone on the desktop in front of me and wonder, of course, how it got in Riley's house. They're right about one thing. If I confront Riley about this, he'll deny it. Obviously. It won't help me gain one bit of information, and it will only serve to make him weirder and more defensive than he already is. There is nothing to gain by accusing him of taking it. I just need to find out for myself what the hell is really going on, and if he is somehow involved.

When the sun starts to set and the girls have fallen asleep on the rec room sofa in front of the Cartoon Network after an hour of video games with Herb, I hear a small tap on the open office door. It's Florence and Herb. I think they might be here to apologize for going behind my back with the Riley interview or what they said about Mack, but their faces are grave, and I instantly know something is wrong.

"What?" I snap.

"Well, maybe nothing," Flor says. "It's just that Bernie said that his church lunch thingy ended at 1:00 p.m. today and he'd be back in time to watch the end of the game and now it's 5:30 and he isn't back. I called Ginny and she said that he said something about him having to leave early, so she thought we picked him up, but we didn't and nobody has heard from him since. His phone goes right to voicemail."

"Well, who else would he have left with?" I ask.

"That's the thing," Herb says. "Ginny said she drove back to the church after we called her and she saw his phone sitting on a folding chair by the dessert table. He left his phone behind and just got up and left. We can't imagine with who and it's fourteen degrees outside, so he didn't get far on his own two feet, that's for sure."

"Well, shit," I say. "There has to be an explanation."

"Ginny said his phone's not locked and she could see an incoming call—a restricted number around twelve forty, and that's about when he said he had to go all of a sudden. She's beside herself."

"Well then, maybe...he must be with someone he knows," I say, but Bernie only really talks to a handful of people outside of his family and the folks at the Ole. Who the hell would be calling him on a restricted or unknown number?

"Okay. Herb, you call the police. Officer Harris is on duty Sunday, so we'll talk to her before Riley can get involved. I'll call Ginny again and see what we can do to help," I say in a hushed voice so as not to upset the girls.

Then a flurry of phone calls are made and, within an hour, after calling everyone in town we can think of who knows Bernie, Officer Harris is sitting in the rec room with us, taking a report, because it appears as though Bernie has vanished into thin air.

I hear Clay's pickup truck pull in front of the glass doors and the girls, who are already bundled up, run outside as I yell "put your hats on" after them. Clay is taking them to Chuck E. Cheese for dinner and Skee-Ball for a couple of hours because I don't want them around this. Even though everyone has been quiet and subtle, there is an energy that's palpable and they're smart, and I can't expose them to anymore fucking trauma, Lord help me. I wave at Clay as he lifts them into the truck and buckles them in. I go back in and sit on the sofa next to Millie. Everyone has a distant, glassy-eyed look, and I keep wracking my brain for an explanation because there must be one. A man doesn't disappear from a church potluck with two dozen people around in broad daylight. Where would he have gone? Who the hell called him?

By 9:30, nobody has heard a thing and half the town is looking for him. The temperature has dropped down to nine degrees and he has no phone and his wallet is on his dresser in his room, so he has no money except maybe the twenty he keeps in his pocket in a money clip for a rainy day.

Millie is hunched over the jigsaw puzzle with a box of Kleenex, crying, and the rest of the gang sit on the sofa, silently waiting for any news. Some of the other residents who are close to Bernie are hanging out in the rec room too, and the only sound is the canned laughter from an old *All in the Family* episode playing on the community television.

Everyone jolts when Clay and the girls come through the front doors. June runs over to pet Gus, and Poppy pauses and hugs my legs when she notices all the sad faces.

"What's wrong?" she asks.

"Nothing, sweetie. It's time to get you guys home to bed," I say.

"Did they find him?" Clay whispers, and I shake my head and give him a look that he understands, and we begin to shuffle the girls back out the door. I hesitate to leave. I feel like we should be doing something more, but what? I guess we let the search party do their job for now.

"I'll be right by my phone," I tell the gang as we head out

and into the pickup coughing out exhaust, idling in front of the glass doors.

As I'm buckling June into her seat, I notice something in the bed of the truck. It's the flapping sound of plastic against the frigid wind that catches my attention, and I can see it's a black garbage bag.

I go to tuck the loose plastic under so whatever he has in it doesn't blow out, and then I see that it's a pile of plastic and wires, and when I flash my phone flashlight on it, I gasp at what I'm looking at. It's our missing equipment. It's all of our security cameras with the wires cut clean, dumped into a garbage bag...in Clay's truck.

17

Florence

The police have advised us all to stay put at the Oleander's for our own safety and security, so of course we all pile into the resident van now that it's morning and there is still no word about Bernie. We wanted Evan to drive us, but Shelby has him staying on high alert at the Ole and is trying to double his hours for a while, if she can get him to agree. I can't say that I blame her. It's a comfort, but one man with a small security guard gun in a building with a questionable alarm system will do little to deter a maniac who has been very creative in their means of attack.

I had forgotten how poor Herb's driving abilities were since we had the luxury of someone else more competent taxiing us around recently.

"Why must you speed up when you approach a stop light only to hard stop behind the car in front of you?" I ask, holding the door handle for dear life as Herb chews on the end of an unlit cigar.

"And why is the window cracked?" Millie snaps. "It's three degrees, are you going through man-o-pause or something? Jeez, Herb."

"Lots of complaining for a couple of fossils with no car," Herb smirks. He hands back a packet of Twizzlers to share, and we all drive in silence for a long while. We pass empty fields of snow, and pine forests with all the tree branches weighed down by weeks of heavy snowfall. The sky is overcast and the air is still, eerily quiet. When we get to town we stop at all Bernie's favorite places—the VFW where Kevin Willits, who has worked there for twenty-three years, polishes beer mugs with a bar towel and watches *Wheel of Fortune* on the TV above the pub tables. Nobody else is there; we go to the Trout but it's closed, then the Cupcake Gourmet, and the bait shop, and then Mario's taco shop where we all stay and have lunch in an old wooden booth near the front window.

Of course, we don't expect to find Bernie just sitting at one of these places in plain sight while the whole world is out looking for him, but what else can we do? We have to do *something*. Herb orders the chicken enchilada burrito combo and chews with his mouth open, but the rest of us just push tortilla chips around on our plates and don't know what to say to one another.

"Who called him? Who would he have left with?" Mort asks, but he's just repeating something we have asked each other over and over already. Nobody has a clue.

"Well, it has to be someone. He wouldn't get too far in sub-zero weather and we'd have found him frozen solid in a snowbank by now within a mile of the church potluck, that's for damn sure," Millie says, but she has already said some variation of this sentiment a dozen times today. Still, we all nod in agreement.

Mort stirs his peppermint tea and Herb doesn't chide him

for ordering peppermint tea at a Mexican restaurant the way he usually would, and nobody gives Millie any sour looks about ordering a margarita before noon. We all stare at our phones or out the window and a sad ballad from the 1990s plays that I can't recall the name of, but it makes Herb push away his plate and dot a tear, although he would never admit it.

Back in the van, the Styrofoam take-out containers fill the interior with refried bean and onion aromas, and Millie is sipping a third margarita from a paper cup. Mort is so quiet that I am beginning to worry about him and how he will handle his good friend missing.

I suggest that we go back to the Ole and record a live podcast where we implore anyone with any information about Bernie Adler to call in, but Herb reminds me that we only have our cell phones to take calls, and the last thing we want to do is get ourselves murdered in our beds because some nutter has our personal information, so we decide against the tip line and go with opening up an email address folks can write in to with information. We all decide this is a sound idea and the best use of our efforts, and so we drive back across snowy roads to the Oleander's, on a mission to do everything we can to find our sweet Bernie.

While everyone is shaking out wet boots and hanging coats and hats on the hooks next to the front windows, I see Shelby through the crack in the office door. She's sitting at her desk and staring down at a garbage bag on the floor. It looks like wires and electrical stuff, and the look across her face is one of despair, I think, but it's just a glance so I can't really be sure. She quickly collects herself and comes out of the office door, closing it behind her. I see Evan at the small computer desk, looking at some video footage on the computer, so I don't disturb him. But even from just his profile, he seems to share the same distraught look as Shelby. I wonder if there has been news. My heart speeds up and I feel a small wave of nausea rise within me.

"His car's gone," Shelby comes out and says before any of us have even sat down. Mort is wiping his glasses and Millie is warming herself in front of the gas fireplace. Herb and I stand in the middle of the rec room staring at her, trying to make sense of what she's saying.

"Whose car? What car?" I ask. Shelby sits on the arm of the couch and sighs.

"Bernie's car."

"Bernie doesn't drive," Millie says unnecessarily loudly and with unearned authority.

"His old Firebird in the back parking lot?" Mort asks, putting his glasses back on. "I thought it didn't run."

"And he doesn't drive!" Millie says again, tipsily, carefully trying to sit herself down on the brick hearth.

"I know," Shelby says, "but it *must* run, because it's not there. And I suppose just because he let his license expire however long ago doesn't mean he's incapable of driving. I just can't imagine the reason behind it—where he would have gone without telling anyone."

"But maybe it's a good thing," Herb says. "If he drove on his own, even for some crazy reason, there's a better chance he's safe."

"I don't see anything," Evan says, hitting Pause on the video and swiveling towards us on his chair. "I think we need to add cameras on the light pole in the parking lot since the ones we have don't catch that dark lot way back there…and it butts up to the woods, so it's pitch-black. See?" he says, rewinding the video as Shelby goes to look over his shoulder and scan the footage he shows her.

"Shit," Shelby mutters at the grainy, useless footage.

"He was here yesterday at breakfast you said, right?" Evan asks.

"Yes," Mort says. "He put maple syrup on his scrambled eggs and I told him he was a Neanderthal." He hangs his head at the memory, and I suppose he wonders if it's the last thing he said to his friend and wishes it were something kinder, even if he was just poking fun.

"And what time was that?" Evan asks.

"Around eight," I say, because I was at the table having my coffee then myself.

"So between 8:00 a.m. and when it was noticed that he was gone, which was 12:40 you said…it seems like that's when he would have taken the car—either before the potluck, or he came back and got it. But I don't even see him on camera walking back that way." Evan scans the footage ahead and pauses on different spots.

"Unless he went out of his way to walk around the wooded area and access the lot from behind if he was avoiding the cameras. Which he probably was if he was planning some strange escape without telling us," Herb says, and I nod in agreement.

"Maybe," Evan says. "But if someone else wants to look through the video with fresh eyes to make sure I'm not missing anything, feel free."

"Thanks, Evan," Shelby says. I walk to the kitchenette and microwave a mug of hot water, putting a Lipton tea bag inside, then sit on the ottoman next to Herb, and we're all quiet again. There is a palpable sense of dread, and even though the car might be a good thing, it's bizarre, and for some reason, I feel this overwhelming suspicion that it's actually very, very bad, and I don't quite know why.

"We thought we'd do an episode this afternoon—a live one, and set up an email address for people to write in with tips," I say.

"Good idea," Shelby says. "Let me know if I can help," and then she stands and disappears back inside the office again, closing the door with a soft click.

We decide to use the computer in the rec room. Evan promised to stay vigilant near the main doors, so Mort shuffles around, setting up mics and untwisting cords, and I can't help but think over and over about that sign-in sheet at the hospital. The whole place is still in the dark ages, so when a visitor signs in, they don't always write down the patient or room number. I can't imagine anyone has even looked at that sign-in sheet in a decade.

The last name Blacklock was signed in many times over the last six months, but often with different first names. Odd first names: Duke, Cornelius, Buster...it was as if somebody was trying to make sure their real name wasn't recorded and wrote down ridiculous fake names, but why, and what does that mean? I went as far as to look up this surname in the town records and I didn't find anything. This is significant. I'm sure Riley is looking into it since I brought all of this to his attention, but I need to understand how it's connected. Blacklock.

"Earth to Flor," Herb hollers.

"Sorry," I say. "Ready?"

We start to record and we don't know what we'll say, but Millie is half-drunk so she starts. "Please, everyone, we are putting a photo of Bernie Adler up on our channel. If you have seen him, please write to us with any information," she manages, but the waterworks start almost immediately, and Mort takes over.

"Hello, everyone. This is Mort from *Mort's Literary Musings*, which you probably know if you are listening right now. We've paused our literary analysis, and now our true crime series, in order to focus our attention on finding our dear friend, Bernie," he says, and I hear his voice crack. I give him a thumbs-up to tell him he's doing well and he continues. He reads out the email address that he and Evan have just created, and it's amazing to me that, just like that, we have a line of communication. Technology never ceases to amaze me.

"mortslit_musings_info@gmail.com," he says.

And even with the heaviness of the moment, Herb can't help

but roll his eyes and say, "At least we know that address hasn't been taken already."

"Well, yes, and actually, Evan and I have decided to partner in the podcast world. He'll be videographer and editor, and I'll be the talent."

Herb sighs. "Uh-huh. Super."

"We're still thinking on our new name and I didn't want to confuse anybody by announcing a change right now," Mort says, looking to Evan for approval, and Evan high-fives him.

"Mort and Evan's show about all things murder and macabre," Mort adds.

"Catchy," Herb says, reaching his limit, so he goes to the minifridge and grabs a Dr Pepper and rolls his eyes to his heart's content out of sight. Truth be told, I think he's a little jealous of the friendship between Mort and Evan, and I suppose between Mort and Bernie, but he'd never admit it.

"Murder and what now? My-Cob? What the hell is my-cob? You can't just make up words," Millie adds. "That title is terrible."

Shelby comes out of the office when Herb hollers for her, and we all take turns talking about things Bernie loves, like feeding blueberries to the pigeons at Sunflower Park, and a good pint at the Trout, and scrambled eggs with maple syrup, and his favorite pendant (which Shelby adds and explains he hasn't taken it off in twenty years, and we didn't even know about that), and pickleball, and his new friend, Gus, who he wouldn't leave behind…and places he liked to go. We read off the license plate of his car and the time frame when he disappeared, and then we wait.

I don't know what I expected—maybe the magic of the ten seconds it took to create a new email address to apply to receiving messages on it, but there is nothing coming in.

After a couple of hours, though, there are nine emails. All of them say how sorry they are for what's going on with Bernie and ask how they can help, to which Herb replies you can help by only emailing if you have something useful to add, which I don't think is at all a helpful thing to do, but I can't blame him. We are all on pins and needles every time the email pings, but nothing.

By 10:00 p.m. Evan is off shift and Heather has taken over for Shelby and Millie has fallen asleep in front of an episode of *Andy Griffith*. The rest of the building is quiet except for the low hum of radios or TVs in residents' rooms down the hallways, and I finally accept that there will be no more news today from police or email tips, and so I go to my room to bed.

I don't sleep, though. I lie awake thinking about Blacklock. Blacklock…and Shelby's phone at Riley's, and Otis's notes, and Leo somewhere deep-sea fishing with all Mack's money, and I especially think about Bernie.

We were all given the password to the new email tip line, so I slip on my glasses and take my phone from the nightstand and log in one more time. It's pushing midnight and I'm certain there won't be anything new, but I feel compelled to keep looking, and when I see a new email, I sit up straight in bed and turn on the light. The sender's address is not Ted Walters or Leslie Katz or Jamie Knutsen from church or the VFW. It's a very scary-looking address with a bunch of numbers and symbols instead of a name.

When I click it open it says, "There is something in the parking lot where Bernie's car used to be. Go look."

I feel my heart beating against my chest and a prickle of heat climb my spine. I shove my feet into the snow boots by my bedroom door and wrap my robe around myself, marching down to Herb's room and tapping on the door.

"Christ," I hear from inside, so I open the door.

"Herb, get up. Let's go," I say, walking over to his bed. I show him my phone and he squints to make out the email, then grabs for his glasses and sits up fully and stares from it to me. He doesn't say anything, just stands and starts grabbing for his coat on the armchair near his bed. Together, we hold hands and walk through the yard, the snow crackling under our feet in the impossibly silent and still night, the light from our flashlight apps leading the way.

When we reach the back lot, I notice that Bernie's car has left a large clearing in the snowy ground, and there is only a chain-link fence and a couple of junker cars next to a shed in the entire area. We flash our lights around, trying to see what this email means—what in the world could be in the spot where Bernie's car was? What the hell does that even mean? The words repeat in my mind as we search. Then, I aim my light down, and I see it.

My hand flutters to my mouth, and I inhale sharply.

"There," I say, pointing to it. Herb turns around, his eyes widening as he sees what I see. He leans down and picks up the shining metal object, holding it up to the light. I move in close to him and we both examine it.

He wipes snow off and reveals the image of a border collie. It's Bernie's pendant.

18

Mack

"Fuck you!" I scream until my voice is hoarse and my throat aches. "Mother*fucker!*" I punch as hard as I can over and over again at the heavy bag suspended from the garage rafters. It hangs like a dead body swaying, and I don't even use the old boxing gloves on the dusty shelf—I just punch until my knuckles are cracking and chafed and then I kick it until I'm breathless and the sobbing stops.

It's close to midnight and the night is perfectly still and silent. I can see each puff of desperate breath in the ice-cold air, but I don't really feel the pain. Too much adrenaline is coursing through me—too much white-hot anger at Leo and his games and his demand that I stop looking for him.

"Fuck you!" I scream one last time, throwing my whole body at the stupid thing, then I hear tires crunching over snow and see headlights flash in my eyes. I freeze. Who would be at my

house at midnight? I begin to move to the wall to close the garage door, my heart racing, my body trembling. Before I can think through whether it's the police with news, or Shelby, or something about the search for Bernie, or a rapist, I see who it actually is, and I exhale. It's Billy. Billy, who I can't fathom having a reason to be creeping up my drive right now.

He parks and turns the engine off, stepping down from the truck in a jacket too light for the cold, and all I can see is a white cloud of breath when he speaks.

"Hey. Sorry if I scared you."

"You did" is all I manage to say, and he must read the look on my face correctly or just notice the dried tears and ruddy cheeks and not know what's wrong with me, so he quickly continues.

"I just—we're all taking turns driving around looking for Bernie. Like a round the clock effort, so I said I'd take a turn after Peggy took over for me at the bar…"

"Uhhh. He's not here?" I say, and Billy sort of snort-laughs at this.

"No, I know. It's just. I was trying to get a hold of you. Earlier…to see if you wanted to join, and when you didn't answer, I mean with everything going on, I wanted to make sure you were okay. That's all."

"Oh," I say. "Well, you can come in for a minute if you want so we don't freeze to death," I say. I see him hesitate and I don't know if it's because it's an awkward request at this hour or because he doesn't want to impose by showing up like this, but I'm too cold to worry about it, so I simply turn and head to the front door and I hear him follow behind.

Inside, I walk through to the kitchen and he stays politely with his boots still within the parameters of the front mat. Linus and Nugget are barking at him and jumping wildly at his legs.

"Can I pour you a drink? You can take those off, if you don't mind," I say nodding to his boots.

"Uh, sure," he says. I shake a bag of treats and the boys come running back down the hall to me. I offer for him to sit in the living room and then I bring over two glasses of red wine.

"It's all I have around, sorry. If I remember, you're a bourbon guy," I say, handing him one.

"This is great," he says. I light the fireplace and sit in front of it on the rug with the boys, who curl up next to me. I look across the coffee table at Billy, and he's probably wondering how the hell he went from a welfare check to having a drink on my sofa, and I'm thinking the same thing myself. It's strange to have anyone other than Leo sitting there. And it might be the last time anyone is sitting on that sofa in this room, since I have less than thirty days to be out of my own home of twenty-three years.

"Thanks for checking on me. No word about Bernie yet, huh? Nothing?"

"Nothing. I mean, besides what's on the news—his car's missing, so some people think he just…" He stops talking and takes a sip of his drink. I can't imagine he wants to say the words. "Some people think he just left on his own—doesn't want to be found."

"Right, I did hear about the car," I say. I pet the top of Nugget's head and take a big swallow of wine. I don't know if it's the chronic loneliness that comes with being abandoned or the arm's-length friends in town that I can't really open up to, which doesn't include Shelby, of course, but considering what she's going through, I can't burden her with all of this… Or maybe the three glasses of wine I had before I decided to punch the shit out of the bag in the garage, or the idea of telling Rowan I've lost everything, or just his kind smile and me having nothing left to lose, but I just blurt it out. I just want to tell someone everything.

"I'm losing the house. I have to be out."

"What?" he says, pausing with his glass halfway to his lips and then putting it down and furrowing his brow.

"I found out there's a second mortgage foreclosure," I say. No need to go into how I found out or the truck stop or Leo's work bag, and God, it's all too much, so I just stick with the basics. Maybe I'm looking for advice or maybe just a shoulder. I don't even know, myself.

"And unpaid taxes...so they can seize the home and sell it, as it turns out."

"I don't understand. You...how could that happen?"

"Leo hid it, made statements digital only, in his name only. He must have forged a few documents to make that happen, but does that surprise you at this point?"

"How much is owed? You've lived here forever—God, can it be that much?" he says, leaning his elbows on his knees like he's in emergency problem solving mode.

"Almost a hundred thousand," I say and he blinks at me.

"Okay," he says, and I know what he's thinking. That I should have that as pocket change and is waiting for the rest of that sentence to be something like "I paid it but it was too late, they had sold it already" but I tell him the truth.

"I don't have it. Leo gambled it away," I say, like pulling off a Band-Aid.

"Oh God," Billy says. "He..." he starts to stutter, so I don't make him sit there trying to come up with a proper response. I just continue.

"I know the talk, so I know people know he gambles, that he got hit hard by COVID with the last couple small restaurants. People felt sorry for him but they still assumed—if all the overheard gossip I get wind of is accurate—that he still had a fortune tucked away from all the prosperous years, but as you might have figured out, that is not the case. If he did, in fact, tuck away a fortune and not gamble it all away, he made sure I didn't know about it and is living large on it in who knows where with it now."

"Oh, Mack," he says. "God, I had no idea." I move to the

couch with a sigh and sit down next to him, leaning my head back and staring at the ceiling, feeling numb and overwhelmed at the same time.

"I don't even know what to say—it's shocking. I'm so sorry," he says.

"I'm sorry to dump that all on you. You didn't sign up for this," I laugh humorlessly.

"It's hard to believe. I mean, all of it is, I guess—he was the nicest guy. It's just never added up," he says. I lean over to pick up the wine bottle on the coffee table, filling both of our glasses.

"A nice guy who I recently found out has been stealing money from the Oleander's."

"I'm sorry, what?" he says, and again, I don't know why I feel the need to vomit out all of this information, but I want to be free from the burden of it. I just need someone to talk to, so I keep spilling.

"I've had a lot happen at once, so that one was just a bullet item on my list of things to dig into," I continue. "But then I found his missing work bag yesterday, and there was more evidence that he is stealing. I found out about some of it recently, but it gets even better… and it looks like he takes a percentage of everyone's Medicare and Medicaid that gets filtered through a bank I'd never heard of till I found the paperwork…after some gets taken out, the rest is deposited to the Oleander's."

"You're kidding."

"I wanted to be certain before I brought this up to Shelby because I thought…"

"She could be in on it," he finishes.

"What? No. No! That's…"

"Oh, sorry," he says quickly, cutting the air with his palm—a "forget I said that" gesture.

"The Oleander's is going under. She'd never let that happen. No way. I just thought… What if someone knows about this? What if someone knows money is being stolen over years and they're fucking pissed and they think she is a part of it?"

"So you mean, what if Leo was a victim, and now Shelby is in serious danger for the same reason—they're thieves together."

"I don't know. I mean, that's a thought, yes. Someone thinks they are working together profiting off the elderly. I don't know. Maybe that's way off track, but I'm just trying to make sense of anything that has an ounce of sense to it."

"I know," he agrees. "It's all so out there. It's hard to know what to think. I had no idea about Leo."

"But you did hear that he gambled, right?"

"Like you said, I heard 'COVID got him drinking and gambling a bit more, but who could blame him?' sort of talk—I never heard any of the things you're telling me."

"I don't know who knows what anymore. Maybe because I don't really know a goddamn thing myself. The money he's taking off the top from the Oleander's checks—it was all carefully and fraudulently crafted so nobody would catch on, and now it's just on an automated system—" I say, but then he interrupts.

"Wait," Billy puts his wine down and shifts his body to face me square on. "You're saying there is still money going into an account that he has access to?"

I nod.

"Holy shit!"

"Yeah," I say, and I know what he's thinking. That this is evidence clear as day that Leo is alive, and not a victim. A minute ago he was *maybe* a victim along with Shelby, and now he's definitely an active criminal. And I know it's a roller coaster, but I think the truth lives somewhere in the middle, despite what it looks like when you sum it up like that.

"And the police can't track him through that account?" he asks. Then he must read the look on my face and his expression shifts. "Oh," he says.

"I'm gonna tell them. It's just…between the phone and finding out about an active bank account, I just—I wanted to try to find him myself instead of giving it to Riley and being told to stay out of the way and just wait. No way."

"I guess," he says, and I can't tell if there is a tone of judgment underneath his words.

"I've hit the end of the road, obviously, so I guess I have nothing to lose by turning this stuff over to the police now. Tomorrow," I say. He picks up his wine, runs his hand through his hair and leans back on the couch. I copy him. We stare at the ceiling and listen to the fire crackle for a few minutes.

"What can I do to help you? Do you need a place to stay or anything? I mean, where will you go?" he asks softly.

I sigh. "That's very nice of you, but I'm less worried about me. I'll sleep in a booth in the cafe if I need to. At least that place is still mine. My main concern is Rowan and how to figure something out before she gets out of school for the summer. I thought about selling the cafe, but then I pay the back taxes—all the debt on the house and have no business. It doesn't make sense. It's not like I have no income. I just don't have that kind of money lying around, not since Leo…" I stop and restart, more calmly. "Maybe I stay at the cafe for a while and find an apartment after I save up…" I'm rambling now, I know it, but it's nice to just think out loud and verbalize everything that's been boiling over inside of me.

"Let me help. Let me give it to you," he says, and I almost spit out the sip of wine in my mouth, but I collect myself and sit up, turning to him with my mouth hanging open.

"You're nuts. No way. I mean that's very kind of you to offer that, but I couldn't possibly."

"Why not?" he asks, brows raised.

"What do you mean why not? Because I can't just take that kind of money from someone," I manage to splutter.

"I'm not someone. I'm a longtime friend, and you need money and I have it sitting in a savings account that made approximately six cents in interest last year. You can pay it back if it will make you feel better, but just…down the line when you feel like you're in a good spot," he says earnestly, and I'm so utterly shocked and moved by this gesture that I don't know what to say. I feel tears threatening to form behind my eyes, so I get up and walk over to the pups. I perch on the edge of the ottoman and pet Linus.

"That's…probably the nicest thing anyone has ever offered," I say, my back still to him. "But I just wouldn't feel right about that."

"You deserve someone to give you a freakin' break," he says. I turn to him and we look at one another for a long moment, then I stand and I think he takes that as a sign to leave, because he stands too, but I really don't want him to leave.

"How about this. Say you'll think about it, and offer's open," he says. I smile at him and nod.

He makes his way to the front door and starts to pull on his boots.

"I said I'd be out looking for Bernie, so I should shove off." Before he can pull on his coat, I move closer to him and wrap my arms around his shoulders.

"Thank you," I say, and I mean it with every bit of my soul. I needed so desperately to feel listened to and heard, and…not like an extension of Leo. Not like someone who is either a victim or might also be guilty, but just to feel like myself again for an hour. I don't want it to end, and I find myself kissing him. Lord help me. *Kissing him.* Right on the lips. He pulls back with a look of surprise on his face, his eyes wide, and then, before I can be mortified at my actions or even apologize, he kisses me back.

For a few moments it's all a blur as I end up with my back pushed against the wall and my hands up the back of his shirt, feeling the warmth of his skin, his breath, his hands on my hips. Exhilaration mixes with profound guilt and the comfort of being so close to another person after all this time fights with shame because I'm still married and the world seems to be falling apart around me and this is the last thing I should be thinking about.

I stop. I catch my breath and look at him as he steps back in the glare of the overhead kitchen light and adjusts his shirt.

"I'm sorry," I say.

"No, I'm sorry. I…" He hesitates and I think about it for a second—about just saying fuck it and inviting him up to my room, but something stops me.

"You should be out looking for Bernie. Sorry," I say instead.

"Right. I should go," he says, pulling on his coat.

"I'll come with you. If that's okay," I say, because as exhausted and devastated as I feel right now, I think a distraction and being of some use will be the best thing so I don't lose my shit completely. He smiles and hands me my coat.

"I'd love that," he says.

We drive the quiet, snowy roads with the heat piping into the truck cab and the radio humming a barely audible Bob Dylan song in the background, and we don't say much to one another. We stop for Styrofoam cups of hot chocolate at the Speedway and wind through the lonely back roads of town, trying to find places we haven't already been. It's solemn business, looking for a missing, elderly man who everyone fears has frozen to death somewhere, alone without his phone or a coat. I feel nauseated even thinking about it. Poor Bernie.

We pull onto a narrow road that hasn't been plowed since last night's snowfall. Billy shifts into four-wheel drive and we rock and sway over uneven ice and fresh snow. I'm looking out the passenger's window into a thicket of pines when I hear Billy take in a sharp breath.

"Holy shit," he says, and I look to where he's looking.

"Oh God," I say, putting my cup in the console and leaning

over the dash to get a better look. It's his car. It's the Firebird they showed on the news. "Oh no, oh my God."

We put the truck in Park maybe thirty feet from where the car is, and can see that it's backed up against a snowbank, and there are footprints in the snow.

19

Shelby

Clay doesn't know how the security equipment got into the back of his truck. He swears to God. He swears up and down and on the girls' lives that he can't imagine how it could have materialized in his possession. He tells me I have to believe him.

I said I did. And then I went to work and brought the bag with me to see if I could cobble any of it back together to work again, because I can't afford a new system, even though we have no choice. But now, a day later, I don't know what I believe. I never thought I would doubt my husband for any reason, but I can't stop thinking about it. One minute I hate myself for even considering he would have any involvement in…what? Terrorizing me? Of course not. That's so absurd. And then the next minute, I cannot think of any way someone else could have accessed all the cameras. And why put them in his truck? Whoever is doing all this is smart, and probably wants me to suspect him. Or maybe *that's* the absurd thought, and I'm blind for not suspecting him earlier.

My mind whirls and my body aches from the ceaseless stress of it all. Early this morning I got news that Bernie's car was found. Mack called to tell me that they found it in a snowbank behind a cluster of pines off a back road while on a search shift last night, and when they called the police, they were told to go home and haven't been given any updates yet. So now, we all wait. Always waiting—waiting tips, waiting on the blood DNA from the snow outside my house, waiting for the psychopath to make contact again. Waiting.

By evening we still haven't heard anything, so when Clay comes home from the bait shop, I ask him to take the girls to my mother's. I say that they should stay with her for a few days because there's too much happening around here and they shouldn't be around it. I just need to know they're safe, and until the new security system is connected tomorrow, and maybe even until things settle down in general and we feel some safety again, they should probably just be there.

My mother gleefully agreed when I called her this morning about it, and she offered to take them to school and back and listed all the cookies they'd make, and snowmen, and crafts, and I stopped her, out of instinct I guess and lied, telling her they have a winter break scheduled so no school, they're all hers. Even better, she said, and when we hung up I called the school and said the girls had some sort of bug and would be out for a few days.

I just can't get past the thought that they aren't safe there— that whoever is doing this tried once to kill our whole family on the ice. Or was I the only target, and it didn't matter who else got hurt? Whoever it is knows where they go to school and where their bus stop is, and when they have recess, and lunch hour, but they won't know they're at my mother's, and she's agreed not to tell anyone they're there, even though I know I've scared her. But she was already scared. All of us are.

My mother still lives in the house I grew up in on a massive plot of land up north that even has a small lake on the property. It's such a good fishing lake that she's always kept it open to fishermen and loves seeing the ice huts dotting the frozen lake top in the winter. As a kid I'd make hot chocolate and set up my stand at the edge of the lake and sell hot cups for fifty cents each. It's the girls' favorite thing to do at their grandma's, so they'll be excited, and that's what I need for them right now— to be completely shielded from all this horror and just happy making pots of cocoa at grandma's.

The girls are all giggles and twirling down the hall in the tutus they're wearing after playing dress up in their room. When I tell them they are spending a few days at grandma's, they're elated. It's like afternoons at the Ole, endless candy and crafts and full-time doting and attention. June asks if she can wear her leotard under her coat on the way so she can show grandma the glittery unicorns on the sleeves and I tell her she can. Poppy packs her Elsa suitcase and asks if they can bring Gus, and I tell her grandma is allergic, and to pull their things into the hall when they're ready.

I hear Clay lumbering around the kitchen and find him boiling a couple of hot dogs in a pan of water. He's still in his coat and boots. I can see the tension in his body just from looking at his back in front of the stove.

"I don't feel comfortable with you here alone while I'm gone," he says. "Not at night."

"It's an hour round trip," I say.

"Still," he grunts.

"Well, I'm meeting Mack for a drink at the Trout anyway while we wait for word about Bernie. I might stay at her place until the security gets fixed tomorrow." I can feel him stiffen at the mention of this, but we don't go round and round about it again since the girls are here. Him asking do I believe him? Me asking how the hell did it get in your truck, then? And then six more variations of those arguments over and over. We just don't say anything else to each other.

When I hear the girls pulling on snow boots and arguing over who gets to sleep on the top bunk in their room at grandma's, I go and kiss and squeeze them and tell them to listen to grandma and not to fight her about bedtimes, and then they pull their things outside and down the sidewalk. Clay looks back at me before he follows behind them. He looks like he's going to say something, but then he just turns and leaves silently.

And then I get to work. I have an hour before I meet Mack and I plan to search every corner of the place I can think to look before I go. I don't know what I'm looking for, but that doesn't stop me from going through all of his things in hopes I'll know it when I see it. He's an outdoorsman, not a man with a home office or briefcase, and he barely gets on the desktop computer. So the only place to even look first is his drawers and his side of the closet which I dig through carefully but thoroughly. All I find underneath T-shirts and underwear is a basket of socks with no matching pairs and old cuff links, earbuds, and a gold watch from a hundred years ago.

In the garage, I stare at the wall of shelving. I watched a movie once where the wife discovered her husband was a serial killer by finding trinkets from all the girls he killed in a plastic Walmart bin he stored in the garage. Trophies, Millie called them. It makes me shudder to think about it now. In the movie I thought the killer was some kind of moron not to be a little smarter than that, but I guess hiding something in plain sight is sometimes not the worst idea.

I open shoeboxes full of old coins and playing cards, and I rifle through storage bins full of everything a person saves over the years for no reason—a cookie tin with a cardinal design, oil filters, and a broken coffee maker. Baby booties and ugly

mugs, wire hangers and tennis balls and a stained glass lamp
from my grandmother's house. I dig my hand down to the bottom of every box full of old paperbacks and rogue Legos and
strings of Mardi Gras beads...for what, exactly? Am I expecting
a used syringe to surface, some suspicious duct tape and zip ties?

After almost an hour, I realize I'm running late to meet
Mack, and that this is stupid. That I'm being paranoid and need
to keep a better head on my shoulders right now. I feel a prick-
ling heat climb my spine as an overwhelming feeling of shame
ripples through me. What am I *doing*?

Of course someone put that stuff in his truck, just like they
snuck into the Oleander's and cut wires, just like they cut the
ice at the lake. "Stop," I mumble to myself. "Just stop." I push
bins back into their spots on the garage shelving before getting
into my car, taking a deep breath, and driving to the Trout.

It's busy tonight. I find Mack at the bar with a stool saved
next to her. She waves and plucks her purse off the seat so I can
sit down. The jukebox plays George Strait and the place is bus-
tling and warm. Hats and mittens are piled on pub tables, and
coats and parkas hang on booths and chair backs. Billy puts a
napkin down in front of me and I order a shot of whiskey and
a glass of Pinot. Mack raises her eyebrow at me but doesn't say
anything. As we catch up, something feels different—distant.
We first talk about the girls and Rowan the way we always
start—kid updates first—but today it's just an avoidance of the
heavy topics neither of us seems to know how to talk about
with one another. We skirt around them, and I get the feeling
there are things she's not telling me.

I, on the other hand, tell her every last detail about Clay
and the cameras and needing a new security system and how I
just want to leave town. How the girls are at my mother's for
a while, and then we order another drink and marvel at how
Riley can have no leads yet, and what to do about it all.

There are only two detectives in our small town so I can't

exactly demand someone else take the case. Jones is the other guy, and he's like an actual lump on a log. He is officially working with Riley on all of it, but says almost nothing and seems to do the bare minimum required of him with zero expression on his face. I didn't know a person could exist in the absence of any personality, but alas, we have Howard Jones.

It's not that he's hard-boiled from a life of seeing the worst in humanity. He may have given Betsy Wisniak a ticket for running the Main Street stop sign or detained Joey Ahlstrom for stealing Tide PODS from Walmart, and that's about as hardcore as it gets…until me, that is.

After I get it all off my chest, I ask what's the latest with her, but again, she brushes it off and changes the subject.

"How's the gang at the Oleander's?" Mack asks.

I shake my head sadly. "Mort is taking it the hardest, and Millie responded by buying a box of merlot and retreating to her room. Flor and Herb seemed to be huddled up with Evan trying to study security footage and discuss everything they think could be clues or evidence and, I guess, trying to not surrender to the idea that anything bad has happened to him. I guess you still haven't gotten any updates?"

"Nothing," she says. She fidgets with her glass for a moment before speaking. "I know it seems off topic, but do any of the residents know that the Ole is in major financial trouble?" she asks, and I'm not sure why she would want to know this aside from the fact that we have just been trying to keep business as usual since Leo's disappearance. Someone could always buy the Oleander's and turn it into an apartment block or bowling alley or something, and Mack wants nothing to do with being the owner of a business that's going under, but I guess she would sort of inherit it if Leo is…well, dead.

I have just been trying to keep it afloat so we aren't in danger of losing everyone's home, but she'll have to be the one to officially make decisions about it at some point if I can't find a way to save it.

"No. I mean, I don't *think* so. I haven't told any of them, but sometimes I get strange comments about saving money or looks of concern around any budget conversations, so I can't be sure. Why?" I ask.

"I don't know—they're going through a lot, and I was just curious if that was another thing on top of it all—if they were worried they'd be homeless or something," she finishes, and I can't help but feel like there's more behind the question, but I don't press.

"I hope not. I'm scrimping and saving and doing everything I can," I say and she squeezes my hand. I know she'd help if she was able to. What a crazy turn of events to be sitting here with Mack, the successful, flashy, wealthy one of us...somehow more broke than me.

Her phone rings and we both look down at it on the bar top to see Riley's name pop up. She gives me a wide-eyed look and answers. She listens for a moment or two, her face falling, and she slowly moves her phone away from her ear and places it back on the bar, numbly, turning to look at me.

"Bernie's dead."

20

Florence

Millie weeps in the armchair near the fireplace as the rest of us stare at the pendant on the coffee table. Herb was smart enough to put his gloves on before picking it up and then putting it straight into the plastic bag it sits in now. I can't imagine whoever left it for us to find was dumb enough to leave fingerprints, but of course, we'll give it to the police anyway.

I have already called Riley, who is sending someone to pick it up, but he said he will need to ask us more questions later. The cops scoured the area around Bernie's missing car—just a rectangle impression left in the snow from where it was once parked—and there was nothing to be found, so somebody purposefully put it there after the fact and wanted us to find it. We told him the story three times. I don't know what else he needs to ask, but for him not to come around in person with his scribbly pad the way he always does makes me wonder if something more has happened that's taking his attention. This is a pretty big clue handed to us, and so after an officer comes and goes with the Ziploc bag containing Bernie's precious pendant, I feel sort of sick to my stomach thinking about what it really means.

We all still sit solemnly around the rec room in our respective spots. Millie weeping, Herb eating a bag of Funyuns and wiping the crumbs on his pant legs, expressionless, and the rest of us just sort of staring around the room, not knowing even what to do next.

"We should tell Shelby about this…" Evan finally says from his usual seat at the computer desk. "Out of respect, before she hears it from…"

"Chipped Beef," Herb interrupts, finishing his sentence.

"Or the news."

"I was gonna say," Evan adds. "Even worse."

"I know…but I want to give her a day," I say. "It won't change anything if we tell her, and I think she needs a moment to catch her breath." Everyone sort of half nods or mumbles in agreement.

"We can put a photo of the pendant on the site and ask if anyone recognizes it—saw who might have had it and could have left it there, and why?" Evan suggests. I agree and send Mort the photo I took of it lying in the snow before we picked it up.

"We'll get it up on the site," Mort says. And then everyone goes their separate ways, except for Millie who has fallen asleep by the fireplace hearth at this point. Evan is making calls about used cameras we can buy for the back lot, Mort and Herb disappear to their rooms, and I sit in the front window on a floral love seat nobody ever uses so it smells of dust mites, but I don't mind today. I sip a mug of Earl Grey and watch the snow lightly fall over the two feet of snow that's already been shoveled this week and sits in piles along the sidewalk. A couple of winter birds hop on a naked tree branch and peck at the seeds Bernie tossed out by the tree.

I think about Bernie, all of the names and clues and possibilities swirling around in my mind, until I find that it's already dusk and I'm startled out of my thoughts when my phone buzzes. It's Shelby.

I find Evan, Mort, and Herb on an old sofa in Herb's room playing some shooting video game and I stand in the doorway, completely numb with the news I've just heard. They pause the game and turn to look at me.

"Oh God," I cry, and I can't help it all coming out all of a sudden. Mort comes to put his arm around me.

"Flor, what's happened?" Herb asks, standing up, the color draining from his face.

"I got the call about Bernie. He was in that car—his car that they found. They're calling it suicide. Carbon monoxide poisoning." Everyone is stunned into silence a moment, and then Mort smashes his hand onto the metal TV dinner tray next to him. It causes a startling crash that makes us all jump because we're already so rattled, and it's also very out of character for him to make much noise or fuss at all.

"No!" Mort raises his voice. "He would never do that. No!"

"That's what Shelby said too. She's at the Trout. Riley's off duty, but called to tell Mack what the coroner's office said, and Shelby's waiting for Clay to come pick her up because she and Mack had a few…and then she's going to track down Riley and get answers, apparently."

"We'll go with her. We have questions too," Herb says.

"Let's hurry," I say, and within ten minutes we are all bundled up and ready to go except for Millie who has moved, but is now asleep in the recliner in her housecoat and slippers. And of course Evan, who has promised to guard the place and whom Shelby would be quite unhappy to see at a bar rather than in the front office of the Ole where he is supposed to be, so it's just the three of us tonight. This is our case now too.

When we pull into the parking lot, I also see Riley and

his wife walking from their car up to the door. That's unexpected. He's off duty, clearly, wearing slacks and a tie. She's in heels and a peacoat, and he helps her balance over icy pavement and inside.

By the time we get our old bones to the front door and go in I see Clay too, standing across the room next to Mack and Shelby, who is gesturing wildly, no doubt telling him more about what's happened. But besides that, the place is as one would expect. A few couples dancing on the parquet square of flooring in front of the jukebox, a few playing pool, people chatting at tables. Clearly, the somber news isn't common knowledge yet.

Shelby sees Riley before she notices us, and it only takes a moment to see her face contort and her loss of balance as she tries to get herself off the bar stool. Clay makes a futile attempt to hold her back but lets her go...she's drunk and he's helpless to stop her without making a scene. I can see that from here, and in under five seconds, she meets Riley smack-dab in the middle of the bar. The three of us shuffle over to the table directly behind Shelby to listen.

"Oh. Shelby, hello there," Riley says after Belinda has sat herself at a table and he's accosted by Shelby on his way up to the bar.

"What's going on? What shit are you pulling?" she hisses at him. I glance at Mack and Clay who can't hear the exchange, but also don't take their eyes off of her.

"Ah, I'm not sure what you mean, but let's talk about it at the station tomorrow. It's not the place. I'm sorry about Bernie—I didn't want to have to tell..."

"Do you pay people off? Or is it you doing all of this? None of it adds up. All this shit keeps happening and you do nothing. *Nothing!*" People are starting to look now. I make a general gesture with my hand like "it's okay" to nobody in particular and a few turn away, but a scene is beginning and I don't think there's any stopping it.

"Shelby. You've had a few drinks. I think you should let me get by, and we'll discuss this at an appropriate time."

"*Suicide?* Are you kidding? We know the Oleander's has been attacked by some maniac and that Bernie's pendant was placed for us to find like a threat—you know there was a call to his phone from an unknown caller and that he didn't drive. How are you accepting this? *Any* of this?" Now pretty much everyone is looking and hushing their voices. Clay walks over to Shelby and tries to gently take her by the elbow, but she pushes him away.

"He was depressed, by all accounts, and found in the driver's seat backed into a snowbank to push the carbon monoxide into the car. Nobody else was there," Riley says in a forced whisper, and Shelby is visibly flustered. Then she fishes her old cell phone from her pocket and holds it up in the air.

"Then explain this!" Now the place is almost silent except for the song playing from the jukebox. "This is my lost phone, and guess where it was found? In *your house*. My residents found it when they were interviewing you. Explain that!"

"Shelby, I beg you," Clay says quietly behind her. Riley gives him a tight smile. A "control your wife" smile, but he doesn't say this. He looks back to Shelby and says: "Let's talk about this at the station tomorrow."

"No. Goddamn it! Who knows if I'll be alive tomorrow, for fuck's sake. Someone is trying to kill me and what are you doing? Why did you have my phone?" He looks stunned and she looks around and addresses everyone gawking at them. "He stole my phone, everyone. Why? You should all be terrified that the detective never has any clues, but shit keeps happening and now my missing phone is found in his couch cushions! Don't you want answers?"

I see Belinda move closer behind Riley and give him a look

like "is that true" and he shakes his head subtly before aiming his attention back to Shelby.

"You're making a fool of yourself. There was no phone in my house. I think it's time for you to get a ride home, Shelby," he says, and since she hasn't registered that we're there, we opt not to speak up right at this moment because it does seem like she should probably get a ride home and not appear so very unhinged in front of half the town. She has every right to be, but it's not a good look.

"Let's go, Shel," Clay says, and she pulls away again.

"Get off me. I'm going with Mack," she slurs, and Clay looks to Mack who leaps off her stool and collects Shelby's things and makes her way quickly across the room to assist her.

"Let's get outta here," she says trying to keep it casual and not trigger any more anger.

"This guy's a fucking crook!" Shelby yells, shoving Riley's shoulder with her palm. Riley plays the victim—the perfectly stable one who has to suffer a crazy woman who's gone off the deep end. Of course he does, how else would he play it? He could probably arrest her, I think, but that's not the play he wants to make.

"A fucking thief, and he's hiding evidence—don't trust him" is the last thing she says as Mack ushers her out the door. And then I see Mack motion to us to follow, and we get to our feet and are right behind them.

Outside, we stand on the porch of the Trout where Shelby is flopped in a wooden rocking chair that's covered in snow, but she doesn't seem to mind. I've never seen her inebriated before, and it would be entertaining if the circumstances weren't so dire.

"That fucker," she mumbles. "Who has a smoke?" She pushes a giant ashtray on a metal table around, which is where the smokers usually congregate, but no one else is out here right now.

"You don't smoke, kid," Mack says and she looks to us, all shivering in the frigid air.

"Sorry. I had a few and I planned to call a cab. Can you give us a ride to my place on your way back? We'll figure our cars out in the morning."

"Of course," Herb says, and we pile into the freezing van, then drive through the dark night to Mack's place. Shelby is quiet now, staring out the window with her forehead leaning on it and tears glistening in her eyes. Herb turns on the radio and nobody says much.

Mack suddenly inhales sharply and holds the dash with both hands. Herb must think she sees a deer in the road or maybe she's having a heart attack or something, and he immediately pulls over.

"What is it?" he asks. Shelby is sitting up and alert now.

"I just remembered something that I didn't really register at the time—all the shock—everything happening all at once, but…"

"What?" Shelby almost screams.

"When we found the car. Bernie's car…there were footprints leading away from it. It was snowing, so they'd be gone now. But…even though everything points to suicide… No. No way. Someone else was there that night."

21

Mack

It's late morning by the time I hear Shelby stir in the guest room. I hear the rattle of the pipes and running water in the bathroom sink, so I pick up the tray of coffee and muffins I made when I was up far too early because Rowan was texting me about some boy she was crying over. I notice the coffee's gone cold, so I pour two new mugs and tiptoe down the hall and tap on her door.

Inside Shelby looks like I remember her in college after a few too many Jell-O shots at a dorm party, and I don't recall even seeing her take a shot of liquor like a twenty-year-old since we were actually in our twenties, but times are tough right now, so I can't say she doesn't deserve to do whatever gets her through.

"Morning." I sit next to her on the bed and hand her a cup of coffee and then slide under the puffy white down comforter next to her with my own mug. "There's a couple ibuprofen," I say, pointing to the tray. She takes them and sips her coffee.

"Thanks, Mack." She leans her head on my shoulder and we are both quiet for a few minutes, looking out the floor-to-ceiling windows at the wind whipping through the tree branches and snow blowing around the deck. I designed that deck that's so lovely, even underneath the two feet of snow on top of it. I'll miss this house.

"I saw a check for an obscene amount of money hanging on your fridge with a magnet...from Billy Curran? I mean it's none of my business whatsoever, but is there anything you wanna tell me?" she asks, and I can feel myself blush.

"I'm not accepting it. He was trying to help with...an expense, but I'm giving it back."

She raises her eyebrows in surprise. "Expense? Everything okay?"

"Yes," I say, with a tone that requests an end to the topic.

"You two seem...close lately," she says.

"Just business. I'm helping him with remodeling ideas," I say, dismissing the topic. "That's it."

"Huh," she mumbles, reaching for her phone on the nightstand and I quickly take it from her and toss it to the end of the bed.

"Nope."

"What the hell?" she says. "I have to tell Clay to pick me up."

"Herb and the gang coordinated to drop your car off last night. They said they had nothing more exciting to do and would be happy to help, so it's outside. So just...no need for your phone yet."

"Uhhh. Why?"

"Just...don't look at Facebook. I know you will, but maybe not *just* yet," I say, and she crawls down and snatches her phone from the puff of comforter that swallowed it.

"Jesus. What now?" She opens her app and scrolls. It doesn't take long before she sees it, but at least I got to semi-warn her.

"Yeah, it appears Riley's wife took a video of the whole thing last night on her phone and took liberties with how she edited it," I say, rewatching it as Shelby plays it over and over. It's less than two minutes long, but her shoving Riley's shoulder is in slow motion and her mouth is twisted and her eyes are watery and bloodshot as she yells *"This guy's a fucking crook! A fucking thief!"* and the caption reads "Mental Health Awareness" and goes on to say that Shelby essentially has lost it and there is no evidence of all the things she's reporting are happening to her and maybe she's lying. That all this is a need for attention, a cry for help, and we should have some compassion and get her the help she needs…not in those exact words, but that's the gist of it.

Shelby stares at the phone screen with her mouth open and an unreadable look in her eyes. She starts to scroll down.

"No! Seriously. Nobody should ever read the comments. Let's just…" but of course she does and one of the comments from Karen Gustafson says "Poor Bernie. It's no surprise he killed himself if this is what he had to deal with from his caretaker." I see tears form in her eyes.

"I'm not even his caretaker. It's senior living, not a nursing home. They don't even…" she begins to say, picking out the wrong thing to defend because she doesn't know where to begin with the real accusations, I suppose.

"Hey, come here," I say, gently taking her phone away and replacing it with her coffee mug. "Karen Gustafson is a twat. We all know that. She snaps her fingers and calls me waitress when she comes into the cafe. And she tips in loose pennies from the bottom of her purse," I say and try to continue offering examples of her faulty character, but Shelby interrupts.

"It has six hundred views," she says numbly.

"It'll pass," I say.

"Does everyone think I'm lying? Is that what people think?"

"No," I say. "Of course not." But the truth is I don't really know what people are saying because I have been so wound up in my own crisis, running to hell and back looking for Leo, decoding boxes of paperwork, and cryptic messages. I have no earthly idea what people are saying about Shelby, but they probably *are* saying that. It's Rivers Crossing. When the gossip gets old and tired, spice it up a bit. Why not?

"Do you think they were Bernie's?" she asks.

"What?"

"The footprints. What if he got out of the car—maybe he checked to make sure the tailpipe was packed with snow, maybe he just walked around to make sure nobody was around, which I guess is silly because that road goes unused for days at a time out there, but I mean, maybe. People were saying Bernie seemed depressed… I don't know." She sighs, sinking down into the bed and holding her cup of coffee on top of the covers tucked up to her chin. She stares up at the ceiling in dismay.

"Maybe, but from what I remember, they were just like… boot imprints leading away from the car. I don't recall prints leading back, but you're right. It's kind of a blur because it was a shock and I wasn't looking for that sort of thing, so when I remembered, it's just a flash in my mind. But I'm sure that's what I saw."

Shelby sighs again, puts down her mug and slowly gets to her feet, pulling on a sweatshirt she left hanging over the chair on the vanity and looking for her socks.

"I have to go and see the girls at my mom's. They're staying there a few days. Maybe longer. I need to call Clay. You know I can already see the look on Riley's face when you tell him you saw footprints. It's sort of like you know he's rolling his eyes internally, you know? That's what it will be."

"I wanna tell you something," I say. She gives me a what-else-could-there-possibly-be look, but when I pat the edge of

the bed, she tentatively sits. I sit crunched up against the pillows in front of the headboard and rest my coffee on my knees.
I take a deep breath.

"I'm losing the house. Leo took out a secret mortgage on it
and it's getting foreclosed on, but please don't say anything about
that. I don't wanna talk about it right now," I say quickly, and
her shocked eyes and open mouth slowly adjust into a forced
neutral expression as she lets me continue.

"He cheated a lot of people. Gambled and stole money from
his staff, partners, and you. Sort of."

"Me?"

"Yes, in a roundabout way."

"Um. Wouldn't that be something I'd know about?" she asks.

"I have something to show you," I say, and she watches me
walk out the guest room door into the kitchen where the dogs
see and start barking until they realize it's just me and go back
to lie down in their bed by the fireplace. I grab some files off
of the kitchen counter and Shelby is already behind me, taking
them from my hands before I can do this gracefully.

"What is it? You're freaking me out."

"I found these in Leo's things." She's looking through the
pages, not making sense of it. "Essentially, he's been skimming
off the top at the Oleander's. There's a secret bank account I
found, so however he set up this…fraud, I guess, it's just auto-
matic now and it filters through this bank, which takes a percentage before it is sent to the Oleander's system, and you would
never know that's not the full amount. I don't really understand
money laundering but that's the general idea, I think."

Shelby sits there with the papers still in hand and a look of
utter confusion on her face.

"This is why we are going under. Why there's never enough
to make the books balance?"

"I mean, yeah. I would think so. I imagine there is a way

to stop it continuing, but if they don't find him it's not like the money can be recovered." She doesn't respond, just pages through the papers in awe.

"I only found out a few days ago. I was trying to see if I could track him down with this information, but it's all been a dead end, so I think I'm just giving up."

"What do you mean? What does that mean?" she asks, putting her hand on my arm and tossing the papers on the counter.

"I'll give all this to the cops, of course. I mean, I was gonna anyway. I just wanted a day or two. And if the house gets sold from underneath me, maybe it's time for me to go. The whole town...it's hard to be here."

"I know," she says, hugging me. And we stay in that glorious hug for a minute before I pull away to wipe a falling tear and apologize.

"It's not your fucking fault," she says.

"I just think maybe it's time to sell the cafe and go to get a little place near Rowan's school. Find a job out there. I just don't know anymore. But the main reason I'm telling you all this is because...what if *this* is why someone is after you?"

Shelby sits on the bar stool at the counter and looks at me. "Because Leo is stealing money?"

"Yeah. Because they think you're in on it. What if they think you have to know since you run the place? What if someone else knows about the fraud and what if that someone else was fucked over—stolen from by Leo—and they think you two are partners in this laundering? I mean, fuck, it's just a theory because why else would anyone be after you? Why not be after me? Maybe they know enough about it all to know he hid everything from me, but they assume you see the finances. I might be grasping at straws here, but it's something, maybe."

Shelby considers this. "Well, who? There isn't one person I can think of that would be capable of this kind of stuff. Unless it's him."

"You think it's Leo."

"Well, fuck, Mack. I mean, you're telling me he's still out there somewhere stealing money from us. Maybe he wants us both dead so nobody else finds out, and he can get away with it all. And he must be alive, because he's still making withdrawals," she says.

I look down at the papers on the countertop and close my eyes. What can I say. She's not wrong, as much as I want her to be. It's just hard hearing another person say it out loud—that he's awful. That he's a criminal. That he's alive, and is letting this all happen to me.

We both jolt when we hear tires coming up the drive, crunching over ice patches and rolling to a stop. The dogs start going crazy and we both stand and look out the front bay window to see Detective Riley and Detective Jones emerging from a police car and walking up the drive to the front door.

"Holy shit," Shelby says. "I just pushed his shoulder and he was off duty. You don't think they're here about last night, do you?"

"I don't know," I mumble as I pick up Linus and shush Nugget. We stand looking at one another, and even though we are expecting the knock, it makes us both jump—the invasive sound reverberating in the silent house.

We both stand in the front hall and open the door to see Riley and Jones, their faces crumpled and grief-stricken as they take their hats off and hold them to their chests upon seeing me. Shelby gasps and holds her hand over her mouth, but somehow it takes me a minute to absorb what's happening.

Somewhere between them asking if they can come in for a moment and the dizziness and someone pulling a chair up for me to sit and my heart in my throat I make out the words—and they try to tell me in a graceful way, but the truth has been uncovered and there is no way to unhear it. There are no threads of hope to hold on to.

The remains of Leo Connolly have been found. Leo is dead. Leo has been dead a long time.

22

Shelby

The officers are sitting with Mack in the living room and I'm putting a pot of tea on because I don't know how else to be of help. My mind is spinning—all this time I've been convinced that Leo must be behind whatever madness has been happening, and he's been dead this whole time. Riley said that the condition of the remains, at first glance from the coroner, are consistent with him being dead over a year. It's probable that he died close to the time he went missing, but they won't know for sure until after the autopsy.

He was found under the ice in a lake, he said—caught on a hook by ice fishers who called the police. They identified him by his clothes and wallet still in his pocket. My God. All these horrible things I blamed him for in my mind, and none of it could have been him. I look through the doorway to see them all sitting there. Mack is as white as a sheet, although she has been preparing herself for this. She's not sobbing. She's just still and shocked.

I carry in a tray with mugs and place the teapot on the coffee table, and I sit. Riley is giving some spiel about how sorry he is to tell her this again, and that they don't know too much just yet, then he looks to me.

"We would like it if you would accompany us to the station so we can ask some more questions, Shelby, if you're able."

I blink at him. "About last night? Don't you think that's a little insignificant right now?" I say, and he clears his throat, giving me a thin, impatient smile.

"No, not about last night. We'd like to ask you some general questions related to Leo." I look to Mack and back to him, confused.

"What are you talking about? What the hell do I know about Leo that I haven't told you six thousand times?"

"Well, since he was found on your family's property, it's only appropriate that we ask you some questions…" he continues to mumble something but I cut him off.

"My…what? You said it was a lake—you mean the lake on my mother's land? Oh my God. What? Wait, my kids are up there right now." I stand, panicked, confused. He stands too, like he's ready to stop me from doing something crazy.

"The lake is several wooded acres from the house. We already talked to her. She knows a forensics team is still there, but the girls don't know anything," he says, and for some reason him knowing anything about my girls that I don't know makes me feel sick to my stomach.

"What does this have to do with me? If you have questions, ask the forensics team."

"I think you might want a private environment…" he starts to say, and again I cut him off.

"No. I don't. Anything you have to ask, fucking ask. Do you think I have something to hide? You wanna ask me how he was found in that lake? You think I would know that?" I'm raising my voice now, and the expression on Mack's face is a look of bewilderment mixed with grief, and I'm so angry at this incompetent dipshit's insinuations that I can barely hold back, but I try to collect myself. Taking a deep breath I sit back down and so does he, and Jones, who never says a goddamn thing, decides to pipe up.

"There are also some potential discrepancies in the details you've given us about the crimes you've reported recently that we'd like to get further insight on." Since I've never heard him string that many words together before at one time, I'm taken aback by how oddly formal he sounds, and also by the way he's looking at me. *Suspicion.* That's what it is. They aren't just being idiots trying to do their job thoroughly, they legitimately think I know how Leo got in the lake.

"I'm sorry. So first the Oleander's gets the electrical burned, and then my family is almost murdered on the ice at the lake, and then I'm attacked at my own home. Are those the crimes you're referring to? Is there some problem with my very thorough reports I have already made that *nothing* has been done about?" I'm so angry that I feel a cold sweat break out on my back despite the frigid temperatures outside, and my heart is pounding in my chest.

"Well, yes, actually," Jones says.

"What the actual fuck?" I say, and Mack puts her hand on my arm in a gesture that tells me to cool down, and I instantly feel guilt that she has to do that when I should be comforting her right now. I take a breath and try to stay cordial.

"What else can I possibly tell you?" I ask as calmly as I am able. "You think I know who burned the electrical panel at the Ole? You want a list of names of suspects? What else can I give you?"

"We'd like to know where you were that night," Riley says, and I feel myself stiffen and my mouth go dry.

"You what?"

"See, we have an anonymous tip that it was you. That you may have been attempting insurance fraud—trying to start an electrical fire to recoup money for the place because it's going under. I'm not saying that's true, now don't get me wrong, but I am saying we have questions," he says, and I can feel my mouth hanging open, but everything else feels numb. I see Mack's hand cup her mouth as she looks from me to Riley and back again.

"You said someone tried to manipulate the ice at your fishing hut, but the holes, upon closer inspection, look like inexperienced ice fishers or teenagers could have been involved rather than a malicious act, and it was your responsibility to make sure the area was safe. Taking kids out there in the pitch-black without making sure it was secure is nobody else's fault," he says, and I feel my cheeks go red-hot. I leap to my feet in defense of my babies.

"Are you out of your mind? Pitch-black? It's pitch-black at 4:00 goddamn p.m. in the afternoon around here. It was dinnertime. We've brought them out there for years with no massive holes to fall through…just like every other family that goes fishing! And you know that. You're blaming me? Now it's also my fault that I was attacked at my own house—strangled almost to death. Did I do that too?" I'm practically screaming now, but the injustice, the absolute shock from what he's saying, is staggering.

"Listen," Riley says, trying to bring a softer tone to the conversation, even though what he says next is the most outrageous thing yet.

"All we have from the night you were attacked is your account. Again, I am not saying that we don't believe you…"

"But you are!" I interrupt.

"I'm just saying there are a series of unusual events with zero proof of anyone else involved. We are still looking into it. It just requires more information from you, is all, nobody is accusing..."

"There were drops of blood in the snow! There was DNA, for God's sake," I say, almost breathless now, dizzy and shaking at this point.

"That did come back..."

"So you have proof," I say, feeling suspended in midair waiting for his response.

"It came back a match to...you. It was your blood."

"What?" It comes out as a stunned whisper.

"You mentioned you were cut on the vase that broke. Maybe it's from that, but again, there's just no other evidence after being investigated. No fingerprints, DNA, no vehicle at your property or tire marks. Even the prints in the snow around the property matched only yours or Clay's boots that you offered for us to compare—I could go on, Shelby. It doesn't add up. And now that Leo's remains have been discovered on your family property, we need to have you come in and answer some questions again. You're not under arrest or anything, we just need your statement on record," he says. "I'm sure you can understand that."

I hold my hand to my heart and try to absorb all that he is saying, but all I see is my life flash before my eyes—a future in a prison cell, a life stolen from me—a life without my girls. How can this be happening?

"You can wait until tomorrow to come in for official questioning if you need to. Like I said, nobody is saying you're under arrest."

"Under arrest," I repeat under my breath. I remember Mort explaining in his podcast that there is a forty percent chance that whoever killed Otis or Bernie or Leo—if it is murder—will get away with it, statistically speaking. That's an absurdly high percentage of people getting away with murder, and with this police force, I can wager it's much higher than that. I wonder what the percentage is for someone falsely accused.

My God, I have to get out of here. This can't be happening. I just need to get the fuck out of here right this minute. I feel the tears welling up in my eyes. I see Mack out of the corner of my eye, overwhelmed and without words, so I just stand up and rush to the door where I grab my coat off the hook and run to my car and I drive away as fast as I can.

I need to go and see Poppy and June. That's all I care about right now. I think about driving to the bait shop to tell Clay about all of this, but I'm so ashamed about what's being said about me. I wonder if he's already heard. I can't face it right now, so I rush home, tears blurring my vision and my head swimming—trying to understand who would be doing this. Why would anyone do all this? For what?

On a windy two-lane road a few miles from home, I stop at a run-down gas station. I stand shivering as I fill up my tank before I go home and grab an overnight bag so I can go to my mother's and be with the girls and get the fuck out of here for a while. There is no indoor section of this place, just a tiny booth with a window you walk up to for cigarettes or soda. There are no other cars, just the wind blowing and the snow whipping. But I think I hear a car idling, even though I don't see anything. It's like somewhere just out of sight, the hum of a motor is present, but I can't be sure because the howling wind is so loud and the pines are thick, so there are so many places a car could be. And now I think I'm being followed and I start to panic. Then, after a few minutes, once I am finished with the gas and sitting in my car, paralyzed in fear, I realize it was a car, and I hear it pull away, and I hear the rev of an engine until the sound disappears down the long road, but I never actually see it. I wonder if I'm going crazy.

Not like you see in the movies. Am I actually mad? Am I

seeing things? No, like I seriously wonder if I've had some psy-chotic break and I can't even trust my own thoughts.

But even if it was my imagination, it's gone now, and I race home to get my things. I rehearse packing in my mind—I'll grab their *Frog and Toad Are Friends* books and Poppy's purple nail polish, and they'll be so surprised. I'll only grab a change of clothes and my charger, and I'll be on the road. I text Clay to let him know where I'm headed, but I don't call because I just need some time alone. To think.

I pull into our drive and turn off the ignition, and in the cold, night air, I think I hear it again: a car idling. But of course it can't be, because this isn't a public gas station. This is my home, and there is nothing but woods around us. The barn and ga-rage, but I don't see anything. *Calm down*, I tell myself. Get inside, lock the doors, get the gun, and just wait. The door is right there. You're being paranoid. Just get inside, and if you need to call the cops, God-for-fucking-bid, then call, but just get safe and then reassess.

It's like running up the stairs as a kid—when you're in the basement and you've pulled the string to turn the lights off and you have to run before the boogeyman gets you. That's how I feel right now. But as ridiculous as it might be, I start to sprint to the front door and I think for just a second that I hear footsteps behind me, but before I can turn around to see, I feel someone grab me from behind. As my phone drops on the ice with a thud, a thought flits across my mind—why would you come here? Whoever wants you dead knows there are no cam-eras here. Whoever wants you dead has just won.

And then, as my head falls heavy into soft snow, I see stars, and everything goes dark.

23

Florence

The sun is setting but you wouldn't be able to tell that from looking outside since these January days are hazy and overcast already. The mood at the Oleander's is a bleak one. Heather is out for two weeks because the stress of it all got to her and she said she didn't think an hourly job barely above minimum wage was worth getting potentially murdered over, and she wanted away from this place, and Shelby, and all of it for her own safety for a little while. I guess that's fair.

Evan has the night off for a bowling tournament, and Shelby said she's stopping in this evening, but there has been no word from her, so I'm starting to get a little worried. The four of us sit in the rec room eating Hot Pockets that Herb heated up for us and discussing the arrangements for Bernie's funeral accommodations. His daughter is doing most of the planning, but we wanted to help so we're coordinating volunteers to set up chairs at the church and serve refreshments.

PBS is playing on the TV in the background, and Bob Ross is painting little clouds in front of a winter moon on canvas, but nobody is watching even though we usually love to get canvases of our own from the craft room and drink chardonnay and paint along on Saturdays.

"I got my permanent today at Frannie's Cut & Curl if anyone's interested," Millie says, picking a pepperoni out of her Lean Pocket. She seems to be in a mood since Herb gave everyone else regular Hot Pockets and decided to give her the Lean Pocket.

"Looks nice, Mil," Mort says.

"That's not what I was fishing for. All the ladies were talking about Shelby and the Trout last night. Where I guess you all went without me."

"You were out. Snoring like a buzz saw," Herb says.

"Anyway, the point is…people are gossiping about Shelby, saying they heard she's lying about all the stuff happening to her, making it up! Georgette said she heard from Barbara Langer who heard from Belinda Riley that the electrical outage here was an attempt at insurance fraud. That Shelby did it herself. That's the talk."

"What?" I snap.

"Yep. Then I stopped at Smokey's for a Juicy Lucy afterward and Candace Walberg shows me a video from the bar last night, which is how I know you old bats were there, 'cause it showed Shelby screaming at Riley, and there your ugly mugs are in the background gawking at the whole thing."

"You were sleeping, Millie. Take a pill," Herb says again.

"You could have woken me up for that sort of thing, Herb!" She sighs the sigh of a martyr and continues. "Anyway, then I take the bus home and who do I see but Gordy Willis, and guess what he wants to talk about? Belinda Riley's video on

Facebook, and how maybe there is nobody terrorizing the town and it's all Shelby, and how she should be institutionalized if that's true."

"Jesus," Mort says.

"Yeah," Millie says, pushing her Lean Pocket away and folding her arms across her chest.

"People are terrible," I add, thinking about poor Shelby and what she must be going through, and again I worry about her whereabouts and quickly check my phone to see if she's responded, but nothing.

"Well, what if it's true?" Herb says, and everyone scoffs at him.

"Herb, that's out of line," Mort says.

"Okay, but hear me out. She's the only one with access to the cameras around here. I've thought about that—watching Evan scan through the footage searching for the tiniest movement that he'll never find because…what if she got to the footage first? I mean, who else would want to hurt a bunch of old folks with a fire? Who else would have a motive if it's not insurance money? What if she—you know, lost a screw when that trauma happened to her last year and she's causing all this… I mean, crap, now that I say it all out loud…"

"No. What's the matter with you?" I ask. "Do you hear yourself?"

"I do, Flor. I'm not making an accusation, just discussing all possibilities. Isn't that what the podcast was supposed to be about? Isn't that what Oleanders do? We stay objective. We solve shit. That's what we all said."

"That *is* what we said," Millie adds.

"See!" Herb says.

"But it's not Shelby," she continues, getting up to dump her Lean Pocket in the trash and pour herself a paper cup of chardonnay from the box of wine in the fridge. "I'd know if she were nuts. I have a sixth sense about that kind of stuff."

"That's helpful," Herb says, flailing his arms and rolling his eyes.

"We know she wasn't here when the power went out that night," I say, as if that's definitive proof of something, but I know it's not. I'm just trying to tick through all the boxes and see what the hell I'm missing.

"And if we tell them that when they ask us, they'll say she could have come back anytime unseen, it's a big enough building to sneak into," Mort adds.

"Well, the one thing she would never do in this whole world is put her girls in danger, so the holes in the ice, that wasn't her. End of subject."

We all stare around the room, no ideas left. The crackling of the fire and the wind howling outside fill the silence. After a few minutes, Millie says she's going to her room to watch *Magnum, P.I.*, and a little while after that, Mort and Herb retreat to their rooms as well, and I sit by myself and watch the snow fly sideways under the glow of the streetlamp in the front lot and think about Bernie some more.

After some time, I realize I have started to doze off, so I get up and make a cup of tea to bring to my room for the evening. It's only just after eight, but everyone is tired and defeated and very sad. I walk down the hall dunking my tea bag mindlessly into my mug of hot water and my mind is very far away until I'm jolted back to the present moment when I pass Herb's room and see something I recognize.

There is something blinking on his television screen. He's fallen asleep in the recliner in his room with his remote in one hand, video game controller on his chest, and a near empty beer in the other hand. I stare at the television, then I push on his shoulder to wake him up.

"Herb. Herb, get up," I say, and he opens his eyes and scowls.

"What the hell, Flor?" he says, wiping crumbs from his neck

and putting the beer on the side table, rolling to his side. "I'm sleepin' here," he says.

"What is that?" I point to the TV screen.

"What's what?" he says, opening only one eye and squinting at what I'm pointing to.

"That! What does that mean?" I demand, pushing on his back. He pulls the wool blanket bunched up at his feet over his shoulders and remains turned away from me as he mutters an answer to my question, telling me to close the door when I leave.

My heart almost stops when he explains what I'm looking at, and how he hasn't put it together is beyond me, but I know what it means. And now I also think I know who's behind all of this—everything that has been happening. I don't know *why*, but I do know *who*. And I can't quite believe it myself, but it's the thread I needed to pull. The culprit got lazy, and just gave me the clue I needed to blow this thing apart.

I'm suddenly very glad Herb is asleep, and I close the door as quietly as possible and go to my room to gather my things. Time is of the essence. If it is who I think it is, they're not at home, and I only have so much time to go and find what I need. I don't know exactly what that is yet, but someone who has wreaked this much havoc and been this destructive— something will be there. The proof I need will be there, even if I don't know what it looks like.

If I tell the gang they will try and stop me and tell me that it's dangerous, but I know that nobody will believe me and nobody else will search this house if I don't. There is no real proof for the police to go on, and I promised Winny, and I owe Bernie as much. I have to go without being stopped. And I need to go right now.

I bundle up in my biggest parka and wooly hat and decide I will call a taxicab to take me to the main bus station because you can wait indoors and there is a coffee vending machine and I can wait for the bus there—the one that stops at Willow Circle, and then walk the two blocks to the house and let myself in while nobody is home.

First I flick through my dresser drawer for the small ladybug box I keep my hairpins in. I pluck two pins out, in case I break the first, and then I sneak down the hall to the main rec room where only Sylvia Waters sits. She's on the sofa with her head bent back and her mouth open and I hear a soft snore, so I work quickly, jimmying the office door unlocked with a well-placed hairpin, and when it opens, I move as quietly as I can, although my heart is still thumping and I can feel a cold sweat forming down my back. There is a nightstick and a Taser and a small handgun locked up for security, and the key is in Shelby's desk. I'm much too afraid to take the gun, but I do help myself to the Taser—just in case. I slip it down inside my big purse and replace the lockbox key in the desk drawer and then I wait for my taxi by the front sliding doors in quite a nervous state, hoping nobody decides to come out to the rec room for a glass of water or something and asks what I'm doing.

What will I say? The reason I'm not taking the cab all the way to the house is because everyone knows everyone and I can't be seen getting dropped off there in case this all ends the way I think it will. So I go over reasons I can tell one of the gang if I get caught standing here. But before I need an excuse the taxi pulls up, and I see that the driver is Lenny Miller as I rush outside. I hop in and tell him to step on it. I'm not usually so bossy, but this is a forgivable exception. I lie and tell him I'm taking the bus to the casino like a lot of the old-timers in town do because they give a free voucher for bus fare, and I leave it at that. He doesn't ask any more questions, thank goodness.

When I get to the bus station it's nearly empty, which is to be expected because a storm is pushing in. Nothing scary, just the usual high winds and blowing snow, but I think I can get there and back to the Oleander's before it hits. Inside the station there is old wood paneling on one wall, and the carpet is royal blue and burgundy with a paisley pattern that looks like it belongs in the hotel from *The Shining*. I look at the schedule on my phone again to make sure there are no delays, and it looks like the bus I need comes in fourteen minutes, so I buy myself a cup of translucent coffee from the machine and a Milky Way candy bar and sit fussing with the wrapper for some time while I think about my strategy.

Where Leo is involved, money is involved, and there is a paper trail here. There must be. Drawers, files, a laptop. I have my big purse ready and my heated electric socks Herb got for me last Christmas, so I won't get too terribly cold on the two-block walk back to the bus station where another bus leaving forty-five minutes after this one will drop me off, and that should be enough time.

The bus is almost empty, and it's chilly and dark inside. The driver maneuvers over lumpy snow and the whole structure rocks side to side, making me nauseated. I could be in my warm bed right now watching *Murder, She Wrote* and could have called the police about my epiphany, but we all know they don't care what we have to say about anything. This is the right thing to do, I remind myself, and then it's only a few minutes before the bus hydraulics hiss and it comes to a stop and I walk off into the icy wind holding my parka closed as I walk against it until I reach the house.

It's a house I know well. I know that the side door leading into the kitchen hasn't had a lock on it in decades, but also, with all of the fear and crime lately, most have started locking their doors. *Not* locking your doors has been a point of pride for most people in the area. In fact, it's a bragging right, and a reason to live here. We haven't needed to, even when the rest of the world seems to be under dead bolts and security bars.

When I walk to the side and turn the knob I don't know what to expect, but it clicks open. Maybe that confirms that I am in the right place—the only person in town who isn't afraid, because they are the one to be afraid of. There isn't even a lock on the door if you wanted to lock it, so I let myself into the small kitchen and stay still a moment to listen—to make sure there is nobody here. And when I don't hear a sound, as I expected, I begin.

I start by rifling through kitchen drawers and cabinets. If I were a killer, would I keep trophies, the way Millie mentioned? When I move into the living room, I stand frozen for a moment, flustered, because this could take forever, and what was I thinking, and I don't know where to look next. I see the door that used to be the guest room is ajar and there's a warm light inside, so I decide that's where I'll go next, and when I push the door open, I gasp. I step back, hand to chest, trying to steady my breath and make sense of what I'm looking at.

It's Shelby.

Photos upon photos, like wallpaper all around the room, of Shelby. A candle flickers on what looks like a shrine, with clippings of hair and small items I recognize as hers—a gold earring, a cotton candy lip balm she loves, a pair of reading glasses; and then I see fingernail clippings in a small jar, and my stomach lurches. The photos around the room are mostly candid shots—pictures taken when she didn't know they were being taken. Some are blurry, like they were clipped from video footage. Most are everyday shots—Shelby eating a scone at Mack's, Shelby crossing the street on Main holding a newspaper over her head, Shelby laughing at the Christmas party with a cup of punch and a Santa hat.

Some are more than that. Some were moments stolen from her: she's undressing, or crying, or mostly nude, sleeping in bed. How were these taken? The whole room is a terrifying shrine that I'm standing in, and I suddenly feel faint—it's more than I was prepared for. I don't even know where to begin. Then I see something in a small bowl next to the burning candle. It's an

ID. I pick it up to see that it's Leo's driver's license. My stomach drops and I know all of my suspicions are true. This isn't just about an obsession with stalking Shelby. It all ties together.

I think to take my phone out and start snapping photos as evidence, because I can't take the whole room with me. It needs to stay in context anyway. My hands shake, and then I realize...I'm not alone.

I feel a presence before I even hear anything, and then a voice behind me cuts through the quiet house, stopping me cold.

"Florence. You shouldn't be here."

But it's too late for me to run.

24

Mack

I identify Leo's things inside a nondescript redbrick building with sterile hallways and bulletproof glass shielding the front desk. I walk out after I've finished with only his wedding ring in an evidence bag, because it's all they could give back to me right now. They didn't really need me for that since he was photographed in the clothes he disappeared in by his friends that night and his wallet was still with him, but I did it anyway, and I feel completely numb. His driver's license was missing from his wallet, though. He had his other ID and cards, but why was that missing? I can't stop thinking about any scenario where that makes sense.

It was him, though. I guess it's not official until dental records come back, but there's no doubt it's him. I'm told it's unlikely they will be able to know the cause of death because of how decomposed his remains were. I'll never know. How is that possible?

When I get in my car, I sit and stare at the gray horizon in the distance and think about what Riley said about Shelby. Someone has done all of this with absolute precision. Someone has victimized her, and somehow made her look like the crazy one. It's been planned and calculated. I'm sure Riley thinks I was second-guessing her when he spilled all of this news in front of me, but he'd be mistaken. I just worry that she can't get herself out of this mess, and I'm concerned. I've called her a handful of times today with no response and I know she's upset, and maybe I should leave her alone for a bit, but my gut tells me to find her.

First I call Clay, who sounds drunk over the phone, and he tells me she went to her mother's to be with the girls. I guess her mom must have picked her up, but he tells me to just leave it...she doesn't want to be bothered, and I think that's an odd thing to say. Why would he not want me to try to contact her? Maybe she doesn't want to be bothered by *him*, but it feels like he's hiding something...or maybe it's just the general paranoia speaking.

I decide to drive out to her mother's place anyway, because I want to see where Leo was. I want to understand why, how in the world he got all the way out here. How he died. I can't accept that I'll never know. He made mistakes. He got in over his head and tried to fix it and win the money back, and in moments where I wasn't busy hating him, I could find a part of myself that felt so sorry for what he must have been going through too. He lost everything, failed his family, lived in a chronic state of stress trying to get it all back and keep it all a secret. And he wasn't the one doing all of these terrible things since. More than anything, I hope he wasn't the one who left Shelby in that freezer that night. His death has to be connected, but I have always prayed that he didn't assault her that night, and that she didn't somehow find him and kill him after. I wish finding him explained something—gave a clue of any kind, but it doesn't do much.

It doesn't even really give me closure, because I still don't know what happened to him...or why. There's still a maniac on the loose. Otis and Bernie are still dead. But I forgive him. Maybe I wouldn't have been able to if it were discovered that he was the one behind all of these attacks, but he was just a man who got in too deep and probably got himself killed.

As I pass over snow-packed roads through miles of thick woods I try to call Billy again, in case I lose service out here. He doesn't even know any of this yet, but I can't reach him. I'm starting to feel like the rapture came and I was left behind. Where is he? Where is everyone?

When I arrive at the lake, I can see yellow caution tape wrapped around a few trees on the icy shore and I expect to see some police or forensic personnel there still, but nothing. Just the flapping of the plastic tape in the wind and a large cut out in the ice where they pulled him out, I guess. I choke down the sob trying to climb up my throat when I think about this.

There are tangles of tire prints in the snow, footprints from work boots and impressions from some sort of equipment I don't recognize, but other than that it's just the same old lake we used to swim in as kids, fish off the docks, canoe across in the summers. It's almost like nothing ever happened. I crouch down and look across the ice to the pines on the other side. I miss him so much, it steals my breath. And I let myself cry because I know now that he's gone, and I cry until my whole body aches, until my hands are so frozen that I can't bear to be out here another minute, and then I drive up to the house to talk to Shelby, whether she wants to see me or not.

When I knock on the front door of their family home I practically grew up in myself, I'm surprised to see Celeste, Shelby's mother, open the door. I figured Shelby would have seen my car and popped out. She invites me in, but I linger in the hallway.

"I have sugar cookies in the oven if you want to come and sit down. The girls helped, so they're a little lopsided."

"Oh, thanks, but I just wanted to chat with Shelby for a quick minute, if that's okay," I say, blowing onto my hands to thaw them and shivering near the drafty front door.

"Oh, she said she stayed the night at your place. Why would she be here? I'm babysitting."

"Oh," I say trying to quickly recover, because the last thing I need to do is to worry the girls and make Shelby's mom hysterical, so I play it down. "She did stay over. But I just assumed she'd be out here, I guess. I came to see..." I stop and make a vague gesture with my hand, and she understands and pats my arm.

"I'm so, so sorry, love," she says.

"Thank you. I'm sure she's at work. I should have tried there first," I say, making my way back to the door.

"You sure you don't want anything, dear? Tea? Something to warm up?"

"Thanks, but I should get going."

"Have her call me, please, when you see her. I told her I'd give her a little space, but still."

"I will," I say, and then I exit back out into the cold and sit, warming my car back up, shaking from the cold, or maybe from knowing something that feels very wrong. Either Shelby lied to Clay or Clay lied to me, but neither one is good right now. And this means she is vulnerable and unreachable and not at home, or here, or the Oleander's, which I already tried before I drove out here. Shit.

I resist calling Billy again, although I could use his help. I could use a friend, if I'm honest. When I dug into things further today after the police left, I realized now that since he's officially...passed, the life insurance will pay out and I can get an extension of payment based on the lump sum pending and I don't need Billy's money, even though I wasn't going to take it anyway. But I have to tell him all of this. Of course I could just rip up the check and leave a message telling him how much I appreciate it, but that, in fact, he's off the hook.

But since I'm looking for an excuse to see him without appearing to be a crazy stalker, I decide to grab the check and bring it to him personally—news that he doesn't have to part with that much money is as good a reason as I can think of to show up unannounced, so that's exactly what I do. Maybe he can help me look for Shelby.

I can't go home and sit in that empty house tonight. I've kept Leo's toothbrush in the cup on the sink next to mine all this time, and I've kept all of his clothes the way he left them in the closet—all of his shoes lined up in neat rows and his favorite mug in the cabinet. Now there is no chance he'll return. Hope is gone, and it's left in its place such white-hot anger that I feel like if I am left here alone I'll lose my mind and rip the place to shreds with my bare hands just so I don't see him in every corner of every room.

I put Linus's and Nugget's little knitted sweaters on them and pluck the check from the refrigerator door, and we all pile into the car for a drive and start toward Billy's house. When I pull into his drive, the house is dark, and I tell the pups to stay here and begin to walk up to the door when my phone buzzes. I look down to see a number that I don't recognize, but I answer it anyway.

The person on the other end is familiar and my heart pounds when I hear the quiet desperation in her voice. It's Flor.

"Help. He caught me. Please help. The address is—" and then I hear a loud smack, like the phone cracking against the ground, and the line goes dead.

25

Shelby

I wake up on what feels like a bare mattress, but there's a blind-fold over my eyes and my hands are tied behind me with something. Jesus Christ, it's my worst nightmare to be bound in any way. The fleeting thought of it can set me into panic attacks, and I can't breathe for a moment. Fear paralyzes me, but I know that to survive, I can't let it take over. I have to force myself to stay calm.

Where am I? It's cold, and the distinct damp and smell of mildew make me think it's a basement. I stand, but I can't see anything, and I don't know what's around me so I sit back down and try to control my shaking. You have to just think and stay in control, I keep repeating to myself. I have to get out of here alive for my babies. Whoever has wanted me to suffer all this time finally has me, and my instinct is to just start screaming bloody murder. *Why? What do you want from me?* But I don't, because I don't want to give away yet that I'm awake.

The constraints around my wrists feel like a silk tie from a bathrobe, and the blindfold feels like fleece or something soft. Part of me wonders if they don't want to leave any marks on me, which seems like there is a flicker of hope that they might not plan on killing me. They might want to release me unharmed. The other part of me fears that this is the beginning of some sexual fantasy about to be played out, and I'm so terrified it seems impossible to control myself and keep my wits about me, but then I hear something—footsteps above me. Very muffled and faint, and I think again that I must be in a basement.

I hear the opening and closing of drawers and cabinets; then it stops. There's a male voice, but I can't make out if it's familiar or not, and then a woman's voice. She yells "No! Stop! I'm just here to talk. It'll be okay if you just—" A door slams, and it's quiet. That's Florence. Oh my God. It's Florence up there. Where the fuck am I? What's happening?

The tears start streaming down my face, and I'm panicking. I stand again and try to force myself into action—anything to keep moving and find a way out instead of buckling under the crippling fear that could easily have me trembling on that mattress until I hear footsteps on the stairs and get slaughtered... or worse.

I think of Poppy and her chipped pink nails and her plastic barrettes she leaves all over, and her Mr. Potato Head she carries around like a stuffed animal. I think of June and her Grover pajamas and her soft curls and her color crayons, and I can't breathe, goddamn it. I can't leave them.

I reach out and feel the brick next to me. A basement wall. I hold still and take three deep breaths. I remind myself that I have survived worse; that I can see my babies again. Then I take a step. If I look straight down, I can see just enough to make out the tips of my boots and the cement floor underneath. I take tiny steps across the floor, and all I see is dust and bits of garbage around the edges of my feet in the tiny slit I am able to see through. A crumpled chips bag, sawdust, oil spots.

"Fuck!" I smack my shoulder into something. I reach my foot out to try to feel what's around me. It's the stairs, I think—jagged, probably old wooden stairs leading up to the main floor, the way all these houses are built. With the toe of my boot, I feel a nail sticking out the side of the second stair. I can use this. I drop to my knees and feel for the nail again with the side of my head, carefully tapping my head against the jagged edges of the stairs to locate the nail. Once I do, I catch the edge of the blindfold on the head of the nail, and I'm able to pull it off of my head.

I feel my chest heave, a sob threatening to explode from within me out of utter relief. I can see now. I calm myself again. I don't let the crying start. I can't.

The basement is not familiar at all. I don't know what I was expecting, but I don't know this place. I look up at the rickety shelves along the walls; boxes and plastic storage containers line them, stuffed with papers and ordinary basement things. Strings of tangled Christmas lights, a deflated basketball, a tire pump, an oil can. It's not filled with ice picks and duct tape or the tools of a serial killer who plans to skin me alive and bury me under the floorboards. There is a moment of relief at this, though I know I'm not in any less danger.

I want to pull down all of the boxes and start rifling through them so I know who the fuck lives here—where I am—but all I need to focus on is getting out, so I scan the room for anything I can use that would cut the ties off my wrists.

It's mostly dark. Now I can see the creaky stairs leading up to the main house, and the only light is filtering down from the cracks around the door at the top of the stairs. It gives just enough light to make out the edges of things. I see piles of boxes in the corner and a lawn mower, some metal ladders, clay pots, and a rusted bicycle. There are tools on a workstation near the back, but a knife does me little good if I can't grip it.

I hear footsteps again from above me, and I squeeze my eyes closed as my heart pounds. "Oh God, please, please, please," I mutter, but I keep moving, rushing around, desperate to find something I can use. The footsteps stop. A door opens and then closes. It's quiet again.

The lawn mower. It's old and crusted in dirt, but I manage to kick it onto its side with my heavy boots, and it falls with a crack on the cement floor. I gasp and hold my breath, staying perfectly still, and I wait. Did they hear that? Is anyone still here? After a minute that feels like days, nothing happens, so I fall to the floor and I sit in front of the lawn mower, pushing my back as close as I can get. I hold my hands out behind me as far as I am able to stretch them until I reach the lawn mower blade.

"Shit!" I almost scream but instead I hiss it to myself when I cut the side of my hand on the blade. I need to stop shaking. I need to pull it together and focus. I shimmy myself back and try again, but the deformity on my hand is not making this any easier. I push the tie around my wrists back until I feel it press against the blade and then I gingerly slide it back and forth, so carefully and slowly, so I don't slice my wrist. I hear the fabric ripping. Oh my God, it's working. I keep going and feel another tear, and after just a couple of minutes, the tie breaks open and my hands are free. They're free!

I leap to my feet and wonder what to do now. Do I try to make a run for it up the stairs? Do I look through the boxes for a weapon? There is an egress window, but it's a few feet above me and it's locked. What do I do?

First, I tiptoe up the basement stairs. I gently place my hand on the doorknob and attempt to turn it as quietly as humanly possible. Of course it's locked, but I had to try. I place my ear against it, and I hear something.

It sounds like someone is in the kitchen, moving around. I hear the clink of ice in a glass, a cabinet closing and a drink being poured. I let go, my hand cupped over my mouth so I don't make a sound. Someone is right there. Feet, if not inches, away from me. Fuck. Who?

I move slowly back down the stairs, carefully, so nothing creaks, and then I look around. I could pick up any number of things—a crowbar, a two-by-four—and wait, but what good is that against a gun or whatever weapon they have? I need to escape. There's no other choice. The wind howls, rattling the narrow window in its frame, high on the wall. The storm is moving in, and I have no idea how far away from anything I am. We could be in the middle of nowhere and I could die out there, but I'll almost certainly die if I stay here, so I move.

I pick up one of the ladders leaning against the far wall and carry it over, placing it underneath the window. This is it. I just have to do it. I can't wait even seconds longer than I have to. Someone could be lumbering down those stairs to murder me any second now. I pick up an ancient fire extinguisher from where it lies in a pile of dust near the damp brick wall. The only thing that is even allowing me to do all this despite the disadvantage of two amputated fingers is pure, surging adrenaline. I hoist the extinguisher up over my shoulder and climb up the ladder with one hand, trying to balance the heavy fucking thing without falling. And when I get to the top, I don't hesitate; I smash it into the glass as hard as I can, looking away so the shards don't hit me in the face.

The glass cracks with the first blow, but I know someone has heard me by now. I bash the heavy metal extinguisher into the glass over and over, until the cracking explodes and it shatters, and I don't even bother brushing the glass away. I'm already in a winter parka, boots, and a hat, so I just push my body through.

Behind me I hear the basement door fling open, and I see the light from upstairs flood the basement.

"Hey!" a man's voice yells. "Hey!" and I know that voice. I finally know who it is. I hear him lumber down the basement stairs, and it's like all of my nightmares from childhood are coming true—the monster is right behind you, clipping at your heels as you desperately try to claw your way to safety.

I scream "Why!" into the night air as fresh tears start to fall, and I grasp the icy ground around the window frame and push myself forward again, trying to get enough leverage to reach all the way through the small window.

I feel him grab at my leg and start to drag me back inside, but he says nothing, which is so terrifying now that I know who he is and I can't understand, still, what's happening—why he could be doing this. I kick behind me and try to pull my pant leg free of his grip. He catches my boot and grabs on harder, pulling me back in with such force, shards of glass around the window tear at the flesh of my hands, and I start to lose my grip.

I'm halfway through the window and it will just take one more hard surge forward to get me out into the night, so I scream with all the air I have in my lungs and kick as hard as I can and I feel the ladder behind me fall. I hear him make a sound—he curses as the ladder hits the concrete floor with a smack, and then with one final heave, I push myself out onto the snowy ground above me. And I run.

I run so hard I'm choking on the freezing air hitting my lungs with a shock. I can see where I am now. I know exactly where I am. But I can't register which direction to go. The snow is too thick. I just need to get enough of a head start that I can at least hide in the pines about a hundred yards in front of me, so I hold my head down against the wind and try to keep going. And then I am in the air as a hidden slick of ice underneath the snow catches me and I slip, and I'm thrown hard against the frozen ground. So hard the wind is knocked out of me and I'm stopped in my tracks trying to gasp for breath, desperate to get the air back in my lungs.

But before I can push myself to stand and run again, he's already caught me. He doesn't even need to attack me or use chloroform on a cloth to knock me out like before. He has control. He's bigger, he's hovering over me, and he has a gun. He smiles down at me.

"Where are you going so fast?" he asks, and I just stare up at his face. I can't believe who I'm looking at. I just don't believe it. Then a swift blow to the head makes everything go dark.

26

Florence

When he says my name and stops me in my tracks, I hold my hands up like I'm being arrested and turn, slowly, to look at him.

"Evan," I say flatly, with forced calm. "I thought you were out tonight."

"What brings you by, Florence?"

"I was just wanting to chat. When nobody answered I let myself in because it's so cold."

"Chat. Oh," he says, and then he smiles at me, looking like he'll lunge toward me at any second. I casually put my hand into my coat pocket and start to press buttons on my phone, hoping to call for help. The last number that called me was Mack, asking if Shelby was at the Oleander's. That was earlier today, so it's the first number my finger finds to press the call button on, and he doesn't notice until I hear her pick up and I pull the phone out and start yelling into it as quickly as I can: "Help. He caught me. Please help. The address is—" and then Evan has me in his grip. He snatches the phone and pushes me into the horrifying shrine room with one easy sweep, locking me inside.

I sit on the edge of the bed to catch my breath. The bed is covered in rose petals. He was planning to have somebody here tonight. Does he have Shelby already? Is that why I couldn't reach her? Oh God. What have I done? I was trying to help, and now I'm in here and can't do a damn thing. I made a mistake coming here. I should have called the police. No. I stop myself. No, I would be some crazy bat making accusations, just like they think Shelby is. They would never have even asked Evan a question. This needed to happen. I can still fix this.

It seems like a very long time that I'm sitting in that room alone, trying not to look at all the photos on the wall, trying not to cry. I do take my blood pressure medicine and open a warm Pepsi sitting on top of the dresser to swallow it with, and then I hear something. A door opens and he yells, "Hey!" and then he runs outside. I can feel the blast of frigid air even from back here. There is silence for a long time, and then he's back. I can hear him humming right outside in the kitchen, and I smell grilled cheese on the stove. He's just going about his business like I'm not even here. I try to run through all the reasons he would do something like this. What does he want?

Then I hear his voice outside the door. It sounds like he has slid down the wall and is sitting on the opposite side.

"Oh, Florence," he sighs.

"I'm here," I say. "I know I shouldn't have let myself in, Evan, but what's going on? I won't tell anyone, Evan. We're friends," I say, and I don't know what my strategy is, but maybe if I can get him to talk I can figure out my angle and talk my way out of this.

"How did you figure it out?" he asks.

"Figure what out?" I still play dumb, but it's clearly not working.

"Can we just cut the shit? I don't want to have to kill you."

"No," I say. "I wouldn't like that either."

"So I ask you again…how'd you figure out it was me?"

After some moments of silence, I make myself speak. "Black-lock. The avatar name you used playing video games with Herb. You signed into the hospital logs with that name. It had to be you."

"No shit? I better fix that." I hear him pull out his phone and tap the screen. "Glad you mentioned that. I deleted it so nobody else would find that. Good catch. Thanks. I knew you were catching on, but I kind of thought you were into it, ya know…"

Oh my God, it's all rushing in—it's all becoming clear that he's actually a sociopath and I am in grave danger of dying in this house and, from his track record, him getting away with it.

"You killed Otis?" I say, my voice cracking, but I try to clear it and stay level. I have so many questions. What happened to Leo, Bernie; where is Shelby? How is it all connected? Why are you doing this? But I'm trapped by a monster, and I don't know what approach to take to make him think I'm not a threat.

"I'm so disappointed, Flor. I liked you. I thought you'd be excited to find out about all this. I thought we could plan our next move together, but you're on their side. I can tell."

"What?" I say. "Excited?" I stutter in disbelief, not under-standing what he's saying.

"Sure. Catching on that Otis was murdered, finding Ber-nie's pendant, all of it—it was thrilling for you. You were get-ting off on all of it."

"No, Evan. I was certainly not," I say, trying to keep the desperation out of my voice, but there is silence on the other end. Then I hear him get up and walk away.

It feels like a long time before I hear footsteps come back near the door, and I'm waiting, shakily behind it for him to come in. When he finally opens the bedroom door, I shove the Taser at him with all my strength and press the button until he's convulsing on the floor. For a minute, I think I killed him.

"Oh God! Oh no," I say, not stopping to check on him but instead stepping over him to retrieve the handgun that dropped from his grip and slipped across the kitchen floor, mercifully not going off.

He moans and starts to collect himself, muttering "bitch" under his breath, and when he finally pushes himself up to sit, he's met with the end of his own gun, which I'm aiming at him. He gives a weak laugh.

"Little, sweet Flor. You don't know how to use it. Let's not do this," he says and starts to stand. I hesitate for just a second, then I squeeze the trigger at the ceiling and I shoot. The noise is deafening and the force pushes me back, but I have shot a gun before. Me and Millie took trap shooting lessons, and I was *very* good.

"Please sit in that chair," I say, nodding to the kitchen chair at the small table next to the stove. He holds his hands up and does so, but still has a smirk on his face that I would very much like to shoot right off of him, but of course I don't do that. I can't.

"Tell me where Shelby is," I say. He smiles at me, and there is a silence that is cut only by the sound of my own ragged breath as I wait for him to respond, wondering if I need to use the Taser again...if I'm capable.

"Pour me a drink," he says back, flatly. I stare at him, my nostrils flaring and my heart racing, and then I pour some scotch that's already on the table into a lowball glass and slide it over to him. He sits and I take a couple of steps back, afraid he could move swiftly and swipe the gun from my hand. I collect the Taser from the floor and back up against the counter where I place it, keeping it close. He watches me. I have multiple ways to hurt or kill him, and I have questions, so he's trapped.

"I don't know where she is. Don't you see the lovely room I

made for her? Don't you think we'd be together in there right now if I had any control over what the fuck Shelby does with her life?" He takes a sip of his drink, and it's like I'm looking at another person than the one I thought I knew. His eyes are dark and his face is contorted, and if I hadn't already seen what he's capable of I would think it's just little Evan Carmichael playing a character in a school play. None of it seems real, or possible, but here he is. A completely changed man.

"Then why did you change your name on the hospital log? Why were you visiting Otis?"

"He used to be a business partner. He owed me."

"Owed you?"

"Yeah. I don't mind telling you, Florence, because I can't emphasize enough how thoroughly every last detail was attended to. You can go to the police right now and tell them I killed Otis or Leo, and they will not find one shred of evidence. Absolutely nothing," he says, and I remember that he was a cop for a long time, and if he planned all this to the letter, what if he's right?

"So why do you have Leo's ID? Why would you kill him?"

"I didn't," he says, and I swallow hard and force myself to cock the gun again.

Evan rolls his eyes. "He had a heart attack. I mean, I did—well, I don't know the right word—kidnap sounds weird for an adult. I *captured* him. And I demanded the money I was owed. We were partners all those years ago and he cut me out of the deal, and now look. Look at all the money him and Otis made—look at the lives they got to have!"

"So that night last October, you were waiting for him at his house and kidnapped him the way the police said?" I'm astonished—to think, Detective Chipped Beef got something right after all.

"I didn't mean for the bastard to die. It was a happy accident. I didn't know about his heart condition. I just went to the cafe and got all of his financials—and got what was mine. I think it's only fair, really. I got a shitty life, living in a studio apartment in the city with a fiancée who was kind of a bitch anyway, because you don't attract good girls when you fail to make lots of money and get shot in the line of duty. They leave, and then you watch these motherfuckers just living the high life with all the money that should have been mine. So no, I didn't feel bad," he says, and I don't know what to do or say.

"You went to the cafe to steal his financial files, and you saw Shelby."

Evan smiles, but it doesn't quite reach his eyes. "Hadn't seen her in years. It all came rushing back—the way she rejected me back in school, how much I loved her back then, and she married fucking *Clay*? Clay, with the fucking receding hairline and dad jokes and the stupid polo shirts? What a joke. I almost finally had my way with her then, but I had a plan, and time was ticking. I had the files and needed the money first, so I had to choose."

"And if you can't have her, no one can. Is that why you tried to kill her?"

"You know, Florence, I always knew you were smarter than the rest of them, but you get in your own way. It's been nice having someone to talk to about all this, finally, but I'm done. I know you won't shoot me and you'll only look like a fool when you tell the police all of this. You'll look just as desperate and delusional as everyone is starting to realize Shelby is," Evan chuckles.

"You don't think the police will see that room you have when I tell them about this and arrest you on the spot?" I ask incredulously.

Evan shakes his head slowly, mockingly. "Oh, sweet, naive Florence. You don't think I have a plan for everything? It'll be like it was never there before they could ever even get here. And they can't search my place on your word, can they? Plenty of time." I can't believe what he's saying—how calculated he's been. All this time, and the truth had been hiding right in plain sight.

I have to find my phone to call the police and have them come while I have him cornered and they can see the room, Leo's ID, everything for themselves, but I don't know where he's hidden it, and I can't leave or turn my back for a second. I look around, scanning the room for my phone, and then I see it in his pocket, sticking out just a hair.

Okay, good. I mean, not good, but I can get one more bit of information I need from him, and then I'll demand the phone. I can Tase his fucking neck until he hands it over. I can get out of this. But I need to know. "Tell me why Otis and Bernie, then. Why?" I raise my voice, and my body is trembling with anger and hatred.

He stands. He takes a step toward me and I hold the gun with both hands and reach it out farther, aiming at him. "I think we're done here. Time for you to go."

"Tell me! Why them—" is all I manage in a cracked voice. I clear my throat and try again. "What happened to him?"

But he doesn't back down and he doesn't answer, and he's two steps from grabbing this gun from me, so I close my eyes and I pull the trigger, aiming the gun down. I hear a scream.

"Fuck! Are you fucking crazy!" He's on the ground now, writhing in pain. The bullet went through his thigh. I cock the gun again, aiming it down at his head.

"Answer me! Why them?"

"Fuck! Otis was dying. Who cares? I told him what happened to Leo would happen to his wife if he didn't give me the money I was owed from what they did to me all those years back—it's their fault my life is a disaster. Fuck!" He holds his leg and moans, continuing when I don't move.

"When I started coming back to town to visit my dad after he got sick I started seeing Otis and Leo around town—living the life, flashing all their money around. Look at this fucking place." He gestures around the room. "It's a hoarder's dump, and this is all I got. They fucked me. He wouldn't budge. He was scared when I told him about what really happened to Leo, but once I said it, once I used it, he had to go. But come on, it was only a matter of days. I did him a favor."

"So what did they do to you that was so bad all those years ago? Bad enough for you to kill them?"

"Not kill, Florence!" Evan growls, clenching his teeth against the pain. "Let's get shit straight. Leo had a heart attack! I just put him in the trunk and drove him out to Lumberjack's Motel so we could discuss the money I was owed, and he dies all on his fucking own! He ended up in Shelby's lake because *fuck* Shelby. She deserves to be a suspect. It's all her fault any of this happened. She fucked me over!" Evan gasps, moans in pain. I don't back off. "They all did, all those years ago. They gave no thought to me! And Otis was a service to him and his family. Bernie too, but he was depressed anyway. I did them both a favor. Just let it go. Nobody cares about these old guys."

"What?" I gasp.

"Help me, goddamn it. Give me some towels, you fucking psychopath."

"Bernie did nothing to you—to anyone. Ever," I repeat.

"Just give me something to wrap this—fuck! To stop the bleeding and I'll…"

"After you tell me what Bernie did to deserve this!"

"He walked into the front office the night before and saw me watching videos I took. Whatever. From the cameras I put in room 128 where Shelby stays the night sometimes—she was undressing and I told him someone from the tip line sent this video to me and we'll take it to the cops, but I could tell he didn't buy it…so he had to go. That's it, now fucking help me!" he pleads.

I feel tears welling up in the backs of my eyes. Bernie. I feel sick. I feel lightheaded, like I could actually faint. The horror of what he's telling me is too much to absorb. My heart feels like it will burst.

I remember, now, with all of these facts flying around me like shrapnel. I remember that he was actually shot in the head, and that he's actually lost his mind. I'm not just dealing with someone who snapped or is inherently evil—he could be brain damaged and completely unhinged—literally a clinical psychopath with no empathy or remorse, and that's very, *very* bad news for me.

I need a moment to think. Do I ask him for the phone and then shoot again if he doesn't slide it to me? I can't get too close. I don't want to shoot him again. I don't know if I can. He's already down. I just need my phone. I grab a couple of towels from a rack next to the oven and take two steps toward him, the gun still pointed at him and ready to go if I need it, but he pulls me. Before I can release my grip on the towel, he yanks the end he grabbed so hard and pulls me toward him and I fall—I crash to the ground, and the gun hits the hardwood with a smack and skids under the table.

I howl in pain. I landed on my wrist, and I heard the snap of bone as I reached out to try to catch my fall, but I still try, in a moment of surging adrenaline, to reach for my phone which has fallen on the floor inches away. I know I can't make it to the gun across the room before him, but maybe I can call for help. I manage to get the phone into my hand, but I'm trembling so violent that I can barely hold it. I steady my hand and tap in 911 and it rings and I hear a voice, but before I can say a thing, I feel a searing pain that steals my breath. There is a blow to the back of my head so hard I see an explosion of stars behind my eyes, and then the world goes black.

27

Mack

I rush directly to the police station when the call from Florence drops. I ask for Riley and I'm told that he's off for the night, but they will take my report, and my blood boils at the lax attitude this is being met with.

"So what are you gonna actually do about it?" I ask. "She's in immediate danger! It should be all hands on deck!"

"Well," a man with a close-cropped hair and unstylish glasses says, and I can hear him trying to keep the condescension out of his voice. "We're sending a squad to look and we'll have Angela call her family—see when they were last in contact, and..."

"No," I cut him off. "Her husband died twenty-seven years ago, and she doesn't have other family. The Oleanders are her family. Did you call them?" and even though everyone knows everyone here, that's only *mostly* true. You can't know every single person, and I only know this officer vaguely. Jerry is his first name, I think, and he's young-ish, so maybe he doesn't know the Oleander's like everyone in town does, because he has a stupid look on his face as I say this.

"Did I call who?"

"Did you contact the senior living facility where she lives?"

"Well, since you just made the report nine seconds ago and you're still standing here, when exactly did you think I had time to do that?" he asks, which is fair.

"Fine. Then I'm telling you that's where to start. And where the hell is the fucking squad gonna start looking? They don't know where she goes, or anybody she spends time with. What's the strategy?" I say, impatient and overflowing with anxiety.

"Again, ma'am. We can work on our strategy if you give us just a minute, alright?" he says. And I know I'm being unreasonable, but there has to be some action here. There's no time to waste.

"What about a silver alert? How do we put out one of those?"

"We don't. We can't do that based on your account of a three-second phone call where you think she sounded in distress. It's just..." And I don't even need him to finish his bullshitty, runaround answer. They think Shelby and her cronies at the Oleander's are completely carried away and causing drama on purpose for podcast ratings, pointing the finger at the wrong people, and off the deep end. I've heard the talk in just the space of a day, and this means they will probably do the minimum amount they have to do here, just to say they did their job. They don't believe there's any danger.

"Where's Riley?" I ask.

"Off. Red Lobster, I think."

"Red fucking Lobster? Did you tell him about this?" I snap.

"Yeah, but it's all-you-can-eat shrimp. And he said to send out a squad and call the family which we are doing, so—" I don't listen to the rest of whatever is coming out of his mouth. I walk out the front doors, to my car, ready to bust into Red

Lobster and flip a goddamn table in attempts to get him to take this more seriously, but then I think of Shelby in the bar and how far that got her. I can't put myself in that position right now. I'm the only one of us they still might listen to, so I drive. I'll go to the Oleander's myself.

I call Riley instead on my way there. He doesn't pick up so I call twice more, and when he finally answers, I can hear the annoyance in his voice.

"Riley," he says, still chewing his all-you-can-eat shrimp.

"Do you know that Shelby is essentially missing and Florence called me? Said someone has her, and she—"

He cuts me off. "Mack. Look. I have some guys investigating the call, okay. Shelby, missing? Come on. She left very pissed off after being called out today. She's probably embarrassed, or is somewhere blowing off steam…"

"No," I stop him. "She told Clay she was going to her mother's, and her mother says she never mentioned coming up there. I've been looking for her all day!"

"Exactly my point. If she's actively lying to get some time to herself, what does that tell you? Clay hasn't called it in," he says, and I realize now that that is because he still thinks she's at her mother's and I forgot all about him once I got frantic looking for her. I never told him.

A call beeps in, and when I see that it's Billy I simply hang up on Riley and his useless answers and pick up the call.

"Billy," I say flatly, annoyed that he hasn't answered my call all day, and at myself for letting it affect me so much, like he's obligated to do so.

"I'm so sorry. I went ice fishing with dad up at Pine Lake, and lost service. I saw you were trying to call."

"Yeah, sorry, I…" I stop for a moment. I'm relieved that in all the chaos, at least he's okay, but I just don't have the time to explain everything to him right now. I'll probably break down sobbing if I start to explain the call from Florence and how terrified she sounded, and how I know something is very wrong since Shelby stopped answering her phone, but I can't lose control and spiral into an emotional wreck right now. I feel the panic creeping in. It's all just too goddamn much, and I don't know how much longer I can go without screaming until my throat is raw and crying until I'm numb and just hiding from it all. I can't afford to do that.

"I'm sorry. I'll call you back," I say, hanging up as I pull up into the Oleander's parking lot and screech my car to a stop. I see inside the front doors that the lights are off. It looks like there is nobody working, which is very unusual. I know Heather is out, but what about Evan? I decide to call him. It rings through. What is going on? I decide to leave a message asking if he knows where Shelby is since I already made the call and I'm trying to deal with two things at once.

I call Herb next, and when he sleepily answers I ask if he can let me in the front door. A couple of minutes later I see him coming down the hall in his big robe and Yeti slippers as I stand freezing in the icy wind that's starting to pick up.

He has a perplexed look on his face as he lets me in, and I follow him into the rec room where he picks up his glasses off a side table and puts them on and looks at me. "What's happened?"

"Florence. When is the last time you saw her?"

"Just earlier tonight. A few hours ago we were all sitting here talking about Bernie's funeral arrangements. Why? What the hell is going on?"

"I don't know yet," I say, seeing his face fall.

"What does that mean? She's not here? She's in trouble or something?"

I tell him about the phone call and he shakes his head and starts heading down the hall. "She was just here," he says as I follow quickly behind. "She was just goddamn here!" He stops at her door and swings it open so hard it hits the drywall with a thwack and creates a little hole, but he doesn't notice. He flips the lights on and we have a shared moment of relief when we see she's right here. She's right here, sleeping.

He rushes over to wake her up and see what the hell is going on, but when he puts his hand on the mass underneath the covers, he discovers pillows made up to look like a sleeping body, and not Florence at all.

"What the hell? She snuck out like a teenager. What in the world? Where? She didn't say anything—she tells me everything, I thought. I don't understand."

"Herb," I say, interrupting his moment of grief and confusion. I pick up a piece of paper I see sitting on her desk. "Does this mean anything to you?" He takes it and squints at it through his glasses.

"Blacklock," he says. "She came into my room earlier tonight asking what this meant. But what the hell? I mean, it's a video game avatar name. I told her since Evan started gaming with me now and then, we sometimes play remotely and that was him logged in as his avatar, Blacklock. What on God's green earth does that have to do with anything? Why would she write that down? She hates video games."

"I don't know, but there's an address. I think it's Evan's. I mean I haven't been to his dad's house since I was a kid, but if I remember right, it's on St. Charles. This must be Evan's address. Why would she go there?"

"How would she even get there?" Herb adds and we look at one another, at a complete loss.

"Something must have happened on the way. Maybe she was followed. Maybe...wait, did you call Evan?" he asks.

"Just now to get let in the building. No answer."

"We have to go," Herb says, grabbing his boots and coat. A few minutes later we're driving through dark, snowy roads to Evan's house, having no idea what we'll find.

28

Shelby

When I wake up, I'm on a bed. I'm not restrained, I'm just locked in a room. I instinctively leap up and rush to the window, and my heart drops when I see it's boarded up. The whole house is in the middle of fixing up, and it's a construction zone. I turn and start to scan the room for another way out, and that's when I see it. Photos of myself, candles, small items that I didn't know were missing. Oh my God. What is this? I still don't know where I am until I hear the door click open.

A figure slips into the room and I don't know what I was expecting but it takes me a moment to register that it really is Evan. I'm not delusional. This is happening and it's Evan. Evan fucking Carmichael is standing in front of me. How is that possible?

At first I think, my God, Florence is somewhere here, and now Evan has been taken hostage too, and I think we must all be in some nightmare—some serial killer kidnapped all of us, and I see he has a wound on his thigh. Blood seeps through the bandages wrapped around it, and I think they've hurt him. And then I know. I *remember* when he smiles the most unsettling smile I have ever seen.

"Hello, Shelby. You're up." I stare back, still trying to absorb that I'm really looking at Evan—of all people on earth—but I can't make sense of it. My head spins trying to piece it all together. He puts a small gun on the dresser and pulls up an ottoman and sits. He gestures at the bed for me to sit and, in a stunned silence, I slowly obey.

"I'm glad you're here," he says.

"I don't understand. What is all this? What do you want with me?" But of course, seeing myself in every image hanging from the walls tells me exactly what he wants from me.

"Do you remember that night you went out with me right before senior year? It was hot. We went to Dairy Queen and sat in the back of my pickup looking at the stars." He smiles and grunts as he shifts his injured leg, repositioning himself.

"Of…course," I stutter, paralyzed with fear and so incredibly confused.

"Best night of my life. The crickets chirped, we had Dixie cups of peach Boone's Farm wine. It was like a country song, wasn't it?"

"It was a great night," I quickly agree, not knowing where he's going but trying to keep him calm.

"Not *great*. I mean, you left me for Clay two weeks later," he says, a shadow falling across his face. "And you couldn't even stay true to him. On again, off again. Even got engaged to someone else at one point. Beer belly Riley. Slut."

And I try to understand what exactly he's doing. I have known him since we were little and I thought he was a nice boy. And when he asked me out it was exciting, but I do remember that night and it felt like he was my kid brother, so even though I remember liking him in a weird school crush way so long ago, it just seemed off. He's bringing all this up *now*? He's been obsessed with me this all this time? I realize, suddenly, all of this has been him. Jesus Christ. *Him.* Him stealing my phone, putting the cameras in Clay's truck, the familiarity I felt—like I knew who it was behind the counter that night last October when it all started. All the attacks. This can't be happening. How could I not have seen any clues? My eyes dart around looking for an escape, even though I know there isn't one. I am not getting out of here. His phone rings. He takes it out of his pocket and looks at it.

"Oh, your buddy Mack is calling me. I guess she's looking for you," he says with the confidence of someone who isn't even worried at all that she'll find me.

"You're upset I ended up with Clay. That can't be what this is about," I say, but maybe it is. Maybe he's so deranged... I stop in the middle of my own thought. Of course he's that deranged. Look around, Shelby! He's lost his mind. He could do anything to me.

"This is your fault," he says and I just blink at him, still in such shock I can't formulate the best way to respond to keep him happy, to buy time.

"I mean, you didn't even check my records—see how long I was locked in a psych ward—that I was let go from the force for...what did they call it? Violent outbursts. That I'm unemployable and potentially a danger to others... I think those were the words. I've been behaving for a long time now, though. I mean, there are records you could have accessed, but you didn't even *ask*. You were supposed to protect the residents, and you just...let me in," he says with a grin, and I feel sick. I feel like I could actually vomit. He's right. I was supposed to *protect* them. But I thought I knew him. I feel shame mixing with terror, and I don't know what to do. I look at the gun, and back to him.

"Nice little weapon, eh? You recognize it?" he asks, and I

look again. I hate guns. Clay has a collection and he's gifted me a couple for protection over the years, but they all look the same to me so I don't know what he's asking, what answer he wants.

"Well, never mind, and don't you worry. The cops can't access any of that information without a warrant, and I've made sure there is no reason for them to ever suspect me enough to order anything like that. When I bury you, they won't find you, or ask me any questions. Can I get you a drink? Vodka? I got it special for you because I notice you getting martinis at happy hours with your girlfriends sometimes," he says, and I feel the panic pushing in. I can't have a panic attack. I cannot let myself. I make myself continue to talk—to keep him talking. Maybe someone will find me if I buy enough time. It's my only hope.

"Why...if you were..." I don't know the right words, so I say something stupid. "If you were so fond of me, why do you want to hurt me?" I say, shaking so bad I push my hands under my thighs so he doesn't see.

He stands, painfully, and goes to the dresser where a little minibar is set up next to a collection of fuzzy handcuffs and condoms. He pours two glasses and hands one to me. I shake my head because I know I couldn't even hold it in my trembling hand if I tried. He shrugs and pours the contents of my drink into his glass.

"Fond of you. That's funny. Cute. *I loved you.* And you rejected me and destroyed my fucking life. You and Leo and Otis. You had these happy lives, and you just pushed me out of it all. We could have been together," he spits.

"I didn't know," I say, because what else can I say?

"You're a liar. But the whole town knows that now, don't they? Fun to watch everyone turn on you. Little taste of your own medicine. Anyway, I tried to move on with my life for a long time and then I saw you at my father's funeral and I knew...it wasn't over," he says, and it's becoming clear. Like any rapist or abuser who kills their wife or girlfriend, the line between love and just wanting power and control are indistinguishable to them in their fucked-up mind. I'm dead. I'm not getting out of here.

I can't control the hiccuped sobs that begin to rise in my chest. I try to breathe, but I'm starting to hyperventilate. He watches me with a gleeful look and then hands me his drink. I force myself to calm down—to not let him enjoy my pain. I sip from the drink because I don't know how he'll react if I don't. Then he takes it back and sits again, crossing his arms over his chest and smiling.

"This is fun, isn't it? I've been waiting for this for a long time. I mean, don't get me wrong. Watching you be terrorized over these weeks has been the time of my life, but this…this is the pièce de résistance."

"Please, Evan. Tell me what you want? I'll…go with you somewhere. It doesn't have to be like this. I didn't know you felt this way, but we can—" I try so hard in this moment to appeal to anything he wants, but the whack of his hand on the dresser next to him stops me midsentence.

"No, you won't. Maybe. Maybe you'd mean that if it weren't for the damn kids. But that's how I know you won't, so don't fuck around with me," he says, and of course he's right. Of course he knows every last detail of my life, because it's been him all along, stalking me, watching me.

"The irony of it all is that you told me everything—well, you told US everything. 'The gang,' as you so annoyingly call them. Mack finding bank paperwork I didn't know Leo had hidden. Of course, I had to put a stop to that. You told us she found Leo's phone, so I had to text it and scare her off. You always told 'the gang' where you were going all the time, so I was always *right there*. It was so easy. You're not careful at all."

"So you were the one stealing the money through Leo's account you accessed, not him. You were the one putting us under. But you were friends with…with the gang, I thought you…" I almost say: "cared about them."

"Oh, fuck the gang! I was there for you!" he shouts, spit flying out the sides of his mouth, and then he stands and he starts to move toward me, and I hear something.

Is it sirens?

There are sirens coming closer. He stops cold, then rushes as much as he's able, hobbling on one leg. He takes duct tape from the dresser top and rips off pieces, taping my mouth and hurriedly taping my wrists to the mirror post on the dresser, and then he rushes out of the bedroom. He takes a moment to stop, turn, and look me dead in the eye.

"If you move even one inch before I get back, your girls are next. Sadly, they're going to suffer a freak accident. You know I'm capable. It will be tragic, and maybe even look like Clay's negligence. It'll be fun. Don't. Fucking. Move. Or that will be my life's mission," he says, and I feel my body heave in fear and disgust.

Then I hear Florence! It sounds like he's pulling her into the kitchen. I hear her scream at the sirens. "I'm here! Help!" Oh my God. Why does he have her too, if I'm his target?

After a brief minute or two, I hear Evan open the door to the police, and what sounds like medics talking, the sound of boots on hardwood and male voices shouting.

"Thank God," Evan says to them. What? What is he doing?

"I don't want to hurt her, but she broke into my house, screaming about trying to find Shelby, and she attacked me. She shot me," he says, and I have a brief moment of excitement knowing that it was Florence who actually shot him, even though my mind can't wrap around the scenario or why she's here or how that could be.

"He broke my arm!" I hear her cry.

"I'm so sorry, Florence," he says, putting on a sweet voice—a pathetic show for the cops. "She came in here waving a gun around. I was just trying to get it from her before she hurt someone," he says.

"No," she whimpers.

Shit. Then the reality hits. He's setting her up, just like he did to me. He's making her look like the intruder—the attacker. I bet he even placed the gun next to her, gave her her phone back—made it all look the way he needs it to. I'm starting to get into his head, see the extreme and calculated manipulation he's capable of. They won't trace that gun to him. I don't know who, but not fucking *him*, because he really does have this all planned out. They won't order a warrant on her accusation. She's lumped in with me and they think we're crazy, fame-hungry, and delusional.

I try to scream, but I can't. If they think she intruded and shot Evan and he hurt her somehow in self-defense, they will take them into the hospital and she'll be questioned. And so will he, but he'll win. And they won't see any of *this*. Me, this room, the broken window, any of it, because they have no reason to search. In moments they'll all be gone and I will be trapped here, just waiting for him to be released and come back.

He'll make his statement, get bandages and pain meds, and be back here to bury me before anyone knows where I am.

I try again as hard as I can to scream, but the tape over my mouth muffles the sound. I pull with all my might to free my hands and the dresser creaks, but it's ancient and heavy and I can't make it budge. I'm trapped.

29

Florence

The call went through. I sit in the dark in a hospital bed with tears in my eyes, thinking about the gamble I took reaching for my phone instead of the gun, and they traced the 911 call even though I didn't get to speak. They still found me. I'm alive.

They're keeping me for a little while because my blood pressure and heart rate are high, and they need to cast my wrist. I asked them to call Herb and ask him if he'll pick me up when I'm ready, but they won't let me go until after I talk to the police and make an official statement. So I wait, worried my blood pressure and heart rate will never come down enough for them to let me go because I'm so worried about where Shelby is, I can't think straight.

My heart pounds even harder when I see Evan. He's standing, talking to a nurse who is handing him papers. Discharge papers it seems to me, and he's freshly bandaged and perfectly playing the victim. I think the nurse might actually be flirting with him. He sees me watching him and gives me a wink before limping over to the elevator. *No.* He can't be released. You have to be kidding me!

Then Riley appears in the doorway and gives a little knock on the door frame before he and Jones walk in and ask if now is a good time to hear my side of things.

"I told the other officer," I say, and Riley pulls up a seat. Jones lingers at the door, looking bored by the whole thing.

"I know, dear, but why don't you tell me again so I hear it from you?" Did he just call me dear? Is there no respect at all? I already know what Evan said. He got to talk first. He got to think the whole thing through and make me look unstable. He got to plot and plan.

"He says you just showed up at his door."

"I did go to his place," I say. "I took the bus because those hospital logs—the ones we gave you—the strange sign-ins. Blacklock. Remember? His video game name was Blacklock, and it was so odd that I thought, well, that had to be him signing in, but why?" I stop. I sound nuts because the whole thing sounds nuts. I'm embarrassed by how it's all coming out.

"He told us that—that's why you said you suspected him of being a...what? A mass murderer? Because of his video game name. He logged into his Xbox app on his phone right in front of us and his name was Evan_Charm75. Not Blacklock."

"He changed it!" I say, louder than I mean to.

"When would he have done that?" Riley asks patiently.

"He did. He told me he did."

"So besides the video game name that made you go over there, what happened?" I can hear the patronizing tone in his voice, and I don't know whether I can fully blame him; this has been masterfully crafted for me to sound exactly like I do right now. Foolish.

"He tried to attack me and take my phone, but then I Tased him and…"

He interrupts me, holding up his hand in a "stop" motion. "So you brought a Taser with you but you are saying you weren't the one attacking him. What about the gun? Whose is it?"

"It's his! I brought the Taser for protection. I didn't want to use it. It's his gun!"

"The serial came back registered to Shelby. Did she give it to you?"

"What?" I sit up and the IV pulls and I wince.

"Take it easy, Flor," Riley says, still in his patronizing, calm-this-crazy-lady-down voice. "I'm not here to upset you even more. Evan doesn't want to press charges."

"What?" is all I manage to cry.

"So you can go home when they release you," he says.

"Well, I want to press charges!" I yell, and he looks to Jones and back to me.

"Flor, I would leave this alone. You took a bus to break into the man's house and you shot him. *Admittedly*. I know you all have gotten carried away on this podcast, pointing fingers every which way, and I think it got away from you, and now people got hurt."

"No," I plead. "I think Shelby is in that house. You have to at least search the house. He has a room with her photos—like a shrine. He has Leo's ID. I was in that room. I saw it. You have to at least look!"

"We will," he says.

"You will?" I say, stopping to collect myself, very surprised.

"Yeah, he said he'd be happy to let us look around."

"When?" I ask.

"I'll send Officer Barlowe in the morning."

"No. You have to go *now*. Please."

Riley fixes me with a stern look. "Florence. I know you're

upset and that you've been through an ordeal, but we can't issue a warrant because you say you saw something funny there and you *think* Shelby is there. Do you know what it takes to issue a search warrant? He said we can come by in the morning, so if he's offering and it helps settle this on both sides, that's the most we can do. We have limited resources here and frankly the lot of you are not making our jobs any easier."

"Please. I'm telling you that it will be too late," I say and he stands and sighs, closing his notepad.

"I'm off duty and Jones is headed to a DUI stop, but I'll see what I can do," he says.

"You have to go now," I say, and he looks at me with pity—an old, confused lady in a hospital bed—and I know what he thinks. I know he won't go.

"Good night, Florence," he says, and then he's gone.

I see Mack and Herb hurrying past the detectives and the nurse's station, into my room.

"Flor," Herb says, rushing to my side. "The bastards made us wait downstairs until the police talked to you first. Are you okay?"

"We got the call on our way to Evan's place," Mack says, pulling a chair up to my bedside. "But then we turned around and came here. We found his address in your room… I mean, what is going on?" she asks.

When I tell them both everything that happened tonight, Herb starts pacing and running his hands through his hair and Mack just sits perfectly still trying to absorb it all—all the stuff about Leo especially, I'm sure.

"A heart attack," she finally says.

"I don't think he'd lie about it because he admitted to everything else," I say, and I hope that it helps her in some way to know he didn't suffer terribly, being tortured at the hands of a madman. It was a merciful way to go, considering the alternative. Maybe slipping something into Otis's IV and carbon monoxide were peaceful ways to go too, both poisoned. That sparks something inside of me. An idea.

"Why isn't he arrested?" Herb asks for the third time.

"Otis was a natural death, Bernie was a suicide, Leo is inconclusive and not able to be determined, and none of it points to him. Not one shred of evidence."

"That can't be. Goddamn. I thought Evan was our friend. I just—" and Herb stops when he looks my direction and sees me carefully untaping my IV and pulling the needle out ever so gently, holding a cotton swab on top. "What are you doing?"

"What they won't do." I stand up and start pushing my feet into my boots. "Let's go. We have to get Shelby."

30

Shelby

The duct tape around my wrists was rushed and there is a piece of it sticking up that has rolled over on itself, and if I could get my mouth free, I could bite it and pull on it enough to tear part of it away and weaken the hold.

There's nothing I can do to get the tape off my mouth, though. I tried dragging the edge of it across the bedpost, but all I got was a mark on my face, and it didn't budge.

"Don't move or your girls are next" is all that repeats in my mind as I struggle to escape. Not if I can get out of here and get to the police before he can get back to me. I have to try. I see the vodka bottle he left open on the dresser top. I know rubbing alcohol removes the sticky residue on tape, so maybe vodka does too. I lean my head down and knock the bottle over onto my hands, and the liquid chugs out of the bottle onto the tape and I can feel it loosening. It's enough to shrivel the adhesive

and create a couple inch gap, enough so at least my hands aren't taped hard against the wood. I can reach down and grip the tape over my mouth with my fingertip and pull it off. I inhale deeply, wincing at the pain, and examine my hands. There is some wiggle room, but I can't pull them out, so I try to bite the piece that's sticking up with my teeth. I pull hard, and it starts to peel away.

I unravel a couple of layers successfully and the tape is weak enough then for me to bite it again and make a tear in the side, which breaks me loose. Oh my God, I did it. I'm free! My heart feels like it will explode it's racing so fast, and I have to think quickly. I push open the door and stagger down a small hallway, and I'm in the kitchen. There's a door, but there is also a blizzard starting outside, and the snow is almost blinding. I need my phone. I need to call for help. I start to look, pulling out every drawer. I look in the mudroom and every nook I can find, wondering where he would keep it. And then I see his coat, hanging by the front door. I rifle through the pockets, and it's there!

He was wheeled off by the medics so fast he couldn't hide it better and he couldn't tie me up securely. He slipped up. That fucker finally made a mistake. Florence threw a wrench in his plans and saved my life. I hope again that she's okay, safe, after whatever Evan did to her. I grab my phone and I don't know where my coat or boots are because he put them somewhere when I was unconscious, but I can take his. Before I can move one inch to grab the coat, I hear a car pull up. I look out to see headlights coming up the drive. Oh God. No.

I watch Evan get out of the back seat. It's a taxi he must have taken from the hospital. I have no choice; I have to run. I race to the other side of the house where there is a back door that leads out to a deck and half an acre of yard butting up against a pine forest. I swing the door open, and I run. Into the impossibly cold, driving snow with no shoes or coat. I push my body against the wind, sobbing with every painful step, and I run until my lungs feel like they're bleeding.

I try to hold my phone with frozen fingers and I can barely see through the snow beating down on me and my tears, but there is still battery left and so I dial, but I don't call the police this time.

31

Mack

When Shelby calls us, we're already on the way to find her. It was hard to understand her through her screaming and the howling wind, but I knew she'd escaped and that she was in danger of freezing to death. Again. At the hands of Evan Carmichael.

We find her on her hands and knees almost half a mile from his house on a two-lane road we could barely even find in the blizzard conditions. Herb was out of the car first, pulling her inside, wrapping her in his coat as I raced along the icy roads to get her inside and warm.

Now we all sit in my living room in front of the fireplace. Shelby is wrapped in blankets in front of the fire next to the dogs sleeping in their beds, and Herb is pouring red wine into glasses on the coffee table. Nobody asks why she didn't call the police. We all know.

After she calmed down she called her mother and checked on the girls. It took all of us to talk her out of going back over there immediately to kill Evan with her bare hands. We need to be smarter than him. Methodical. She said she'd be up there in the morning and now we're all quiet with a drink in front of us, not knowing what else to say. Not knowing how we got here—in a world where sweet Evan Carmichael is really a complete monster and where he is so good at it, he has turned the tables to make it look like he's the victim and has nothing for the police to arrest him for. As we speak he is free, at home, probably with a shredder or a maybe a fire blazing, getting rid of the traces of evidence he has carefully controlled and had plans to destroy when the time came.

"He said my kids are next if I escaped," Shelby says.

"We won't let that happen," I say, kneeling next to her. "Have you called Clay?"

She shakes her head. "I can't yet. I know if he ever found out who it was, he'd be over there with a shotgun. He'd either take his shot and make it, or miss and be dead, but that would be it for him either way. I just can't yet," she says.

Florence picks up her wineglass and leans back in her chair. "For all the reasons you didn't go to the police because they would never believe you, just know that there is another reason to add to the list…the gun I shot the bastard with came back registered to you," she says, and we all turn our heads and look at her. "Riley told me."

Shelby breaks down, head in hands, sobbing. "I'll never be safe again—my girls! It's like he's spent an entire lifetime setting this up. I should just call Riley now and make the report. Even if it's a formality that they file it—just keep making reports. What else can I do? There's no getting rid of him," she cries.

Florence puts down her glass. "Unless there is," she says.

"What are you trying to say, Flor?" Herb asks.

"Don't tell the police or Clay or anyone you were there—or

what he did, or about that room, any of it. It doesn't go outside of this circle right here. You start pointing the finger at him, after how they dismissed me? That won't do a damn thing but make things worse for you. We all know it," Florence says.

"I want you to know something. I don't call myself a Buddhist but I very much identify with the principles, and peaceful means are always the answer. I don't even kill the odd cockroach I find in the kitchen in the summer. I capture it in a cup and take it outside. All life is to be respected. But even the Dalai Lama said that to kill out of absolute necessity to stop a tragic, inevitable chain of events is sometimes justified. I'm paraphrasing, but what I'm saying is..."

"Jesus, Flor. We know what you're saying, but you can't be serious...and I *knew* you used my mug for that cockroach. I asked you about that too. You said you didn't," Herb says, staring at her in disbelief.

"Flor," I say. "This man has set us up so well that if something happens to him, don't you think me and Shelby will be the only suspects?"

"Use me," she says.

"Florence," Herb says, eyes wide.

"We gave Evan an oleander plant when he started working there. It's one of the most poisonous plants in the world. A few leaves boiled and poured in a drink and he wouldn't hurt anyone else...ever again."

"Or get away with what he's done," Herb says slowly.

"Until they do the autopsy and tox report and it's...of all things in the world, oleander? Are you kidding?" I ask, but Florence is calm. I can see she's thought about this.

"I have a good friend, Alice Wadoski, who's a retired homicide detective in Milwaukee, and last time she visited she joked that I could get rid of Herb by doing this exact thing—boiling some oleander. Herb was being especially annoying that day and she was just joking of course, but..."

"Jeez, Florence," he interrupts her to emote how offended he is, but she waves her hand at him.

"Take a pill. She was kidding. Anyway, I said to her, 'Don't worry, Millie will talk him to death and Mort will bore him to death without my interference.'"

"Good one," Herb interjects with a shrug.

"And then I added... 'Plus, I am not going to prison for killing Herb. That wouldn't be worth it, now would it?'"

"I'm right here, ya know," he says.

"And *she* said they would never know. The tox reports cover all the common toxins, but in a million years they would never test for oleander unless they knew that's what it was—like the person said they ate a weird flower. Even then, the money and resources to do that kind of testing? Never. So she said, if you ever decide to kill Herb, that's the way, and we laughed and drank mint juleps and played gin rummy, and she was only kidding, Herb. She likes you."

We're all quiet for a few minutes, but Shelby has finally lifted her head and seems to be entertaining this.

"I mean, do I need to say out loud how crazy this is?" I finally say.

Shelby sits up suddenly. "'When a man is denied the right to live the life he believes in, he has no choice but to become an outlaw,'" she says and Herb stops midsip of his drink to give her a confused look. "That's what Bernie said before he died," she says. "He was telling me to defend myself, in his own Bernie way."

"Well," Florence says. "Even if the manner of death isn't caught, me and Shelby would still be suspects, probably be the only and total pariahs in this town—more than we already are, I mean, as if that were even possible.

"That's why you use us. We're invisible. That happens to a person after a certain age. You'll have alibis. Shelby is going to her mother's. She'll get receipts, make sure to appear in front of a security camera or two—take the girls to Dave & Buster's or whatever and be seen by a bunch of people all day thirty miles north of town. You can do that, can't you?" Florence says, and Shelby nods.

I start thinking about this as a real possibility for a moment and I feel like I'm in a nightmare. But I feel like there is no other way out of it either.

"And I can fly out to see my daughter," I say quickly, before I lose my nerve.

"Good. Airtight," Florence says.

"And Evan might write a final note expressing his guilt for what he's done. A suicide note, maybe," Herb says, apparently to Florence's utter surprise, because she almost spits her drink out but then collects herself and shoots down the idea.

"We can't have handwriting involved, they can figure that out," Florence says, shaking her head.

"I know the password to his laptop. It's Porkchops…named after a dog he used to have. He let me use it once to play *Minecraft*," Herb says. Florence pats Herb's leg and gives him an impressed look.

"And Herb will drive me. I know my way around the man's kitchen now. It's the only way," she says.

"Oh God." Shelby holds her head in her hands again. "She's right."

"It's a terrible thing, I know, darling," Florence says.

"Lesser of two evils, though," I say, coming around to the idea that she's right.

"He'll kill my girls. He promised they're next. He won't stop until he's caught, and when will that be? I mean, eventually there will be evidence. Eventually he won't be able to keep getting away with so goddamn many things, you would think—but when? Who else will have to die first? Not my kids. If he's dead, they'll dig into his records, right? All the psychiatric stuff proving he's psychotic, and that will really seal the deal. Right now all that stuff is sealed—needs a warrant there is no reason for them to order. But this way…along with the note we'll write for him, confessing to everything…it will show we've been right all along. It's the only way. She's right. Florence is right." Shelby sounds almost hysterical, but she has more to lose than the rest of us. We all sit with this for a minute. I take a sip of red wine and stroke the top of Nugget's head and wonder if we could really pull this off. It's so unimaginable, but it's really Shelby's life at stake.

"Nobody outside of the four of us can ever know. Four people keeping a secret is already statistically fucked," I say. Everyone nods in agreement. I start searching on my phone to see ticket availability to Boston for early tomorrow.

"I can fly out before 9:00 a.m.," I say. "And Clay thinks you're at your mother's—that she picked you up. That's what I thought when I called him."

"That's the last thing I told him. That's good. He assumes she picked me up, so he's not worried. He goes to work in the morning and one of you can drop me off and I'll take the car up—just call and say Mom picked me up yesterday because she was in the area shopping and it was easier, but now I am staying longer than planned so I need the car after all. He won't ask questions and I'll make sure to stop for gas, at a restaurant, keep receipts. Just in case. And I'll take the pups while you're gone," she says to me.

"It sounds like we're all really doing this," I say, starting to feel hot and a little shaky.

"And no phone calls between the four of us. No texts. No speaking about this ever again. If this goes right, just keep an eye on the news. If it goes wrong, that's the only time I'd call, but only to make plans for coffee. To meet and only ever discuss in person no matter what happens. We never say anything about this over the phone," Florence says, and we all nod.

"Yes," I agree.

"How the hell will you be able to do it? How will you even get in?" Shelby asks, and Florence turns to Herb, and then we all turn to Herb.

"We have a way," Florence says.

Herb raises his eyebrows. "I guess we're all outlaws now."

"Yeah. But he made us this way," Shelby says, and we're all quiet for a long while, staring at the crackling fire, collectively terrified and exhausted. And together, about to kill a man.

32

Florence

We watch from a distance the next morning, me and Herb, as the police enter Evan's house, and after about thirty minutes inside, we watch them exit, giving Evan a handshake and back pat. They all laugh together about something, and then the police leave and Evan goes back inside.

Herb and I brought sandwiches for our stakeout. We told the gang he was doing a kindness, taking me antiquing today to cheer me up after all I went through in the hospital, and that ensured nobody else would ask to come. They only know I fell and broke my wrist. The rest of it we keep close to our vest, so now here we are with a thermos of coffee and some cheese sandwiches, hoping Evan leaves the house today. We'll try as many days as it takes because as long as our eyes are on him, he can't be up to no good.

Late last night, I found a couple of small oleander plants

around the rec room and in a resident's room who is no longer with us. Everyone gives them to us as a little joke for our namesake so there were plenty to choose from—plants that wouldn't be missed because I don't want noticeable cuts to the one in Evan's house...if he even kept it. Not that it's something Riley would catch if his life depended on it, but one can't be too careful. The plants I found were abandoned and some of the leaves had dried right up, so I was able to grind the leaves into a powder using a coffee grinder under the sink in the rec room, but of course I washed that and then threw it in the dumpster because, again, one can't be too careful. Now the ground leaves are in a Tupperware container in the center console of the van that I handle with rubber gloves. It all feels very wrong, but we've set the plan into motion. No turning back now.

A couple of hours go by, and we're not feeling very hopeful. Maybe he is keeping off the radar for a while. Herb changes the station on the radio and tries to find some music to pass the time, but neither one of us is listening. He stares out the side window and I close my eyes and mentally rehearse my plans A through C, considering every scenario. Then I feel Herb take my hand and hold it.

"You sure about this?" he asks, still looking out the window and not at me. I squeeze his hand back.

"You're a good friend," I say in response. And then we see movement. Evan's garage opens and his car backs out. He pulls onto the street, and then he's gone. We give it a few minutes, afraid he forgot something and will come back or just making sure he didn't see us and could creep back around, but after ten more minutes, we decide the coast is clear.

The weather has calmed this morning and the fresh snow is light and glistens in the sunshine. Sun we haven't seen in weeks, and it feels so happy and so incongruous with what we're doing. We park in the cluster of trees to the side of the house. A path has been shoveled in the front and a makeshift path has been cleared on the side of the house that leads from the kitchen door to the detached garage. We walk hastily toward the side door which doesn't lock and let ourselves in. I pause inside the doorway and I shudder being back in this house. Herb places his hand on my back.

"It's okay," he says. "Let's hurry."

The plan is to find his scotch bottle while Herb looks for his laptop. Herb was much closer to Evan and tells me he's a scotch guy, and I do find three different bottles on the countertop next to a rusted-out toaster oven. I carry them to the kitchen table. The sun streams in through the window above the sink, and I sit down and carefully get to work, pouring more than is necessary into the bottles. You don't want to take a shot like this and miss, even though it takes very little to be fatal. The more that's ingested, the faster the whole ugly process will be over.

Herb comes out with Evan's laptop after a few minutes. He found it twisted in the blankets on his bed, so I instruct him to open a document and write.

I tell him what to say, revealing the details he disclosed to me but that the police wouldn't even hear. I make sure that the money trail and secret bank account are mentioned, and even though I don't have numbers or names, with Evan gone they will finally investigate what they would never touch with him alive and a good ole boy like them—one of their own.

All of the "zero evidence" to justify harassing this man, as the police said, and hidden records will be blown wide open. I do hesitate a few times though—wondering if I can really do this. Is this who I am? But I know that I am doing the world a kindness. I know this will save more lives than not and I rest on that, keeping my trembling hands steady as I twist the tops back onto the scotch bottles and we finish up writing the final apology note to the world from Evan Carmichael.

The laptop needs to go back in the bed where we found it so it doesn't raise suspicion when Evan comes in, if he might even notice such a thing. And we need to get back into the van before we overstay our welcome and Evan returns.

We sit in the van another hour and a half before we see first the garage door open and then Evan's car coming around the corner and pulling into it. The garage closes, and I look at Herb.

"I'll wait for the phone and then I'll be listening," I say and he understands. Taking a deep breath, he calls me and I answer. Then he slips his phone in his pocket with our call still connected so I can hear everything going on in the house. He picks up the bag he brought and exits the van. I see him pause, but then he walks up to Evan's front door. I can't see him once he turns the corner of the house, but I can hear everything.

"Herb?" Evan's voice says, surprised.

"Hey, haven't seen you in a few days. I tried calling so I thought I would stop by because *Final Fantasy* 7 came out this week. I borrowed my grandson's copy," he says, keeping his voice light and friendly, and I hear him rustling around to pull the game out.

"Oh, no shit. Wow."

"So I brought it over, thought you might want to play. I mean, no worries if you're busy, I can head to the VFW for a beer if you have plans," he says. *Way to play it cool, Herb.*

"Oh, uh. I guess I thought—isn't Florence injured? I thought I…I thought you'd be…" I can hear it in Evan's voice. He's confused, of course, as to why Herb is so clueless, even though Herb is often clueless, and I mean that in a loving way. He must be sure I told everyone I was held by a serial killer—who wouldn't?—so he needs to know Herb hasn't heard yet, and maybe he even thinks he already won since the cops left with a handshake. And maybe he thinks I won't tell anyone, because some victims start to shrink with every new person who doesn't believe them.

Nevertheless, Evan is going to get a show from Herb.

"I got a call she was still in the hospital—that she broke a wrist. She'll be okay, don't worry about her. I'll stop by to see her with some tacos later," Herb says.

"Oh. Glad she's recovering. She didn't say what happened?"

"Uh. No," Herb says. "But I haven't talked to her directly."

Evan seems to perk up at this. "Okay, well, come on in. I have a little time," he says.

Yes. We're in.

"I was gonna bring you the scotch my son got me for Christmas. It's just a mini bottle—stocking stuffer—good stuff, though. You'd appreciate it more than me, but I totally forgot. Next time," Herb says, and he's sounding a bit shaky.

"Well, if it's scotch you want, I have some great stuff," Evan says. Good, get right to it, I think, but I also know this approach is a risk. If Evan tells him to try it first or waits, expecting Herb to sip it and react, this could blow up.

"Great," Herb says in reply. Then I hear liquid being poured into glasses.

"Cheers!" Herb says, and I hear two glasses clink so I assume they take a drink—Herb will fake it, but will this fly? Will Evan notice? He only needs a sip or two to do the job, but the next step is for Herb to get his phone. Not only can we not have him call for help in time to save him, Herb can't just toss it out into the snow or something. We need to secure it, keep it away from Evan, and then replace it neatly before we leave. Untouched.

"Xbox is this way," Evan says, and I hear footsteps. Okay, he couldn't tell Herb didn't drink. This is good. I know there are wires and gaming gadgets in the living room because that is where he kept me the second time, after the shrine room, so that must be where they are headed to play. I feel a wave of nausea as I think about being trapped in that room with a broken wrist, in searing pain from a blow to the head. I squeeze my eyes closed for a moment and keep listening. Evan is still fishing to make sure Herb is as clueless as he seems.

"Mack called last night looking for Shelby. I hope she's okay. Anyone get in contact with her?" he asks.

Pathetic, I think. He doesn't know if she died out there. He's just waiting for a news story to show her frozen to death or possibly another call from the cops with more, fresh accusations he has to answer to...and then subsequently get away with.

"Oh, I hadn't heard that. She called this morning to say she'd be at her mom's for a few days with the girls, so someone must have heard from her. She's fine."

"Oh. Well, that's good. I didn't get a chance to return Mack's call."

"Check this out," Herb says, and I hear trilling video game sounds. He's expertly changing the subject. "You only have one chance to get Pandora's Box in this one," Herb says, and I guess he's talking about the game. "In the whole thing, just one chance. Brutal, right?"

"Love it. I like a challenge," Evan says, and I wonder if they are sitting down to play yet. I feel a surge of adrenaline thinking about Herb's safety and what will happen when Evan starts to feel the oleander take effect.

"You okay?" Herb asks. *Holy crap, I think. It must be working.*

"Yeah, just a little..." Evan trails off. "Fine."

"Cheers," Herb says again, I guess encouraging Evan to drink so he can be done with this horror show and get the hell out of there. Get the phone, Herb. Get the goddamn phone.

"They almost cut Yuffie and Vincent out of this one," Herb says, and I know he was memorizing facts to discuss in case he got nervous so I guess this means he's already using them and is pretty freaked out right now.

"Oh, no shit? That would have been a mistake," Evan says, and he doesn't sound right. "Excuse me just a moment," and I hear footsteps and a door close. Evan must have rushed to the bathroom. Okay, shit. This is feeling real.

"The phone is on the coffee table. I'm coming out with it

now," Herb whispers, and I leap from the van and run up to the kitchen door where Evan's phone is placed on the window ledge where the snow is scraped off. I snatch it and rush back to the van. Then there are a few silent minutes. I hear the sounds of video game music repeating, like the game is on pause, and then a door slams open.

"Fuck, Herb. I'm sick. I'm sorry man. We gotta…" Then he stops talking and I hear the sound of vomiting and heaving. It's horrifying. I hold my heart. *Get out of there, Herb.*

"Oh Jesus."

"Oh God, should we call for help? Are you okay?"

"Get help," Evan wails.

"Holy shit, buddy. Okay, I'm calling now," Herb says, and Evan sounds like he's stumbling because I hear some shuffling and a bump into a wall and then more vomiting noises. Then I hear a scream and moaning so wretched I put my hands over my ears, tears streaming down my face. *What have I done? What have I done? What have I done?*

"What did you do?" I hear Evan scream to Herb, figuring it out, putting it together. I jump from the van and rush inside to see Herb standing in the hallway off the kitchen and Evan on the floor. It looks like he's having some sort of seizure.

"Oh God. Oh my God," Herb says, tears in his eyes. "We have to call for help. This was… I can't do this!" Herb cries.

"Okay. Yes. No. I don't know," I say and then Evan's writhing body is still. I run to Herb and hold on to his arm and we stand frozen a moment, and then Evan sits straight up and I see the blood vessels in his eyes are all broken and there is blood seeping from his mouth, and he looks like every monster you might see in your nightmares. And he is.

He screams a terrifying, guttural scream and reaches out to us.

"What did you do? Help me!" I hold my chest—I can barely breathe. "You fucking bitch!" And then he falls again, this time his head hits the floor with a hard crack and he is motionless. Lifeless.

Herb and I stand still, paralyzed in guilt, in fear, in relief. We don't even look at one another. We can't bear to. After a few minutes, Herb silently moves to Evan's body and takes his pulse. Our eyes meet. He doesn't say anything, just gets on with the rest of the plan quickly. We collect the scotch and the two glasses along with the video game and push it all into a grocery bag that I pull out of my purse.

Then we place Evan's phone on the kitchen table. Herb gets his laptop from the bed, opens it to the document we created earlier and leaves it open on the table. And then we swiftly move out the side kitchen door, back to the van, and Herb pulls out as quickly as he can. In minutes we are on the main road and headed back to the Oleander's like nothing at all happened. Nothing, except that our lives are forever changed and the horror of what we just witnessed will never leave us alone.

33

Shelby

Three Months Later

The snow is beginning to melt. Spring is coming. I wave at Mack when I push through the doors of her cafe, and she waves back. She looks like a different person with her hair swept up and a smile on her face for the first time in as long as I can remember. She's packing boxes and getting ready to move everything out for the new owner.

"Looks like you're making progress," I say as she stops pushing boxes around and sits at the counter, pouring us both a cup of coffee.

"Almost done."

"So how long do you think you'll stay?" I ask.

"Well, I'm moving Row into an apartment after graduation in a few weeks, and I don't know. I'll stay there until…"

"Until you know," I say, and she smiles.

"I just want to be with her. She needs me after all this. I

mean, at least I got to give her closure—no more always wondering, always hoping. She gets to move on with the rest of her
life now, so I'm happy for that. I just don't really know what
to do with myself now," she says just as Billy walks through
the front doors.

"The mugs are in the pantry," she says and he comes over
and gives me a side hug and kisses her on the cheek.

"Thanks. I'll be back in a bit," he says, grabbing a box and
exiting back out the front doors again into the sunny afternoon.
I raise my eyebrows at her.

"Just donating some things to the bar," she says.

"Uh-huh. So does Billy have any plans on visiting Boston?"
I ask with a smirk.

"Actually, he's driving me up on Friday. We're gonna eat
clam chowder and go whale watching and do all the cliché
things, and then…"

"You don't know yet," I finish for her.

"I just don't know yet," she says.

"And that's totally okay." I stand and give her a hug. "We're
off fishing for the weekend, just the four of us, so I might not
see you, but I'll call. You're getting out of here just in time.
Carolyn Walterman is bringing her Jell-O salad to the annual
potluck next week."

"She'll force that shit on you and hover until you're forced
to eat it and say it's good," she says.

"She will. And you can't gag."

"You cannot," she says.

"I love you," I say, hugging her one more time, and then
I walk out and drive the two-lane roads past the thickets of
pines, melting in the spring sun, and head to pick up the Dis-
ney Princess custom fishing poles Clay ordered for the girls.
He really wants them to like fishing. He really wants to mend
what's broken and help me heal, even though he didn't have

the privilege of killing that bastard himself. I think about that a lot—that what-ifs.

When the news started unfolding the story of Evan Carmichael, it turned national pretty quickly. It started as a local suicide under unusual circumstances and then they unearthed his mental health records, the money he was stealing from the Oleander's, the shared history between Otis and Leo and their business dealings. Although there is still no way to prove any of the three deaths were murders—although everyone has come to accept they are—there is also no way to prove his death was a murder.

The locals are beside themselves that a killer was in plain sight all this time. They've all forgotten I was treated like a madwoman only a short time ago and now I'm almost a local hero—the woman who escaped the grips of a serial killer and lived to tell the tale. I'm called brave and fearless…and lucky. I'm given free meals at restaurants and have doors opened for me wherever I go. People nudge one another and point at me in public, and I try not to hate every single person in this town for turning on me when I needed someone to believe in me. I tell myself it's human nature—it makes more sense to believe I'm traumatized and lashing out in all the wrong ways than that there is a mass killer in our small town. I can give them that, I suppose. Some days anyway, when I'm not *as* angry. Some days, maybe I'm even…grateful.

I tell myself he was so brilliant at crafting every single moment of this nightmare that of course people questioned me. He made them. How could they not.

Sometimes I want to leave like Mack is doing—just drive, just go. The memories of my daughter's hand disappearing under black water and the tape around my wrists, and running and crawling for my life, and his face—it all lives here, and I can never really escape it.

But a whole life before that lives here too—my girls running

SERAPHINA NOVA GLASS

through the sprinkler in bare feet, sledding down Buck Hill, growing tomatoes in pots on the back porch, sewing mermaid costumes for the school play, sitting under the lights on the baseball fields at night, and the corner Dairy Queen and the church potluck and soaking in the gossip at the Cut & Curl. Our whole lives that I don't think I can leave behind for him.

I wish I felt a sense of guilt sometimes for what we plotted—what we did. But I don't. I have to live with the toll that keeping a secret like this takes on a marriage. We all have to live the rest of our lives looking over our shoulder, even though he's gone. There's not a day that will go by for the rest of my life that I won't harbor some fear that the truth could be uncovered, and even though maybe some would say it's justified, the law won't.

We're all outlaws now.

34

Florence

We had a hunch that the Oleander's was going under, but Shelby did a good job keeping from us how grave it was—that we might have lost our home and been scattered about in different cities at state-funded institutions. So when the call came that not only would all the money Evan stole from cooking the books be recovered from his estate, but that he also made far more than he told Mort about from the podcast, it felt almost poetic. We found out we were safe, even though we didn't know the extent of how insecure the whole thing really had been.

There was even a little leftover money to buy a foosball table, of all stupid things, but the gang loves it. It causes a lot of arguments and Millie spills a lot of chardonnay on the little plastic men, but all in all, I think it's an asset to our little rec room. Mort is covering *Moby Dick* on his *Literary Musings* podcast, and he's invited us all to discuss it in roundtable fashion the way we did with the missing person cases, but nobody is interested so he's grappling with his drop in ratings, but many people still tune in, to Herb's utter disbelief.

Gus doesn't leave Herb's side. It's almost like he knows Herb needs him, but I suppose that can't be true. I like to think so, though. There was a story about a little dog who went to sleep on his owner's grave every night after the man died, so you never know, do you? They sense so much.

I don't sleep anymore. I knew what I was doing when I did it, but I didn't know that I'd never be able to live with myself after. I thought I could put it away somewhere in my mind and rest, knowing that I did the world an enormous kindness, but I can't.

Herb is always with me now. The others notice sometimes, how we're always together—always whispering. I try to separate myself from him sometimes so they don't wonder, but we need each other, and maybe folks know the loss of Bernie changed us all and don't suspect anything odd is happening, but I guess I can't really worry about the talk. It will always be there in one way or another.

I text Herb late at night most nights, and he comes over to my room and lies in bed with me. Some nights he makes popcorn and puts on *The Three Stooges* and we try to laugh and forget about what we've done, and other nights I cry and think about a man writhing in his own shit and vomit, with bloody eyes, dying in front of me while I did nothing, and I just can't take it. No matter how evil he was, it wasn't a humane thing to do.

Herb stays with me and he holds me against him as we lie side by side. Some nights I know he cries too, because I feel a tear land on my neck, but I don't say anything, I just hold his hand, and we try to make it through the night.

As weeks pass and the scent of lilac bushes stream in the open screen window of my room, the world begins to feel a little bit different. We have a cookout planned in the yard and I arrive early to set up the croquet set and Herb and Mort arrange plastic tablecloths on top of folding tables on the grass. Millie pours vodka into the punch bowl, and Shelby starts the grill.

Many of the residents' families come for the occasion—Mack sits at a weathered picnic table and picks at potato salad, Mort is reading a book in an Adirondack chair in the corner and scowling when folks are too loud, and Shelby is laughing as Clay hugs her from behind and takes over the grill in a playful argument. *Shelby's laughing*, I think again. Then I watch Pops and June run, skipping over the lawn and blowing soapy bubbles from a toy wand with Gus chasing behind, biting at the bubbles in the air.

I hold a small glass of very strong watermelon punch on my lap and smile at the scene in front of me—the shouts of laughter, the pop song playing on one of the teenager's phones—Jeffry Patton's grandson, I think. The smell of fresh-cut grass and charcoal burning, the hiss of the sprinklers—summer in the air.

I see Herb crossing the lawn in my direction. He stops briefly to look at Millie, who is already tipsy and trying to balance a paper plate of food in one hand, unsuccessfully. He gives her a smirk and I hear "Up yours, Herb" as she waddles her way to a picnic table.

Herb pulls up a metal folding chair next to me and puts out his cigar, waving away the smoke for my benefit. He has brought me a glass of punch and sees I already have one, so he shrugs, gulps down one of the glasses in his hand, puts the full glass inside the empty and sits next to me. I raise my eyebrows at him.

"Woo!" He shakes his head, not expecting it to be so strong. We both chuckle at this. We stare out at the backyard party and watch Poppy and June tire of their bubbles and pull at Shelby's dress asking for ice cream sandwiches, and I feel my heart leap. We're safe. All of us. It's over.

Herb puts his hand on top of mine and squeezes it, and I know he feels the same thing—that it wasn't until today, maybe even this moment, where we could say it's really over—that it will be okay. That now the air has changed and life has continued and…we had no choice but to become outlaws. We did the right thing.

★ ★ ★ ★ ★

Acknowledgments

Thank you from the bottom of my heart to my biggest supporter, Mark Glass. To my agent, Sharon Bowers, you are simply the best. Thanks to my wonderful editor Sara Rodgers and to Leah Morse and the whole team at Graydon House.

Of course, thanks to my family, Dianna Nova, Julie Loehrer, and Mark & Tamarind Knutson.

A very special thank-you to Tonya Cornish, and to retired Omaha Police Department detective Tammy Mitchell for all of the research help and for answering all of my twisted forensic questions. And to all of my dear friends who continue to support my work and cheer me on.